LAZARUS

The Untold Story

by

Pete Murphy

**Grosvenor House
Publishing Limited**

This book is published by
Grosvenor House Publishing Ltd
28-30 High Street, Guildford, Surrey, GU1 3HY.
www.grosvenorhousepublishing.co.uk

A CIP record for this book
is available from the British Library

ISBN 978-1-906210-82-3

Dedication

I started this book because of my ex-Wife
I completed it for my Son
I would now like to dedicate
it to my Mother,
Monica Murphy

Acknowledgements

As Lazarus tell us in this book, every morsel of information we possess in our subconscious mind we have accumulated over the years from other sources, e.g. school, books, television and obviously the very latest form of information gathering, the internet. I have used all these mediums to help me write this book. As for the fiction and fantasy, well that came from the dark corners of my oh-so-warped imagination.... or did it?

I would like to take this opportunity to thank my Brother Phil, Sister Angie, Cousins David, Jane, Laura, Paul, Sarah, and Tez for their help and support, their constructive comments or quite simply for just putting up with my constant intrusions into their lives. I would also like to thank my nephew's wife Becky Davies, for the comments she made after reading chapter twenty (Willie McBride). She said, "It was so sad, it made me cry." I was flattered although a little surprised, as I believed the only way to make a woman cry was to take away her credit cards. So on that sexist joke I will stop before I alienate a large proportion of my potential readers. All that remains for me to say is I hope this book gives you as much enjoyment when you read it as it gave me when writing it.

Pete Murphy

The most famous mind of his time, indeed some might say of all time, the man who worked out the laws of gravity and was at the forefront of unravelling the motion of the planets wrote, after studying the Book of Daniel, *"The bible proves that the world will end in the year of our Lord two thousand and sixty. It may end later but I see no reason for its ending sooner."* He also wrote that the end of days would see *"the end of weeping and of all troubles, the return of the Jews from captivity and their setting up a flourishing and everlasting kingdom."*

Sir Isaac Newton - 1704

Contents

THE PLACE: London, England
THE TIME: The Year of Our Lord Nineteen Hundred and Ninety

The rain slapped down hard onto the car window, almost obscuring the view, and as Frank Sinatra sang "I'm walking behind you," the American crooner's dulcet tone drifted melodically out of the car stereo. I thought to myself how appropriate the words were, for I have walked behind Larry for such a long time. As I watch him try to relax and he submerges himself into the deep leather seats of the car's interior I think of the long road we have been down together. Have we really come to the end of our journey? Well we shall see.

The vehicle he travelled in belonged to the British Government so, Larry was being chauffeur driven, and this was a luxury Larry wasn't used to. It was not intended for someone as insignificant as Larry, it was for the personal use of his friend John, who had kindly offered to give him a ride home today as Larry's BMW had been at the Doctors all day. The principal dirty faced surgeon had informed him that the knocking sound he had asked him to look at was far more serious than first thought and if left unattended the long term prognosis for the vehicle was unfavourable, so a very expensive part had to be fitted. He admired this black nailed technician for how he delivered his verdict with such a straight face, even Dick Turpin would crack a smile when he said his immortal line "stand and deliver," as many a lady confirmed afterwards. Larry was not feeling worried because he felt he was being overcharged by the "*oh so honest*" BMW specialist; no, he had far more important things on his mind. A few weeks after the Brighton bombing, all top government buildings had metal body scanners installed, this in turn dictated to him that he could not take his prized possession whenever he visited these places. It made him feel uneasy and he felt naked without it. John dropped him off outside his apartment and said goodbye.

Larry knew something was not right as soon as he entered the elevator. He alighted at the third floor and walked down the corridor. He could see his door was slightly open, but he knew for sure the apartment was empty. For you see, Larry was not your average civil servant. He was tall, tanned with a good looking Mediterranean appearance about him. He seemed to be in his mid-twenties but, in actual fact was so very much older! He had seen the sun rise and set far too many times to be a normal human being.

Larry pushed open the door to his apartment to find the place had been totally ransacked and along with a few personal possessions, the spear head from the crucifixion of Jesus of Nazareth had been taken. Larry knew this was not an act of an opportunist burglar but, most definitely the work of the agent of the Anti-Christ. For it is that sacred relic that helps him to locate the demons sent from hell to undermine this world and to bring it to a premature end. Larry decides to put pen to paper, as it just may unlock his memory and help him find a way to locate the demon before it is too late.

As we leave Larry writing his memoirs you may now be wondering who I am. Well my name is Cevat, I am an angel. I was on the right-hand side of Archangel Gabriel, when both he and the Archangel Michael vanquished Lucifer and cohorts from the everlasting kingdom into the darkness. I am not, nor have ever been, a human being, although I have come in contact with your kind through the years when discharging my responsibility to "Larry," for you see I am his Guardian Angel. I have no dominion over him, I can only guide, but I do possess many powers. I can almost see the smirk on your face as you read this, for you feel you are a superior intellectual, you sit there in your nice safe central-heated home in the twentieth century thinking you know everything. A long time ago you consigned God, the devil and angels to the realms of fantasy along with Father Christmas and the tooth fairy. Allow me to inform you, not only do Guardian Angels exist but you also have one, he is now standing at your right-hand shoulder and it was actually he who guided you to read this. So just maybe you are the very person who could help save this world!

I will say no more on the subject and let you read and digest Larry's own words.

Yours

Cevat

Prologue

"I am the resurrection and the life."
When he said this he cried out in a loud voice,
"Lazarus come out!"
The dead man came out, his feet and hands bound,
with bands of cloth round his face. Jesus said to them,"
Unbind him, let him go free."

John 11-1-45

My name's Lazarus but you can call me Larry. Who am I? Well at the moment I am what you call a Spin Doctor, I've got the ear of the British Government. If I say so myself I look pretty good for my age, not a grey hair on my head and I am nearly 2000 years old. No, before you say it, I am not some kind of creature that needs human blood to survive. I am a human being, a selfish human being, like all mortals.

Even after all the atrocities over the centuries that I have seen, it is my own personal loss I feel most. My father was a proud man; he waited until he was on his death bed to tell me he loved me and ask for a kiss. My mother, the stories she would tell at bedtime, I tried so hard to stay awake but her voice was hypnotic and would drag me off to sleep. My sisters to whom I am eternally grateful for taking me to the Master, would have made good mothers if they had not sacrificed their lives to preaching the Lord's word. So I am a Human, I feel loss.

I think about the boy I adopted on the Isle of Cyprus who as an old man, I held dead in my arms. When I think of what he achieved in his short life, I feel proud. So I am Human, I feel pride.

Like most men, I have fallen in love. I can still remember the first time I met my wife at the harbour of Ephesus, she was a slave girl. They said she was an Angle with her gold hair but, she was more like an Angel to me. I can see our final moment together when she was taken away by pirates; she smiled that magnanimous smile and pointed to the sky with her hand. Was it a sign for me to keep my spirits up or was she saying she would see me in the next world? Deep down in my heart I knew then that it was the latter. So I am a Human, I have been in love.

I go back in time and see myself watching my Master being dragged through the streets of Jerusalem and doing nothing, cowering with fear behind the crowd as they beat him and spat at him. When he died I was watching John standing strong and tall holding Mary the mother of Jesus, in her hour of need, and what did I do? Run away and hide. So I am a Human, I feel shame.

After all this time I feel all my own pains, so I am totally selfish and that definitely makes me a Human.

On another level, although my body doesn't need substance like other mortals, I enjoy Chinese food, a nice bottle of claret and of course my Havana cigars; and if I were to make love to a woman I dare say I would enjoy it but I don't need these things to survive. It is as though the animal has left my body.

Why then after all this time have I decided to put pen to paper? Well the end is coming and the world hasn't changed. Take my birthplace, Jerusalem. They changed the Roman soldier for the Israeli, the Palace Guard for the Palestinian police – it is still two sides that hate each other, trying to take control of the population. It is like a never-ending circle. Well where should I start? At the beginning, that's always a good place!

CHAPTER ONE

In the Beginning

I was born in the year of the Great Census, eight years after the Master. My family comprised my father named Caylus, my mother Martha and my two sisters, Mary and little Martha. Our home was in Bethesda, a small village on the outskirts of Jerusalem. It was here that I enjoyed a happy childhood and then a contented youth, working alongside my father as silversmiths in our family business. The goods we made were either sold in the small store at the front of the workshop, or in Jerusalem where we would travel to, on market days, to trade our wares in the temple.

I must confess that the first twenty years of my life passed by relatively uneventfully. However, all that was to change on the death of my father when suddenly the welfare of my family fell onto my shoulders. Bearing this new mantle of responsibility, I threw myself into my work with a vigour and enthusiasm that surprised everyone. Things went well and it was not long before I decided to expand by leasing a bigger shop in Jerusalem. Although at first, my mother was against the idea I was able to convince her that we would get more trade and this would ultimately be beneficial to us all. The new shop also had an upper room, which we would rent out for wedding parties and other such festive events. Initially I would work for four days in the shop with my manservant and would then return home to spend the remaining three days, including the Sabbath, with my family in Bethesda. As the business prospered so my commitment to it increased, and soon I found myself spending the whole week in Jerusalem, and subsequently celebrating the Sabbath became less important.

The less I saw of my family the more I sought solace elsewhere, the drinking houses and brothels of Jerusalem almost became like home to me and the Roman soldiers and the city's undesirable misfits, with whom I mixed, became my friends. As the business became more successful, I was able to delegate the running of it to my servants leaving me to do whatever I pleased. Like most mortals, I never even considered the future for my eternal soul; I lived purely for each day, believing that because I ensured that my family enjoyed a comfortable lifestyle, I was fulfilling all my expected responsibilities. What I could not see was the distress that I was causing my mother with my avaricious and selfish lifestyle.

All too quickly, I was to rue the errors of my ways and words cannot describe my feelings the day I received the news of my mother's death. Her loss simply left my sisters and I absolutely devastated. Finally, following months of mourning, we got some respite from our desperate grief when Martha told us about the stories she had heard of a new Messiah. His name was Jesus of Nazareth and his teachings spoke of eternal life and of a re-union with departed loved ones through the resurrection on the last day. Martha pleaded with me to go to one of his gatherings, although at first I must confess that I was, like most people without faith, extremely sceptical. I had already lost my own religious belief and I certainly wasn't looking for another one. However, I decided to go if only to please Martha. What I witnessed at that gathering was to change my life forever, only at this moment in my life I didn't realize just how long forever was going to be.

From that moment on, I gave up my errant ways and became a devout follower of Jesus of Nazareth. I rekindled my relationship with my sisters and went back to my original work pattern of four days at the shop in Jerusalem, ensuring that I always spent the remainder of the week at the family home. We always attended the public sermons given by the Master and we soon came to know his close attendants, or disciples as they are better known. It was not long before Judas, who was, to coin a phrase, the self-appointed financial guardian of the organization, sought me out and encouraged me to help the cause with a monetary contribution. I willingly arranged to donate fifteen percent of my income to help with the Master's work in easing the burden of those less fortunate.

Around this time, Jesus would often frequent our home to escape the hustle and bustle of Jerusalem and we would often, after supper, sit and talk for hour upon hour, sometimes even until sunrise. Our discussions were not always on theological matters; Jesus was a very entertaining man who could freely discuss any number of subjects to keep his audience captivated and enthralled. Although viewed as a serious preacher, Jesus could easily lighten the atmosphere with his acerbic wit and humour.

It was about two years after meeting with Jesus of Nazareth that I suffered my illness. Martha said I had contracted some kind of fever, which had me slipping in and out of consciousness, and the doctors of the time did not know what to do for me. At this time, the Master was away in Galilee preaching to the masses and despite Martha sending a message relaying my poor health to Jesus, I passed away before he was able to return. For my part, all that I can remember of my time of illness was falling into a deep sleep. Three days after my death, Jesus, along with my grieving sisters, made his way to my tomb. Again my only recollection of that instance was the feeling of utter confusion at hearing the Lord's voice inside my head repeatedly whispering my name, and of then eventually finding the strength, even though I was swathed in bandages with my legs and arms stiff and aching, to somehow stand up and walk out of the tomb.

My sisters then took me home, still sobbing - only now their tears were tears of joy, and though I had so many questions to ask, I could not think clearly nor could I get the words out of my mouth. At home, my sisters lovingly nursed me back to full health, and I was eventually able to sort myself out and ask all the jumbled questions that had been running through my mind. When I received the answers, I was utterly astounded at what I heard; that Jesus had given me a second chance through resurrection. It was just as he had promised in his teachings and now he had delivered. Was it all real, was I dreaming, or had my Master proved he was the real Messiah?

I pondered on these questions, trying to make sense of it all, continually; and it was only when Jesus came to visit me several days later that he finally gave me all the answers and assurances I needed.

Following my resurrection, many things in my life changed. Take, for instance, the bare essentials of life - food and drink. I never seemed to hunger or thirst which was both very strange and surreal; I simply ate and drank to appease Martha who, quite naturally, insisted it would make me strong again. I also remember walking in Jerusalem, shortly after my recovery, and passing two Roman Soldiers, who I was certain, were defeated Syrian soldiers, more than likely forced to fight for the Roman Empire in return for their lives. I assumed they were speaking Aramaic, for I could understand every word they spoke. What I didn't realize it at this time was that along with my new life I had been given the gift of tongues. The effects of these and other changes all became much clearer to me later in my life.

My priorities in life also changed after the miracle, and I decided, along with my sisters, that I would give all my family's wealth to the Master. I employed a young man, Jacob, who had a young family, to look after the shop in Jerusalem and this then allowed my sisters and me to devote ourselves to the Master and follow him everywhere we could. Whatever profit the shop made after paying Jacob and taking out our living expenses, we gave straight to Judas. It was through this time that I built up a friendship with Judas, the much maligned and misunderstood character from a historical point of view. Yes, he did betray Jesus and he was driven by his own greed but are we in a position to judge? Would we not be lured in the same way as Judas by the promise of wealth, merely for placing a kiss on the cheek of a friend? Another question that has remained unanswered in my mind is: Did Jesus in fact orchestrate his own capture and was Judas merely a pawn in this plan? For it seems that with or without the kiss Jesus would have been captured, as he never hid himself away or disguised himself. Jesus was proud of who he was and would have stood up in a crowd of people and said, "I am he, Jesus, the Son of God."

On the night of the festival of the Passover, Judas came and said that Jesus wanted a room and a meal with his disciples; I said the best place would be at my shop in the upper room, it's peaceful and they wouldn't be disturbed.

Later that night they all arrived and everything was laid out for them, I was downstairs with the servants bringing the best food and wine for the meal. At about nine, Judas ran down the stairs and straight out of the house, slamming the door on his way. A short while later the remainder of the assembly came down the stairs followed by the Master. Jesus kissed and embraced me, far too long for a simple goodnight, and he then whispered in my ear, "Keep the wolf from my sheep as long as you can, Lazarus." I didn't understand the meaning of this at the time but I do now. Jesus then said out loud,

"We are going to the garden on the hill to pray, keep a light burning for me my good friend Lazarus."

I took this to mean he was coming back to stay the night, so I told the servants to clear the upstairs room and prepare the sleeping quarters for everyone.

I was determined to stay awake and greet their return. Sometime before dawn, I fell asleep but I was awoken by a frantic banging on the door. It was a distraught Peter; he told me he had denounced the Master, no matter what I said I could not comfort him. Although I was inwardly thinking that I could not disown the Lord and run away, I said to Peter,

"Come on, we will go and find Nicodemus and see if we can somehow buy Jesus his freedom."

When we arrived we were told he was in a meeting with the High Priest at the palace. Eventually we managed to get a note to Nicodemus and we met outside. We explained that we had gold to buy Jesus of Nazareth back. He said,

"You don't understand, this meeting has been held over the festival because not all the council are here. The moderates and the supporters of Jesus mostly are away holding family festivals. Unfortunately, this is not a case of *will he die* but *when will he die,* and how many will die with him."

At that moment the bravado left me and my right arm began to inadvertently shake. I staggered out and stammered,

"I must go and save my sisters."

"Yes, go and save yourself," hailed Nicodemus.

CHAPTER TWO

The Red Rocks

I see that Lazarus has finally heeded my suggestions and started to recollect his life in order to get back a full perspective of his life's purpose. I must say that I love him like a father loves a son, but I have got to admit even as a child he was never the sharpest tool in the box. Just reading his story, like you are, amazes me how long it took him to work out his destiny. Had I not pushed him forward at the crucifixion he would never have picked up the spear to comply with his mission.

Before I continue, it would probably make sense to inform you of my involvement in his life. As I have previously mentioned I am his guardian angel, so allow me to explain a little bit more about guardian angels, who we are and what we do. You all have a guardian angel, some of you realize it and some don't, but we are with you from birth to the grave. Our role is to guide people throughout their life on earth. We are, if you like, the inner voice in the back of your mind telling you to take or not to take the chances in life. I'm sure you've all heard of stories, in which the person or persons in question, relate the unusual circumstances which prevented them from getting on a plane or train or how at the last minute they just decided, for some unknown reason, not to make a journey and then subsequently found out that there had been a crash and that they were lucky to be alive. Well believe me, there is no luck involved, it's the work of their guardian angels either creating a series of events to stop them, or subconsciously telling them not to make that journey. Or how about the stories of people who in times of crisis perform amazing feats - like a mother who, after seeing her child being rundown in a road accident, is suddenly able to lift off the car which had been slowly crushing her child to death? Experts say it is the inner strength of a mother but trust me it's not, it's the power of the child's guardian angel working through the mother.

These things are done to ensure that those for whom life on this earth is not yet complete, do not get embroiled in accident/events which have been scheduled to claim the lives of those who have completed their pre-set objectives. We act, if you like, as spiritual traffic lights to prevent wherever possible the untimely collision of souls on their journey through the crossroads of life.

However, you need to be warned; your guardian angel can only intervene once in your lifetime. Following an intervention to prevent an untimely demise, the soul of that person then becomes susceptible to possession by unclean spirits or demons who scour the earth, as agents of the devil, looking for such unprotected souls - and your guardian angel can do nothing to prevent it. Sadly, in the multi-media world of today, there are far too many stories of young innocent children being kidnapped, tortured both physically and sexually, and even murdered. Although horrible acts have happened many times since the dawn of time it would seem that thanks to mans desire for twenty-four-hour news channels, free newspapers, the internet, etc., every gory detail of the victim's ordeal is graphically relayed and this has no doubt led to these types of atrocious incidents taking place on a far more frequent basis.

Why, I hear you ask, does their guardian angel let this happen to them? Well, there are two reasons why they have to stand back and live every painful moment with their charge. Either it's because it was their pre-ordained time to go, or their angel has already had to act in their short life, and is therefore helpless to intercept. One thing I would say is, do not feel sorry for the child, because they leave this world for a far better place. No, your heart must go out to the parents, for they must carry the scars of such tragedies for the rest of their lives. Even feel sorry for yourselves for you have to endure this now mad world a little longer, and most of all feel for Lazarus because he has to walk this world alone witnessing the evils of his fellow men till the end of time.

While Lazarus records the events in his life, I would like to tell you what happened to the spear head after it had been taken from his apartment but first I must take you back sixteen years for another example of a guardian angel in action; it is relevant to my story.

This tale involves four seven-year-old boys, all the best of friends. They had all been born at the same hospital, Stepping Hill, where their mothers had all become great friends so it was almost inevitable that they too would end up like brothers. Their names were Stephen Stanton (Stanie), Terrence Carlton (Tiger), Jamie Bredbury (Jay) and Dave O'Brien (OB). The world, for these boys, was centered in the Heaton Norris area of Stockport, a large town in the Greater Manchester conurbation. As far as these seven-year-olds were concerned London, Paris or New York might as well have been on another planet. The most exciting place in Heaton Norris was the recreational park, known locally as the 'Rec', and the favourite parts of their playground were the Red Rocks.

The park grounds were laid out on a slope overlooking the town. At the top were Crown Green bowling grounds, the preserve of the retired folk and, as far as the lads were concerned, far too boring to bother with. After the Crown Greens were the tennis courts, alright for mucking about on during the summer when everyone wanted to play tennis for two or three weeks until Wimbledon had become a distant memory, then further down the sloped hill were playing fields marked out as several football pitches, the domain of the Sunday leagues footballers. Finally, there was a stretch of unkempt land which was fenced off from the main park for safety reasons; the ground soon gave way to the red sandstone cliffs that had given the area its nickname.

The rock face plunged down onto the new motorway which followed the route of the old railway line and split the Rec off from the town centre. It was here that the lads had made their secret territory. They knew that they weren't meant to play there but how many seven-year-old lads did as they were told. And the fact they weren't meant to be there only added to the excitement.

Our story starts around dusk on the 1st November. The boys were excitedly anticipating bonfire night only four days away. The anticipation unfortunately had proved too much for Tiger who had taken the fireworks hidden in his father's workshop; he knew there would be hell to pay when he was found out but he just couldn't help himself. The fun and respect he would get from his mates far outweighed the negatives and he would just have to deal with the consequences of his actions at a later date. The fun soon wore off after the first ten or so repetitious fireworks had been let off on the park.

"Let's make a genie," suggested Tiger to keep the attention and admiration of his mates.

"What's a genie then?" quizzed Stanie.

Tiger explained that if they emptied the contents of three or four fireworks onto the ground and then lit it, the resulting explosion would look and sound like it did when the genie appeared on stage during the Christmas pantomime they had seen at the Davenport Theatre the year before. Stanie, who was always the sensible one, was unsure but kept his reservations to himself to prevent the undoubted ribbing he would receive if he said anything that made him seem like a spoilsport. Instead he just stood and watched together with OB, as Jay and Tiger broke open the remaining fireworks and poured the contents onto a flat stone they had found lying close by.

Tiger stood looking toward the football pitches and he could just about make out the outline of the tennis court on top of the hill in the fading light of dusk. Stanie stood to his left and the other two lads were facing him and the town centre below. All four lads stood staring at the small pile of dark dust piled onto the stone, and nobody spoke for what seemed like hours but it must have only been a couple of minutes, if that. Before Jay or anyone could change their mind, Tiger pulled out a match and struck it against the box; he smiled at his friends then dropped the match. All four sets of eyes were fixed on the match it as it slowly tumbled toward the stone, in what seemed like slow-motion mode.

As the match hit the gunpowder, the explosion and flashes of light were far greater than any of them had expected. All four of the young boys were forced back due to the intensity of the explosion. Unfortunately for Tiger, he was pushed over the edge of the rocks, it was then that something astounding happened; as Stanie watched and saw his friend's body disappear over the edge of the Red Rocks to his certain death, he leapt like a cat and grabbed hold of Tiger's left ankle. 'He was like Superman flying through the air!' OB said later. Stanie held onto his friend with all his strength. The energy he expended in his actions was far beyond that of a seven-year-old boy, the power surging through his body stemmed from another source. When the other boys had regained their composure, they helped Stanie pull Tiger back over the edge to safety. All four boys sat on the ground for several minutes staring at each other, not speaking.

When Tiger had finally recovered from the ordeal of staring death in the face, it was Jay, who broke the silence.

"God you were just like a bird flying through the air. How did you do that? You saved his life you really did," he said, looking intently into his friend's eyes. Tiger chipped in almost breathlessly:

"I'll never forget that for the rest of my life, you saved my life."

Tiger had acquired his nickname when he was about five; Jay had christened him with it after seeing him playing out in his new jumper his Gran had knitted him out of leftover orange and black wool. Like all his Gran's creations it was two sizes too big. 'Plenty of room for you to grow', was what she always said as she forced oversized garments on her grandchildren. Following his near-death experience on the Red Rocks that November evening, the nickname became more appropriate as he began to live up to the nature of his namesake. He became unpredictably wild and vicious; the only person exempt from his fierce temper was Stanie. It was, as you have no doubt guessed, due to the fact he had lost the guidance of his guardian angel.

I must now take you forward fifteen years from the adventure on the Red Rocks. It's a cold and wet Saturday night in January. Stanie, OB and Jay were walking up the A6 back home after a night on the beer. They were all walking with their heads down into the fierce wind and rain when a BMW pulled up beside them.

"Jump in lads, I'll give you a lift home," shouted Tiger from behind the wheel.

Without asking, the lads knew it was a stolen car. It wasn't the first time he'd done it and they had all readily accepted lifts in the past. However, on this occasion they all hesitated.

"Are you coming or what?" he yelled in anger.

OB and Jay looked towards Stanie for guidance. However, he just stood and stared at the car. The rain was starting to pour down now and they still had another ten minutes of drunken staggering up the hill against the rain, which seemed to come at them horizontally, before they reached home - but Stanie stood there and said nothing. What was wrong with him? Tiger was his best mate and he'd never before questioned his actions but as he later discussed with OB and Jamie, it was as if someone was telling him not to get into the car. Tiger half expected that reaction from Jay and OB but not from Stanie. Stanie had saved his life as a kid and Tiger had always looked out for him ever since. He felt betrayed by what he thought was the closest person to him.

"Fuck off then," he shouted as he revved the engine. "Get pissed wet through, see if I'm bothered." With that he closed the window and sped up the A6 towards Hazel Grove.

The three friends stood there in the rain watching the lights of the stolen car disappear into the distance, and then continued on their way home without speaking.

Stanie was awoken from his drunken slumber early the next morning when his mum burst into the bedroom. She looked pale and it was obvious she'd been crying.

"What is it mum?" he asked.

"Oh thank God you're here," she cried as she dragged him from his bed and held him tightly. "I didn't know if you'd been out with Tiger last night," she sobbed as she kissed his head.

"Mum, have you been at the cooking Sherry. What's going on?"

"It's Tiger love, there's been an accident."

That afternoon, he was sitting in the snug of the Railway Inn, their local since they'd looked old enough to drink. All three friends talking about the night before, thankful that they hadn't got in the car and been involved in the police chase and subsequent crash that had killed their friend. A few hours later, they had caught a 330 bus and laid flowers at the scene of the accident in Bredbury, a few miles away from where they believed was the last time they had seen Tiger.

CHAPTER THREE

The Crucifixion

I don't know how long it was or what path I took, but I found my way back to the family home. I was incoherent at first, but after a little while I managed to come out with my story. To my amazement they were very calm and collected; I was confused by their manner.

"Don't you understand? We have got to get out of here!" I said. "We could go and stay with relations in Petra, we have just got to get out of here and wait for this to die down."

They would not hear of it. I loved my sisters equally but when Mary asked for anything I could not refuse. She took hold of both my hands and with her big brown eyes looked into my soul. She had an air of quietness about her, and when she spoke people listened.

"Dear brother, I love you with all my heart but if you were to die tomorrow it is one more day that the Master has given you. Have you forgotten so quickly, you were dead Lazarus, this is not your time anymore, it belongs to him."

So I set off back to Jerusalem, to what? I didn't know. Not long after leaving my sisters I lost my resolve and the fear returned. It was after noon when I reached the outskirts of the city. As I got closer I could see a crowd was gathering by the garden gate entrance to the city. I reached it just in time to see a sad procession coming through the gate. I could scarcely believe what they had done to him; he looked directly at me, and never before or since have I seen such sadness in someone's eyes. In my shame I turned away. I was now looking directly at a smiling Roman soldier but it wasn't the smile that caught my attention but his eyes. They were blood red and pure evil. At first I thought it was a trick of the light but it was no optical illusion. It was the beast. In those days he didn't hide from me, in fact he did not know I existed. I suppose he couldn't miss the chance of seeing the Son of God being put to death. I watched that sad procession make its way up the hill to Golgotha. Tears stung my eyes. What could I do? I have had more than a lifetime to contemplate what I should have done, but to my shame I did nothing.

My Master's journey to the cross has been well documented over the centuries but one particular incident stands out for me. The Master had fallen yet again and was being beaten by the soldiers who were being led into a mad frenzy by the soldier with the red eyes, the beast. From my vantage point I should not have been able to hear what was being said but somehow I could. The beast was taunting the Master,

"Where is he then? You're the Son of God, he should be helping you," he said.

The Master looked but said nothing.

The beast then said, "You are on your own boy, but I can help you. I can stop all this if you were but to say those few words."

Out of nowhere came the Centurion; he hit the beast and threw him to the ground. The look of complete shock soon turned to anger and then changed to willful defiance towards his superior officer. For a moment I thought he was going to retaliate but then he seemed to get a grip of his composure at the last minute and began to smile.

"Luceus, you are the son of an evil bitch but even you have surpassed yourself today. This man is to be put to death by Roman authority not tortured and murdered by the road side. Do you forget yourself man and the uniform you wear? You are a Roman soldier and you represent the Roman people, you are not a barbarian. Get control of yourself soldier or you will end up on a cross of your own," the Centurion said.

He then addressed another soldier, "Nereus, get someone from the crowd to help him carry the cross before we have a dead man on our hands."

He then turned to the Master and said in a whisper, "You are a brave man my friend, do not worry it's not far to go now, your suffering will soon be over."

There was a definite sign of pity in his expression when he said those words. So there you have it, someone who was supposed to be his enemy and was putting him to death showed him compassion in his hour of need. Me, his so-called friend, what did I do? I even kept quiet when they asked for a volunteer to help him carry the cross. I knew I should have offered my services but fear had taken hold of me. Lord, even now as I write these words I beg for your forgiveness. As the crowd pressed together for a better look, the Saviour of the World was nailed up high. I stayed at the back filled with fear and sadness, crying for him and also for myself for my shame. I was feeling sorry for myself but not for my Master. After all they had done to him, he was not thinking of himself. He cried out to his father to forgive them, and then he gave up his spirit to his father. The Centurion came forward and took a spear from one of his soldiers to pierce his side. With horror, I watched as water gushed from his side; they had literally bled him dry. At that very moment, at three in the afternoon, it went completely black. The Centurion threw down the spear and it broke. I heard him say,

"This truly was the Son of God."

In the darkness I came forward driven by a force that was unknown to me then. I picked up the spear head and put it beneath my cloak. I took one final look at my dead Master and departed that sorrowful place. My eyes were now adjusting to the dark as I was going down the hill towards the city. All at once, there was a flash of lightning, instantly followed by thunder. The heavens opened and within minutes the hillside was like a gushing stream. Every so often when lightning struck I could see the people ahead of me being tormented by the thunderstorm which made them panic even more than the darkening did. They were slipping and sliding, some were even falling down the hill in their panic to get away from this place of death. It was like the hounds of hell were running after them. I could hear some soul lamenting,

"This is God's wrath raining down on us all for killing his prophet," shouted someone.

"This is the end of the world," screamed another.

I thought to myself he could just be right. I needed to go back to my shop to get out of the wet things so that I could gather my thoughts, then I could decide what I was to do next. I knew there was no point in trying to get back to my sisters in this storm. I would try to get some sleep then set off at first light in the morning. When

I arrived back at my shop the place was closed and all the doors were bolted. I rapped as hard as I could. There was no answer at first so I banged once again; there was still no answer, so I shouted out as loud as I could trying to make my voice stand out above the storm. With the thunder still roaring the noise was deafening. So when the storm abated for few moments I called out again,

"Jacob are you there, it's me Lazarus."

This time I was in luck for after a short recess I could hear the bolts being lifted at the back the door. As soon as the gap between the door and the jam became wide enough for me to pass through I went inside. The first person I saw was Dorcas, Jacob's wife. Her face was pure white and full of fear. When I was fully inside, the door was instantly bolted by Jacob who now stood directly behind me as I moved further into the room I was met with a surprise for my sisters were there along with Peter and his brother Andrew. Everyone's face seemed to be etched with fear, apart from Mary. She was playing with Jacob's two young children, Amos and Tabitha. They were laughing uncontrollably because Mary was tickling them; their gleeful screams of joy were in sharp contrast to the others somber mood. I embraced everyone individually, but not before picking up Amos who had jumped off Mary's lap and come running to me. He was three years old and had always been the apple of my eye since Jacob had started to work for me. His obvious joy to see me was comforting in some way, and helped calmed me down. Once I had calmed down I explained what had happened to the Master. When I finished my account of how he had died, there was a great air of despondency about the place then all at once Andrew spoke up,

"How could Judas have done such a thing, after the way the Master had been so good to him?"

Then my sister Mary jumped in, "Because he had to do it. If he had not betrayed him how else would Jesus have been put to death, for without dying he could not fulfill his prophecy that he will rise again."

It was said in a bright and happy tone, not in hope but with unshakable faith and conviction. Everyone to a man turned to look at her in total disbelief, even Martha came in from the kitchen to hear her sister's words.

"Mark my words well he will be back," Mary said.

Right at that moment there was an almighty bang on the door. Everyone jumped out of their skin including the children, then Jacob slowly moved to the door with trepidation.

"Who is it?" he said.

"It's Thomas, let us in quick."

With him was Mary the Master's mother with John close by her side. As you can well imagine Mary was in a distressed condition. John told us that Nicodemus had gone to the Romans to ask for permission to take the Master's body to a tomb owned by Joseph of Arimathea, although they found out later that Caiaphas had a large bolder put in front of the entrance of the tomb once the Master had been laid to rest, because he had heard of the story regarding the resurrection.

"He obviously thinks we are going to do something," Peter said.

"We should gather what money we have left and get as far away from this place as we can before we are all arrested like him," Thomas said nervously.

"No, we can't go anywhere until the Master returns," my sister Mary said in a soft but assertive voice.

There was once again a collective look of disbelief on the majority apart from the Master's mother. It seemed my sister's unshakable faith gave her comfort. Over the next few hours and at different times of the day and night the rest of the company returned. By the first day of the week, all of the close followers of the Master were there. It was then decided a meeting would take place where we would all vote on what to do next.

CHAPTER FOUR

Heaton Norris Boys

I don't know about you but I am really enjoying Lazarus' account of his life. It's almost cathartic for him; he should have done it about a thousand years ago. As he sits at his desk depressed because he believes the spear has been destroyed, he's desperately thinking of another way he can save mankind. I will tell you of the whereabouts of the relic, but first we must go on our travels again, back to Stockport and our gang of childhood friends.

This time it's only two nights ago, a Saturday night to be precise. The Heaton Norris Boys were having a right old drink, or at least two of them were, and that expression most of you use 'As Full as a Gun' springs to mind. Stanie had been pacing himself as he had things on his mind that he wanted to discuss with the lads, plus they had a big football game in the morning. It had been over a year since the tragic accident that had taken Tiger from them. At the time of the accident all the lads had blamed themselves, they never really spoke about it but each of them when they lay awake in the middle of the night asked themselves why they hadn't stopped him. This played on Stanie's mind, more so than the other lads.

Since the incident with the firework he had tried to watch over Tiger. He was the only one who could calm him down when he "Went off on one."

The sands of time had eased the guilt for Jay and OB and whilst they never forgot their friend, and still several times throughout the day they would see and do things that reminded them of Tiger, the guilty feeling had thankfully faded away. Unfortunately for Stanie this was not the case and even now over a year after the crash that killed Tiger his guilty feeling where strong, maybe even stronger than originally. He should have done something, he was the sensible one he should have stopped him, even if it meant dragging him out of the car. He'd had these thoughts every waking hour since the accident; his only escape was when he eventually dropped off to sleep at night; however recently he hadn't even had that luxury. For the last few weeks he had had a recurring dream, in which Tiger had been pleading for help. He couldn't tell in the dream what was wrong with Tiger or why he needed help; all he ever remembered was his screams for help. Did the dreams mean that Tiger was not in peace even in death?

After OB and Jay were suitably oiled Stanie plucked up the courage to tell the only people he could openly discuss the dreams with, Jay and OB. They both laughed it off and told him to ignore it, however deep down both of them resented Stanie telling them his dream, it only helped to resurface the guilty feeling it had taken them months to suppress.

The three lads sat there enjoying the atmosphere of the busy pub. Stanie was sure it was the combination of alcohol and the jovial laughter and drunken banter that filled the smokey pub, but for him it was the relief after telling his friends about the dream. After he'd told them, there had been an awkward minute or so where all of them were too scared to speak in case someone mentioned Tiger again! In a strange way it may have been a good thing talking about Tiger because for the first time since the accident all three of them where enjoying their Saturday night pint.

Last orders had just been called and OB was getting to his feet to avoid the rush to the bar when Stanie stopped him.

"Come on lads we've got a big game tomorrow, don't you think we've had enough?"

"You've only had a couple Mr Sensible," OB replied.

OB looked at Jay. They knew he was right, he always was.

"Well you're not stopping me going to the chippy captain Sensible!"

The three lads finished their pints in silence then made their way through the still busy pub to the exit. On the way out OB and Jay stopped to take the mickey out of a mate out on a blind date. Stanie was unaware the others had stopped and he was alone as he stepped out of the White Lion. As he stood on the pavement, the cold air filling his lungs, he heard someone shouting.

"Stanie you midget."

The voice seemed to be coming from across the road. It seemed familiar and as he focussed his eyes he was sure he could make out the shape of someone standing in the doorway of the bank. He'd been meaning to go and get his eyes tested for ages, he was sure he was short-sighted but vanity had always stopped him going to the opticians. As he strained his eyes the shape slowly started to take form. Just then the door opened and OB and Jay staggered out. As the cold air hit Jay in the face he lost his footing and barged into Stanie's back.

"Watch it you moron," Stanie snapped at his mate and quickly returned his gaze to across the road but the shape had gone.

Stanie decided it must have been the lack of sleep, beer and the wind that had played a trick on him, he apologised to Jay and the three lads set off to the local Chinese chippy for their supper.

When they got there they hadn't beaten the rush and the queue made its way around the shop and out of the door. The three mates huddled together and Stanie and Jay looked at each other both thinking the same thing, how long it would be before OB shouted "Sore Finger," and burst out laughing. No matter how many times OB heard the elderly Chinese man ask his customers if they wanted 'Salt and Vinegar' he couldn't resist shouting out 'Sore Finger!' He still thought it was funny. If his mates found it tedious imagine how the old man must have felt. Within seconds of finally entering the warm chippy, true to form OB shouted 'Sore Finger' and he had to be held up by Stanie and Jay as he collapsed in fits of laughter. The proprietor seemed relieved when the lads were served and they were on their way out of his shop, he was used to dealing with drunken Englishmen but that boy really was annoying.

The queue at the chippy had been longer than they realised and by the time they were staggering up the A6 eating their chips it was nearly midnight. OB was having none of it when Jay pleaded with him to get a new routine. Stanie just laughed to himself, he knew it was pointless trying to change his mate; anyway his corny jokes were what made OB such a loveably fool. As they approached Belmont Bridge he knew he would be subjected to another one of OB's standard comedy routines. For you see that was the predetermined point where the boys separated. OB and Jay would go to the right as they lived four doors away from each other in a row of Victorian back-to-back terraced houses. Stanie went the opposite direction, to the large semi-detached house his family lived in. Usually at this point OB would come out with another of his stand up routines and true to form as they got to Belmont Bridge OB said,

"My Mate Stanie is a posh lad, lives in a big house, he even gets out of the bath for a pee."

As the three lads laughed they all heard someone shout.

"Stanie you midget!"

They all stopped and stared across the road where the voice had emanated from.

"Come across then, I haven't got all night," said the voice.

As they started to cross the A6 to see who was shouting to them Christ Church clock started to strike midnight. This was impossible as the church had long since been demolished, all that was left of it was the folly of the shell of the clock tower, but the clock and bell had been removed in the seventies.

It was now exactly twelve months to the day of Tiger's cremation, you can well imagine the collective shock of the boys. For when they crossed to the other side of the road, they encountered once again the celebrant of the anniversary they were to commemorate.

CHAPTER FIVE

Risen

Before noon on the first day of the week Mary Magdalene paid us a visit, she was looking for Peter.

"Come in, he's inside," I said.

Mary excitedly began to say, "He's here, he's here."

"Yes I told you Peter's here. He's just coming," I said.

"No, no, he's here. He's here," she repeated.

I was totally confused. She seemed incoherent, I just couldn't understand her. I thought to myself, this has been too much for her. She's on the edge of a breakdown. Then Peter came into the room.

"What is it Mary? What can I do for you?" Peter asked.

She was stammering and could not get out what she wanted to say. My sister Martha came forward with a cup of water, she took the cup with both hands and drank the water greedily. When she had finished, Mary put a comforting arm around her, this seemed to help. She stammered again but this time she managed to tell us her story.

Early that morning she had gone with friends to visit the Master's tomb. When they arrived at the entrance of the tomb they found the boulder had been moved. They went inside and found the remains of the burial cloth were on the floor of the cave. All at once there was a flash of light and then a brighter light came from the back of the tomb. As the light grew more intense, a figure appeared dressed all in white. She said it was hard to keep focussed on the man as the light was so intense. He was the most beautiful man she had ever seen. The man told them that the Master had gone; his voice seemed to come from all around the cave. She felt if she had listened any longer her eardrums would have burst. They went outside as they could not stand it any longer; there they met a man whom they assumed was the gardener. As their eyes had not adjusted from the bright light they did not recognize the Master and asked him where they had taken the Master's body. Before he answered, Mary realized it was him. He told them he had come back from the dead as he had foretold them he would and that he would see us all very soon.

When she had finished her story Mary said, "I told you all he would come back."

Thomas interrupted, "She is totally mad. The woman has gone crazy. Nobody can take the ranting of a mad woman seriously. I for one will not believe he has come back from the dead until I can feel the holes the nails made in his hands and put my own hand into his side where the spear has been."

His conversation was brought to an abrupt end when the Master's mother walked into the room. She was informed of Mary Magdalene's story and it was decided that Peter and some of the others would go to the tomb to investigate. If you have read your bible you will know the outcome.

After that there were many more sightings of the Master, including many by straight-thinking men; people you would not assume to be taken in easily or to tell such a far-fetched story if it were not true. Thomas would still not believe and not only that, he would belittle anyone who did. I had always liked Thomas, he was a good looking man with a great dress sense and a wicked dry humour, but he was now definitely getting on my nerves. Up until this time I had not seen the Master, if I was to put my hand on my heart at that time I could not have sworn that I believed Jesus of Nazareth had risen from the dead. I wanted to believe but I was not one hundred percent sure. I did think that if people believed they had seen him who was I to doubt them, at the very least they were getting comfort from this at a difficult time. What annoyed me was Thomas, what right did he have to belittle them?

That night, after our evening meal, the same old question kept coming back. What do we do? John spoke up, "We should go out and tell people that he is back."

Before the crucifixion, John's opinions were never sought and when occasionally given, were never held in high regard. He was the youngest of our group and so he was looked down on a little. 'You've a lot to learn young man', I heard on many occasions.

However, after the way he conducted himself at the crucifixion, the way he stood tall and firm looking back at the mob as if to say, 'I am a follower of Jesus come and do your worst,' and holding Mary as she watched her son die on the cross while the rest of us were conspicuous by absence, this time the people were listening when he spoke. But not Thomas, he was still denouncing it all. Then, all at once, the Master appeared. It was impossible, there was no one downstairs and the front entrance to the shop was locked, the door to the upper room was bolted, no one had moved from the table but somehow the Master was in the room with us. To say we were startled was an understatement.

Peter spoke, "Master, is that really you?"

"Yes Peter, I am here." Jesus looked around the room, his gaze stopped at Thomas. "Thomas, I think you wanted to ask me something. Is that not true?"

There was complete silence; you could have heard a pin drop. He repeated the question.

"Is there something you wanted to ask?" Again silence. "Don't you want to put your fingers into the nail holes in my hand? Don't you want to put your hand into my side where the spear has been?" He then looked directly at me, I instantly flushed but he just averted his eyes back to Thomas.

Thomas ran towards him crying and said, "My Lord and my God."

Jesus just said, "You have seen, happy are those who have not seen, yet believed."

When I look back on that time, from the point when Mary Magdalene first met him at the tomb till the night that he appeared in the upper room, I believe it had been a deliberate test. He had only come back to a chosen few at first; he had wanted to test the rest of us to see if we believed he was back without actually seeing him. If it was a test then to their credit, my sisters had passed; I again to my shame had failed.

So how can I now criticize you who have lost their faith or never had faith in the first place? Because I was brought back from the dead and I still doubted. So for those of you who believe with all your heart without the proof for your own eyes, I salute you and envy you, for your place is secure in the everlasting kingdom. After that night, there was no doubt in our company at all. We didn't realize at the time that the Holy Spirit had put his hands on us. We all knew what we had to do when the Master was gone, so at that time we were enjoying his company, it was as you say a learning curve for us all. Eventually, the Master did return to his father on the day of his ascension into heaven. There was no sadness on my part just gratitude for the knowledge he had given me, the privilege of having known the Son of God when he walked as a man on this earth.

A week after the ascension turned out to be the final day I was to see my sisters in this life. It was planned that I would travel overland to the sea port of Caesarea and then take the first available boat to the isle of Cyprus. My sisters were to stay in Jerusalem in my shop with Jacob and his family. The shop was to become our link with each other when we would reach our individual destinations. We were to send regular correspondence regarding our progress back to the shop where Mary and Martha would copy the letters and send them back to everyone. That way, we would know how everybody was getting on with our own ultimate goal of converting people to the ways Jesus had taught us in the places we were sent. It did not matter how long it took, we were not to leave our given destination until the goal was completed.

Before I left for Paphos, I completed the sale of our family home in Bethesda, the proceeds going to our newly formed church of which Peter was now the head. I was sad to leave my sisters, especially Martha, we had always been close, and to know I would not see them again for a long time was hard to bear. If I had realised then that this was to be the last time I would see them it would have been impossible to leave. After saying goodbye to my sisters and my friends, there was a little sadness in my heart but also excitement as this was to be an adventure and I would be doing the Lord's work. It took me almost all day to reach Caesarea and another two days to arrange passage to Cyprus. I arrived at the little man made harbour at Paphos just before sunset. The island looked really beautiful in this light. I was looking forward to starting my work but the first thing I needed to do was to find somewhere to sleep. I had been befriended by a young sailor whose name was Edom. As if he read my mind, he asked if I had anywhere to stay. I told him no but that I would find an inn. He wouldn't hear of it.

"My mother would enjoy meeting you, come and stay with us," he said.

So when the boat finally docked, I went off with my new-found friend. It didn't take long to reach his home, a lovely typical Cypriot house set back from the harbour. Edom's mother met us at the door. She was a little woman, dressed head to toe in black. I guess like many women of these small fishing islands she had been made a widow by the sea. She hugged him for a long time. Eventually he pulled away and said,

"This is my friend Lazarus; I have invited him to stay with us."

She looked me up and down and said,

"You have got a kind face, I like you and any friend of my son's is a friend of mine. Come in my dear boy and sit down by the fire, it gets very cold this time of year when the sun goes down. You must be hungry; I'll fix you both something to eat." She was as good as her word and the food was excellent.

After our meal, we sat by the fire and chatted. It seemed that Edom's mother, Centura, was the island's 'wise woman' or what you would today call an herbalist. When I informed her of my mission she just laughed out loud.

"Not more Gods, I'm sick of Gods. I don't believe in Gods, I believe in Mother Nature. If you respect her she will look after and feed you. Even when you are unwell, she supplies the right plants to heal you."

"I see I will have my work cut out with you." I said jokingly.

It was decided I was to lodge with Centura for a while as Edom was to go to his boat early next morning and would be away for a week or so, as they were sailing into deep waters and when they had made their catch of fish would sail on to the mainland to sell them. He told me it would be a personal favour to him if I would stay on and look after his mother. So over the next few days I got to know Centura. One evening at our evening meal we sat by the fire talking when a visitor came, Centura's services were required. A child in the next village was very ill and needed her help. I told her I would come with her to guide her back.

"You guide me back on my own island? That I would like to see," she said with a smile.

It took nearly an hour to reach the small village as most of the journey was uphill and hard going on the small donkey owned by Centura. When we did eventually arrive, the child had grown worse. Centura got to work at once while I saw to the donkey. When I returned, she had made a quick assessment of the child and discovered an infected wound on the young girl's leg. In Centura's opinion, the poison had gone too far in the child's system and the only solution was to cut off her leg. Even then she was not sure the child would live, she only knew the girl would die if she did nothing. When Centura told the parents, the mother cried out but seemed resigned to her daughter's fate if it would keep her alive. The father would not hear of it.

"How will I marry my daughter off with only one leg?"

"If I do not take off her leg, you will not have a daughter at all to marry off," Centura replied.

"Then so be it, she is in the hands of the Gods," the girl's father said.

"You stupid man, why have you sent for me if you won't take my advice? You may as well pray for your useless Gods; I give up with people like you." Centura stormed out of the house towards her donkey, and I ran after her.

"Can you not save the child; is there nothing you can do for her?" I asked.

"No, unfortunately that tantrum by me that you witnessed in there was my last gamble, I had hoped the father would come after me," she replied.

"What about the plants you gave me to put into my bag?" I said hopefully.

"You're right Lazarus, the herbs. We can't save her but we could ease her passage into the land of the dead, go bring them to me and I will get a pot of boiling water," she said.

I ran as fast as my legs would carry me to where the donkey was grazing. I stopped for a moment when I realized she was going to kill the child. How could I let that happen? Then again how could I watch the child die in agony? I prayed quickly to my Lord for help. Then I put my hand blindly into the donkey saddle bag to obtain my own bag and walked back to the house. Centura had the water boiling on the fire. I put my hand into the bag; to my surprise the herbs were wet. Something in my bag must have leaked. For the life of me I could not think what it was. The bag was full of my silversmith tools and a small amount of silver. Don't ask why I had brought them with me on this errand of mercy, but I did. As I passed the herbs to Centura she said,

"There is blood on these herbs, have you cut yourself Lazarus? Never mind, it does not matter about the blood for what I'm going to use these for, it will be of no consequence."

I was still looking for where the blood had come from as she took the rest of the herbs. I went to the other end of the room where there was another light but could not find a wound or open sore on my person. I emptied the contents of my bag onto the floor. As I had thought the bag had contained the tools and silver but I had forgotten about the pouch with the spear in it that had pierced my Master's side. It was covered in blood. I checked the outside of the bag, thinking maybe the donkey was injured, but the outside of the bag was clean. The blood was coming from the pouch. It can't be my Master's blood, I thought, there wasn't that much blood on the spear. I couldn't think straight. I put all the contents back into my bag, set it down and begun to pray.

After a time, I went over to see how the child was doing. Centura looked perplexed and as I looked at the child, I understood why. Far from being on the brink of death, she was sleeping peacefully. Centura excused herself from the parents and came towards me. She indicated for me to go outside with her.

"Are you a sorcerer Lazarus? If not, then I have no explanation for what just happened in there. I gave that child enough poison to kill a camel and yet she is not dead, far from it, she is sleeping peacefully. That wasn't blood on the herbs was it?"

I explained the story regarding the spear. When I had finished she said nothing, she just turned and walked back into the house. I followed and watched her go over to the child and take off the bandage covering her leg. She then let out a gasp, and her hands were shaking.

"I don't believe what I'm seeing."

I moved forward to look at the child's leg. The wound was no longer there. Centura came to me, held my bag with both hands, kissed it and said,

"Your Master truly was the Messiah."

That night I told Centura and the family the complete story of Jesus of Nazareth and we stayed the night at the house. The next morning, the villagers woke thinking they would be attending a funeral but instead witnessed the first set of christenings on the island. Centura and the family became the first people I had the pleasure and privilege of converting into followers of the teachings of Jesus of Nazareth, the Son of God.

The word of miraculous recovery spread like wildfire all over the island. Every illness and injury was brought for my attention; even sick animals were brought to be cured. It seemed like every week I was performing christenings and afterwards families in question would hold a party. So yes, nearly two thousand years ago, Cyprus was definitely a party island; what with visiting the sick of the island and holding christenings all the time, I scarcely had time to write to my sisters regarding my progress, or read the letters they sent from my fellow missionaries. Although, I always found time to read the personal letters from my sisters. I was really enjoying myself on the island, but I did miss my sisters, especially Martha. The stories she wrote me about Amos, the things that the cheeky chap was getting up to - it was definitely true, you don't realize what you have until it's gone.

One day, Centura said to me,

"I'm going to take you on a trip to the top of the island. It's lovely there this time of year and you can meet a friend of mine who's a shepherd. He lives there with his young son."

The journey on the way up was hard but very rewarding because the higher we got the better the view. I marvelled at the stamina of my companion, she was definitely a tough old bird. When we came across the first stragglers from the flock, we could tell something was wrong. As we travelled further we found carcasses that the wolves had left uneaten.

"Oziel must be very sick to let this happen," Centura said.

It didn't take long to locate the problem. We heard the barking of one of Oziel's dogs, we homed in on the sound and followed it to the edge of a small cliff. The dog was obviously upset, barking and looking down over the cliff. While Centura was settling the dog I looked over the edge and saw a small lamb that was bleating. It was perched on a small ledge just out of my reach. I stretched over and to my horror saw the body of the shepherd below. From my vantage point, I knew he was dead. It was the terrible position his body was in, and next to his side was the body of one of his dogs. By the look of the trail of the dry blood, the man must have fallen trying to rescue the lamb and the dog followed him. Injured, it dragged itself to his Master's side. I went back to Centura to inform her of what I had found.

"The spear, what about the spear?" she said excitedly.

I knew instantly that even this most sacred relic didn't have the power to bring anyone back from the dead, only God can grant that.

"What about the child? We must look for him," I said changing the subject.

So we left that sad scene for the time being. We made our way to the shepherd's home not knowing what we would find. As I opened the door, the first thing that hit me was the stench of urine and faeces. I half expected to find the child dead; we had no idea how long he had been alone in the place. At the end of the room was a large cot or what you would call a playpen today. My heart was in my mouth as I took the small journey across the room followed by Centura. To my relief what I saw was the most beautiful baby I had ever seen, with a mop of thick black hair, a pair of big, wide, beautiful brown eyes and a smile that went from ear to ear. From my limited experience with babies, I would say he was not a year old. The first thing he did was to lift up his arms to me and from that moment I knew I would love this child for the rest of my life. Centura came from behind me and took hold of the child.

"Come here my little love," she said taking him into her arms, "let's get you into some clean clothes and get some food into your belly."

Once again Centura took charge of the situation. It was decided that I would go and fetch the child's father and bury him next to his wife behind the house. But first

I was to milk a goat and slaughter a lamb. The child had no living relatives, so it was up to us to look after him and the flock. When the time was right, we would take the sheep to market and get the best price for them, as this was all the child had left in the world.

I got some rope I found in the shed, gathered food for the remaining dog and set off back to the cliff. When I arrived, the dog was still barking, it must have been exhausted but it had never left its Master. I gave it food and tried to settle it down as best I could. Now my problem was how I was going to get down there to the shepherd and retrieve his body. Luckily there was a sturdy tree not far from the edge. I could use it to secure the rope and lower myself down. With the help of the donkey I could create a pulley system to retrieve the shepherd's body and the lamb. I decided to rescue the lamb first to see if my idea would work. I lowered myself down, taking a second rope with me to tie around the lamb; I climbed back up, placed the rope around the tree and attached the end to the donkey. It was successful but getting down to the shepherd's body wouldn't be that easy. I eventually got down to the dead man but not without a few hazardous moments. I secured the body with the rope and climbed back up. It was hard going in the heat of the day. I did as I had done with the lamb and slowly brought the shepherd's body to the top of the cliff. I placed it on the donkey and was about to leave when I thought about the dead dog. I looked over the edge at the pitiful creature and thought its attempts to reach its Master should be rewarded with at least a burial, so I repeated the operation again to retrieve it.

When I returned to Centura and the baby, we buried the shepherd next to his wife who had died giving birth to the child. It was such a sad scene, the child played innocently unaware that these were his parents and he would never know or remember them. Life can be so cruel and although I had never met them, I could imagine them and the hopes and dreams they must have shared for their son. I prayed to God to take them into his care and let them know that as long as I live their son would know the love and protection of a parent. From this day I was a father. It filled my heart with such love; some things in life just feel so right. As I carried the boy back to the house he lay his head on my shoulder, for he too felt the bond.

I played with the baby as Centura set out the meal. I was really looking forward to it as I had worked as hard as my body would take. I could almost feel hunger and the need for a rest, something I hadn't felt since my resurrection. Whether this was real or psychological I do not know, I just knew that I had never had a craving for anything before, but there was no time to rest. Centura gave me a large sheep fleece made into a coat.

"You will need this tonight because it will get very cold out here while you keep the wolves from the sheep all night."

When she said those words it was like ice cold water had been put into my veins because it made me recall what the Master had said to me the night before his death. 'Keep the wolves from the sheep as long as you can Lazarus.' Surely this was not what my Master had in mind.

All through the summer, I worked hard but enjoyed it. During the day I would play with the baby, who was also coming on wonderfully under Centura's watchful eye, and at night I would look after the sheep. Every now and then, I did lose one or two sheep to my adversary, the wolf that is, up until that fateful night when I had a very hair-raising experience. Fighting off a pack of those big hairy animals was bad enough but when one of their members included a demon from the underworld, it was almost impossible.

Now when I look back on that occasion, I realise that it was the first duel with an unclean spirit. You see, the devil not only knows about every evil thing that is being done in the world, but every good thing. It seemed I had obviously come to his attention as he had sent one of his minions to destroy me and take the spear. After that I would always hide it on my person. One night, I was by the fire with my dog, who I had named Antonius because he reminded me of a Roman. He would go mad if you took anything off him, especially food, but he knew his duty, very Roman like. He stood to attention with his ears pricked up.

"What is up boy?" I said.

Then from out of the shadow of the fire came about ten wolves. The sheep were behind me so they were safe in a rock-made corral. The only way they could get to the sheep was to come through the fire, and that was the one thing they were scared of. At the helm of the pack was what I assumed to be the alpha male. He was terrifying, but it was his eyes that gave me the scare. They were blood red, like the Roman soldier at the crucifixion. At the time I thought it was fear or the fire light playing tricks with my mind! He came so close to the fire that his fur should have been scorched. He was making a very low frightening growling noise and the rest of the pack was howling. In one quick flash of a moment he had jumped over the fire and was on top of me before I could arm myself. I could hear the yelping sound of Antonius; he was being attacked by the other wolves. I thought 'this is where it ends being eaten alive'. It felt so disappointing to die like that, not to see my sisters again, and I felt a great sadness that I would not see my baby growing to be a man. I had grown to love him that much. The pain from the wolves' teeth become too much to take; there seemed nothing I could do. The alpha male was pinning me down to the floor but I managed to reach out my arm to my bag. I fumbled around and found the spear. It may be too late to save me but at least I could send this demon back to hell, how apt. I took hold of the spear and with my remaining strength, plunged it into the wolf's side. It let out an almighty yelp and then fell off me. At that instant, the rest of the pack stopped their attack and retreated. Then up trotted Antonius; none the worse for his battle, he began to lick my face. 'What use was that, to a dying man?' I thought as I lay there for a few moments not wanting to touch my wounds? When I did eventually pluck up the courage to feel them, I didn't have any injuries at all, only torn clothing where I had been bitten. I turned to the dead wolf to look at its eyes but they were normal and more to the point looking right back at me, it was still alive. The eyes were no longer frightening, they had a look of apathy about them and I was surprised to find the animal was not injured. After what seemed like a long time, it got up and trotted out of the camp. I did see it again but it never went for my sheep, in fact it become an outcast from the pack. I even tried to feed it but it just refused all offers of food.

When the time came to move the flock down to market, I went to the town to recruit some men. With their expert help we had no trouble in bringing down the flock. When we arrived at the market, Centura introduced me to Nicholas, who was a larger-than-life character, very bubbly with long hair and a beard.

"I have heard about you, you are the man with the magic spear? Could you use it on my wife to make her beautiful? No, don't tell me. It's powers are not that strong?" he said laughing.

Centura informed me that Nicholas was the head man of the town, or what you would call today the Mayor. He was also an expert when it came to sheep, so we put them in his capable hands and hoped he would get the best price for them. Once again, Centura was right; Nicholas achieved a really good price for the flock.

A meeting took place about the child's future. All the elders of the village were present and it would be up to them to decide what was best for the child. I spoke to them and told them how I loved the child and wanted to bring him up myself. They were all quite surprised as it was very unusual for a man to request this. They were not keen on this as they thought that every child should have a mother.

"Yes, where possible I agree but surely the most important thing a child needs is love and I do love him with all my heart," I said.

I began to panic at the thought that they would take him away from me. It didn't seem to matter what I said, they were not very keen on the idea. It's funny how no one questions a man's love for his natural child even if he is not a very good father, but if they could have felt what I did for the child they would have known there was no difference to me. Just when I thought all was lost, Centura spoke up for me.

"You all know me," she began, "I'm no fool, I've been with these two all summer, watched them together, seen the love and bond they have developed. Lazarus is a good man, no; he is an exceptionally good man. I'm as sure of him as I am my own son. He has become like a son to me and I too love the child like he was my grandson, so he will not be short of a mother's love. I ask you not just for Lazarus but for me too. The child has already lost two parents, don't let him lose another."

As she ended her speech, I looked at her, smiling - she was right. Over that summer we had become a family and as happy as any other. Eventually, after much debating, I was allowed to adopt the child, I was his father and no one could take him away. We held a big party; everyone on the island was invited. In front of all the villagers I christened him Nathaniel. In my eyes, no man in the history of the world could have had a finer son than that boy. Now it was my job to make his nest egg into something worthwhile. With the proceeds from the sale of the flock I decided to buy a house with a shop. I was no shepherd, farmer nor fisherman, the only way I knew how to make a living was as a silversmith, so that's what I did. When Nathaniel was old enough I would teach him the trade, he would be secure. Centura came to live with us; she sold her house and gave the proceeds from it to her son to put towards the purchase of a boat of his own. The rest of the money he needed came from Nathaniel's inheritance. So at the grand old age of two, he was the co-owner of a merchant vessel. Edom was the captain and the boat was named the Paphos Fish. The fish was a reference to the Christian connection. With all that was going on, I had not forgotten about my mission.

Donations were made by islanders and with that I started to build a church.

As the weeks turned into months and the months into years, I watched my son grow. Never a day went by when he would not do or say something that would make me proud. I know I sound like an overbearing father, but I say to you if you are a parent, 'Cherish every minute of every day that you are with your child because you are a long time without them.' I miss the good man Nathaniel turned out to be but I miss the child more.

I wrote regularly to my sisters regarding the process about the church and their new nephew. They both longed to meet him and how I wish now that they had taken the time to make the journey, why do we put off things we should do until another day? Take a bit of advice from a very old man, live each day as you were going to live for hundreds of years but also as if each day could be your last. I was so busy with the church and the business that I couldn't spare the time to go visit my sisters. 'Maybe next year,' I would say. Edom's boat business was going great. He would take all kinds of cargo from island to island or to the mainland just as long as it made a profit and it did. After three years, Nathaniel had doubled his initial investment.

Then one fateful day, I received a letter that would change my life completely. Through it I gained the love of my life but lost the childhood of my son. Even now my heart grows heavy at the thought that she is not here. It was one of the best and worse things that could have happened to me. All because of one letter. The contents of the letter appertained to Paul and although I had never met him, I read his letter that my sisters had sent with great interest. It seemed Paul had been imprisoned in

Ephesus; a fight had broken out after one of Paul's lectures at the Great Theatre of Ephesus. I had to go and see if I could help, so I left the shop in the capable hands of Tolga. He was in his late forties and had been a shipmate of Edom's for many years. Their seafaring life had become too much for him and he needed other work. He was from the village in Tarsus and had been originally trading as a silversmith before the lure of the sea had called. I had worked with him for over a year now, he was a natural, and he had not forgotten anything. He could easily manage the business on his own and if needs be he could train Nathaniel. So that was sorted. I said my goodbye to Centura but the hard part was trying to say goodbye to my son.

"Please take me with you father, I can protect you and fight off your enemies," he pleaded.

It would have been so easy to take him, I wanted to be with my son every hour of every day but in those days the world was a very dangerous place. Making a journey didn't always mean you would reach your destination. More importantly though, was that Centura loved Nathaniel like a son. She had already lost her own son to the sea and you can not in all honesty deprive a mother from her son. So with a sad heart, I departed from Paphos. What I did not realize was that I was departing from my son's childhood forever.

The sea journey to Ephesus turned out to be uneventful. It was my first visit to the city and to see it was breathtaking. Jerusalem was a busy city but nowhere near as cosmopolitan as this. The magnificence of the Roman architecture could be seen way off from the shore. As we came into the harbour I was fascinated by the people. There were so many different races that it seemed as if there was a representative of every nation on the earth.

"They are mostly slaves doing the household shopping," Edom said.

Then my attention was caught by the most beautiful creature I had ever seen. She had light coloured hair that when the sun shone on it, it would look like gold. Edom said,

"She's probably an Angle or a Celt from the far north."

But if you were to ask me then to describe an angel then it would have been just like her. Before my Master had called on me from my tomb, I had been a user of women, what today you would call a lady's man. I could have never settled for one woman. If I saw a young woman I wanted I had to have her, whether she was high born, low slave, free, married or single. The act of copulation drove me on, some were easier than others to seduce but in the end they would all eventually fall for my charms. I am now bitterly ashamed of the way I behaved and the hearts that I broke. If I could speak to those girls today I would beg for their forgiveness. There is a saying, 'What goes around, comes around.' For however long they carried their broken hearts, I have carried mine for nearly two thousand years, so I have got what I deserved.

In all the years since my resurrection, I have never had a sexual feeling. I did like the chase and was still a flirt, old habits die hard. But unlike the hungry fox, I would always let the chicken go after the chase, before she came to any harm. But the feelings I felt for this young girl were different. She took my breath away, even on that first day if she had asked for the world and I would have give it to her had it been in my power. Through the ages I have known people who, because of love, have given up their families, even betrayed their country. I knew one man who gave up his throne. The sad thing is love can exist one-way; it's wonderful if it is returned but it can still survive on its own.

'Pull yourself together, you are here for a purpose and even if you were not, she is far too young for you, you are in your thirties and by the looks of that girl she is not yet twenty,' I said to myself. You can give advice to a person and if they are sensible they will digest your information then act accordingly, but not to a person's heart, it is a stubborn organ, with what seems like a mind of its own.

She was with two small children, unlike her; they were well dressed and high born, probably the children of her master. I could tell by the way they looked at her that they loved her and she loved them in return. I had to get this girl out of my mind and do the job I had come to do and get back to Nathaniel.

There was a Christian community in Ephesus; it had gone underground since the riot. Edom, like his mother, took charge of the situation. He had a contact named Quintus Memmius; he was the chief scribe to the Roman Procurator and also a secret Christian. He lived in a fashionable two-storey house in a district where only high level citizens lived. The house over-looked the site of the new theatre. Quintus took us out onto a fine terrace overlooking the construction. We were given food and wine.

"Can you imagine what it will look like when it's finished, but unfortunately we will not be here," Quin-tus sighed. "Now gentlemen, what can I do for you?"

We told him why we were there, he in return informed us about Paul, who was now safe and had left Ephesus. The problem was started coincidently by a silversmith named Demetrius who caused the riot for commercial reasons. Demetrius made his living making silver images of a female deity. If a new religion flourished, he thought he would be out of work. He hired some ex-soldiers to start a fight. To regain order on the street, the Roman Procurator decided there should be no more Christian gatherings.

"A bit of Jewish diplomacy was needed," I said.

So armed with a bag of gold, I went off to see Demetrius, using the directions given to me by Quintus. I found the shop and went inside; I can only describe him as an ugly old man, small with a large protruding nose rather like the stereotypical Jewish minister you see now in films. I took off my silver chain which had a silver fish hung on it; I had it made in my shop. I asked him for a price to make ten exactly the same.

He said while examining it, "Ten dinar. What is it by the way?"

I informed him that it was a Christian symbol and that I usually have five hundred made but it seems it's being made illegal for me to preach here.

"It's a pity, for the more I convert, the more money you would have made. Not to worry, I'll just have to go somewhere else and make them rich instead," I said smiling.

I went back to Quintus' house and informed both him and Edom of what took place. I told them there would be no more interventions by Demetrius.

"It seems you have ensnared a fox. I will see the Procurator first thing in the morning. He is a good man and not unsympathetic to the Christian cause but by

Roman law he has to keep the peace. I am certain now that we can guarantee there will be no more trouble, he will lift the ban. But now gentleman, will you do me the privilege and be my guest while you are in Ephesus," Quintus said.

Now fate or God played its hand because in walked the young girl from the harbour. It seemed Quintus was her master. My legs went weak, my heart fluttered and I think I flushed a little. Why was this happening to me at my age? I was acting like a teenager. She told me her real name, Orpha, but at her christening by Paul she had taken the name Anna. She had been made a slave at the age of about five, and she could still remember seeing her father being killed, then she was dragged from her mother's arms. I felt so sorry for her. If I could have gone back into the past and stopped it from happening to her, I would have. I yearned to put my arms around her and never let her go. She came to all my lectures and would sit in the front and hang on my every word. I think she was as taken by me as I was with her. When we were back at her master's house, she would ask me to tell her more about Jesus and about Nathaniel.

Paul had left Timothy in charge of the church at Ephesus so I was not needed. The time had come for me to return to Nathaniel, I missed him so much. I also felt I could not leave Anna. I knew it would be selfish to ask her to marry me, I would be taking away her youth but I could not help myself; I wanted to be with her for the rest of my life. When I asked her to marry me, she accepted and with Quintus' blessing she became my wife at the age of twenty.

The day after our wedding we set sail for Cyprus and Nathaniel. On the voyage back, we kept very close to the shoreline. We had heard there were pirates operating in the area. It would take longer but if we did spot pirates, we could move into shallow waters where they could not follow. You see, the Paphos Fish had a flatter bottom than most boats. During the day, Anna and I would take in the view. It was like a honeymoon cruise, and I would lie at night and watch her sleep. I'd smell her hair and marvel at how beautiful she was. How I wished I had never had any other woman in my life. At the brief moment in time I had never been more content. I was doing the Master's work; I had a beautiful wife and a wonderful son. I felt so happy my heart could have burst, everything in my world was right so I say to you, dear reader, look at a beautiful rainbow and enjoy it while it lasts. Don't go through your life moaning about what you've not got, just look at what you have and enjoy it because I'm afraid, my friend, nothing lasts forever. Even I will die one day soon but I look forward to it because if I go to heaven, I think I will recognize one Angel at least.

On the third day, we left the shoreline and headed into open waters for the final leg of the journey but this is when the devil intervened. Out of the sun, like a big black bird of prey came the pirate's ship. She was on us before we could change course to head inland. Edom and his crew put up a good fight but it was impossible for us to win. We were outnumbered five to one, and I was knocked unconscious early on in the engagement but not before seeing my good friend Edom go far too early to meet his maker. When I came to, I was lying on the deck being attended by Balaam, Edom's second-in-command, and there seemed to be only six of us left. We were surrounded by a bunch of mean looking pirates. I wanted to get up to find my Anna but I was restrained by Balaam.

Two pirates were having a big argument at the far end of the ship.

"I thought you were dead. The blow you took would have killed most men. See the big man over there, I think he wants to kill us all, he's the one that hit you, in fact he killed nearly everyone single handed. I have never seen anything like it in my life," Balaam whispered.

I had an uncomfortable feeling that I knew this man. I was wondering where Anna was and as if to read my mind, the big man turned to me and smiled,

"Don't worry Lazarus, I will find her a good home."

I couldn't understand, it was the Roman soldier from the crucifixion, the beast. How did he know my name? I looked in the direction he was pointing and saw Anna, she was still on the Paphos Fish. I was on the pirate's vessel. The big man wanted to kill us before he left but the captain needed us as his galley slaves.

"No doubt we will meet again," he shouted as he jumped aboard our boat.

They say the eyes are the window to your soul and as I looked into his I somehow knew he did not have one. As I looked across at Anna, I am not ashamed to say I cried. I have got to be honest, I did wonder if Anna married me for love or to escape slavery. That terrible day I found out the truth, I know that she loved me up till the end of her life. As any bereaved lover will tell you; while the thought of knowing that you were dearly loved will not mend a broken heart, it certainly eases the pain a little. How did I know for certain she loved me? Because as she was being dragged away by the pirate, I could see her lips moving. I had thought at the time I was lip reading but I could hear her voice as clearly as if she was whispering in my ear. She was praying to the Lord asking nothing for her, only for me and Nathaniel, 'Lord, whatever fate awaits me, let your will be done. But I beg you, don't let them hurt him and one day please return him to his rightful place, beside his son.' When she had finished, she blew a kiss and pointed upwards with her hand. I was never to see her again in this life.

We were dragged off to the bottom of the ship and chained to the oars. Each day we were fed stale bread and a sort of soup made from left over fish heads. Once a week we were taken from the galley up onto the deck and washed down with sea water. Our captain was not being humane; there was no philanthropy about his actions. He was a realist, the healthier his galley slaves were, the faster his ship would go. This enabled him to avoid the Romans' warships that patrolled the area, as even the predator can become the prey. It was at one of these weekly inspections that I lost another friend, Balaam. After being washed, he was found to be suffering from a skin infection. Whether they thought it was contagious or they just needed a victim for their games I do not know. They tied a rope around Balaam's waist and his legs were slashed with a knife. Then he was lowered into the water and it didn't take long for the sharks to sense the blood. In those days 'Mare Internum' which is the Mediterranean, had its fair share of sharks. Man's inhumanity to man never ceases to amaze me. To kill a man is one thing; to make a sport out of it is cruel and evil. Eventually, all my companions died either by being thrown to the sharks or from natural causes. New faces came and died including the crew, I completely lost track of time. I had no idea what year it was. My only hope was that a Roman warship would come along and catch us. We would be sunk and although it would result

in the end of my life, it would be the end of my misery...
or so I thought.

My day of deliverance did eventually come; it started
with us being whipped to increase the speed. I could hear
the panic-stricken voices above. The next thing I felt was
an almighty jolt, then a crashing noise and then I saw it,
the front end of a ram which was attached to the bow of
a ship. It was in the shape of some Roman god. So I knew
who the vessel belonged to. I could hear the screams as
the water level rose, but for the first time in my life, I was
not afraid. I said a prayer to my Lord and prepared to
meet my maker. I know what you are thinking, how long
did it take for the penny to finally drop with me? Right?
I had been brought back from the dead, I met with
demons, and I had seen miracles, everyone around me
died. Why could I not see? Because I tried to rationalize
everything. I was not dead; I could have been in a coma.
The Roman soldier could have deserted and joined the
pirates. I must have only winded the wolf with the blunt
end of the spear. I can only say in my defence, what if
Jesus came back today, would you believe? If he told you
he was the Son of God and performs miracles on live television, I bet ninety-five percent of you would say it was a
trick of the cameras. Don't you see, life is a test to see if
you truly believe without definite proof. Take the last
millennium, I witnessed rich men give away their
fortunes because they thought the end of the world was
coming, only to want it back when it didn't. Life is like a
plane flight, some people like flying, some people worry
themselves sick. It's just the journey; it's the holiday destination you are going to that's important. So I say to you
enjoy your life but don't cling to material things of this
world; your house, your car, your holiday home. Don't

cheat people; if someone does you harm you think the big man among you will sort them out and make it right, but the biggest man among you will forgive. That's the only way to stop the cycle. I don't profess to know all the answers, I don't know the secret of life, and I wasn't given a manual with this job. If I have a problem I can't phone head office, I can only pray to be guided on the right path, like you can. I don't even know why God gave me the love of my life only to be snatched away. Maybe he wanted me to really love someone from outside my family. I feel there is only one kind of love. If you really love a person you would die for them and you would forgive them anything, like the saviour of the world did for us. Love is such a misused word. I heard the story of a woman who loved her husband and children up to when he had an affair, then she went out, bought a gun and killed him making her children fatherless. In the eighteenth century, I was once a defence attorney in France. My client told me he killed his wife because she was going to leave him for another man. He told me he loved her that much and that if he could not have her then no one could. You don't keep a beautiful butterfly in a jar because it will die; you admire it in your garden for however brief the moment and you let it go. Don't get me wrong, I've been no saint, I've misused the word love too. I once told a young married woman that I loved her but if I had I would not have made her an adulteress; I would have let her go.

The only thing I know for certain is that on the day when my ship was sinking, I wanted to die. Like a plant in the desert craves water I craved to die. Through the centuries when things got too much for me, I would find a cave to hibernate like an animal. I would come out after a few years when I smelled the dew on the grass, could see the lambs in the field, feel the sun on my face, the wind in my hair, see a fantastic sunset, sit up all night watching the stars in heaven, then everything would be surpassed by a magnificent sunrise and I would be very glad to be alive but always wished Anna could have been by my side. Someone said, that when God made the earth, he created man so he could admire his design or just maybe he didn't like to be on his own. I tended to breeze into people's lives when I need company and then blow out like the wind before I could put down my roots. During the centuries I have flirted with young women, and even contemplating remarrying, but how could I stand in front of God and pledge my heart and body to someone? It would not have been a marriage only a facsimile because there would be no heart in it. That was given to a young girl with golden-coloured hair over a thousand years ago. But what I did notice was that when I came out of my self imposed hibernations more than a normal amount of natural disasters had taken place. Perhaps this was my test. The more dismayed I become about my fellow man, the more the earth turns on herself. Did my Master mean this when he told me to keep the wolf from his sheep? If that is the case, Lord send some-one else more worthy than I because I'm too old, too tired and too weak. If the fate of the world has to rest on one man's shoulders, let it be a better man than me.

CHAPTER SIX

The Out of The World Overhead Kick

Now where were we? Yes that's right, the boys had just re-met their long lost old friend, the friend they thought had died in a high speed police chase in a stolen BMW, the friend whose body had been fried like a crisp in the burnt out car, the friend whose body they believed they'd watched disappear behind the curtains at the crematorium twelve months previously. Although their eyes were taking in the image of their friend it had not quite registered with their brains. We know that twelve months ago they had all lost the guardianship of their Angels, although they had not been totally abandoned by their Sentries, who would still be whispering words of warning. Unfortunately only one of the young men was listening.

All three lads stood transfixed to the spot unable to move or speak, and after a few moments Tiger or the thing they believed to be Tiger broke the silence.

"Suppose you're wondering what the hell's going on?" he asked followed by an almost silent chuckle.

The barely audible laugh sent a chill down Stanie's spine and he assumed it had a similar affect on the others as still none of them were able to speak.

"Well I'll take the silence as a yes then," Tiger said.

He then leant back against the phone box that was on the bridge and started to regale his boyhood friends with his version of the events on the night of the accident.

He said that they'd pissed him off big time when they'd refused to get in the car. He decided to go 'posh' so drove off at speed up the A6 through Stockport Town Centre towards Hazel Grove, as there would be less police presence in that direction. When he got up near Stepping Hill hospital he'd noticed a hitchhiker at the side of the road, and feeling like a bit of company after the rejection from his best mates he pulled over and picked the lad up. The hitchhiker explained that he'd been on a night out with friends from work who'd left him behind when he'd got lucky with a girl in the Bamboo nightclub. It was only when the girl failed to return from the toilet that he realised that she'd had it off with his wallet. He lived in Buxton and was genuinely relieved when I told him I was heading that way and would be delighted to drop him off home. As we entered New Mills he'd spotted a police car starting to tail them. Knowing my recorded I knew if I got caught I'd be looking at a stretch in Strangeways so when the police car started to flash me I had no option but to put my foot down and try and shake them off. As the thing inside Tiger was talking, in the boys' mind a film was playing. As the tale was being unfolded, it was so real, it actually felt to the boys like they were there. It was being narrated directly into the boys' subconscious along these lines.

The chase seemed to last for hours but in fact it must have only been twenty minutes or so, while his reluctant passenger sat silently beside him. The roads were quiet at that time of night as they sped through Offerton, Marple and Romiley. He managed to lose the Police car as they entered Bredbury and for the first time since it started his passenger spoke.

"Drop me off anywhere mate. I've had enough fun for one night, I'll make my own way back to Buxton," he'd said.

Tiger told them how that had pissed him off, he was doing this lad a favour and that's how he repaid him. He agreed to drop him off in Stockport Town Centre but for one last thrill he put his foot down as he sped down Stockport Road on his way back into Stockport Town Centre. Unfortunately this rush of blood to the head had been his downfall, and as he reached the lights at the entrance to Vernon Park at the junction of New Zealand Road and Newbridge Lane he lost control of the car. He tried to brake and steer the car down Newbridge Lane but he'd taken the junction too fast and the car hit the railing and headed towards the Goyt River. There hadn't been much rain recently and the river was low, there was a sandy bank exposed in the middle of the river and unbelievably the car landed upside down there. He was fine, just a few cuts and bruises.

"Bloody Hell that was fun wasn't it," he'd said to the hitchhiker. "In the words of Elvis himself, I'm all shook up."

He'd laughed at his own joke but stopped as soon as he turned and looked at his passenger. The impact of the crash must have broken his neck or something because he was dead. Tiger sat hanging upside down in the wrecked BMW when he formed one of his cunning plans. The lad was about the same height and build as him. If he was to put all his own personal belongings on the body, then move it over to the driver seat then set fire to the car he'd be out of bother with the law and it would gets some very heavy people off his back.

Tiger then told his mates about a drug deal he'd been mixed up in that had gone pear-shaped. He was into this gang for thousands of pounds and if they caught up with him it would have been curtains for him.

He knew he had to act fast so he released his seat belt then did the same with the dead lad. It was easy to shift the body beneath the steering wheel; it would look to the police like he'd not been wearing a seat belt. He removed all the lad's personal belongings and replaced them with his own, then crawled out through the window into the ice-cold river. Although the river levels were unusually low the current of the Goyt was still strong as it headed towards the River Tame to form the River Mersey, and he had to hold onto the car as he fished around his pocket for his lighter. He could smell petrol over the stench of the river so he knew it would be easy to torch the car if he could find his lighter. He eventually did then struggled to his feet on the bank, stood as far away as possible then tossed the lighter onto the petrol tank; the explosion forced him backwards like the firework all those years ago. He smiled and looked at Stanie.

"Only you weren't there to save me this time mate."

He must have blanked out for a few minutes, probably a combination of the accident and the explosion because the next thing he remembered was clinging to the far side of the river bank with the heat of the fire searing the hairs on the back of his neck. He managed to pull himself up and slip away before the emergency services arrived. The body in the car was burnt to a crisp so badly that his Dad only identified it as Tiger by the rings and chain on the body.

As the film show stopped playing in Stanie's mind he felt like he had just been short-changed at the cinema (great action, but just too unbelievable to be real)

To Stanie now, what was more incredible than the film show he had just seen in his mind's eye, was the reaction of OB and Jay. They seemed to have swallowed this garbage hook line and sinker!

"What about fingerprints or dental records?" Stanie remarked sceptically to the thing pretending to be Tiger.

"What about fingerprints and fucking dental records - you joined the C.I.D. since I've been away?" said the thing inside Tiger menacingly.

For the first time in his life Stanie was genuinely scared of Tiger. He stared into his eyes and for one brief moment he could have sworn they were red with anger. Something was definitely not right here and he now realised it would be prudent to keep his thoughts to himself until he had a chance to talk to the boys on their own away from Tiger or whatever was pretending to be Tiger. OB had always been gullible, easily led, a sandwich short of a picnic but surely Jamie would realise that what they just been told was a load of rubbish.

"I'm like the Phoenix that rises from the bleeding ashes, back to me best mates and all you can do is quiz me about fucking fingerprints and shit," bellowed doppelganger staring directly at Stanie.

Almost as quickly as the rage had appeared it disappeared, his smile returned and he stepped forward and hugged Stanie.

"God you don't know how much I've missed you, you little bastard," he said still holding Stanie tight to his chest.

Stanie was rigid with fear at first but not wanting to antagonise Tiger he returned the hug and smiled back at him. He looked at Tiger's smiling face and for one brief moment he was happy to have his friend back, then he remembered the story and the feeling soon faded. Tiger released Stanie from the hug but placed his arms around his shoulders and began leading him to Stich Lane. The other two lads followed them to the end of the road where they stopped next to a top of the range BMW, you could tell from the gleam of the metallic green car that it was new.

"It's for you Stanie," said Tiger, "a thank-you for saving my life all those years ago."

Stanie's stare alternated between the car and Tiger.

"You haven't changed have you Mr Honest," teased Tiger "Don't worry it's all above board, look your name's on the log book," he said as he opened the passenger door and leant into the car to open the glove compartment. "Jump in lads and I'll fill in the blanks from after the accident to now."

As all four lads settled into the BMW, Stanie behind the wheel with Tiger next to him and the others in the back, Tiger continued his story. He told them that after he'd fled the scene of the accident he'd started walking, trying to gather his thoughts. By the time he'd come to his sense and his clothes where dry he was at Stockport's main train station. He waited for the ticket office to open then took the first early morning train to London. He didn't want to bore them with the details but he'd got involved in several lucrative business opportunities, he didn't say it but they knew that these opportunities must have been dodgy. The outcome of these business ventures was that he'd become involved in some serious London gangs and also he'd made wads of cash, hence the BMW. He then told them how he wanted to share his good fortune with them! His gang had become too notorious in London and they needed some fresh faces to nick something off a guy, something that was rightfully theirs anyway. They would each receive thirty hundred each; they could also help themselves to anything else that took their fancy in the guy's apartment.

He then took out a mobile phone as if from nowhere and handed it to OB. All three looked at it mesmerised, it was the first time they'd seen one in the flesh. Stanie knew that if there were any lingering doubts in OB and Jay's minds they'd evaporated the minute Tiger produced the phone. They were seeing pound note signs and an escape route from their hum drum mundane lives. He then said he would meet them at the Scratchwood Service Station at the end of the M1, he would be waiting there for them at noon on Monday, with details of where they were to go and what they would be looking for when they got there.

"It will be a piece of cake, the easiest three thousand pounds you've ever earned," he told his friends. "Now I need to be back in London to tell the gang that you're on board, so will you drop me off at the station Stanie, I need to catch the late night train back."

Even though he had had a few beers Stanie didn't want to anger Tiger so he agreed and the four lads set off for Edgeley station. The five-minute journey to the station was made in silence. When they reach the station entrance Tiger alighted and made his goodbyes to the others. Stanie reversed the car and made his way down the station approach, then just as he was about to turn left onto the A6 and return home to Heaton Norris, Jay shouted,.

"Stop!"

Stanie's mind had been racing away with everything that had happened in the last hour and he was so startled by Jay's outburst he did an emergency stop in the middle of the road. Luckily at that time of night there was no other traffic on the road so the only casualty was OB, who was thrown against the seat in front of him by the force of Stanie's emergency stop.

"Fuck man what was that all about?" OB asked as he felt his head to ensure there was no permanent damage.

"There are no trains to London tonight," Jay told them. "They are doing track maintenance all weekend; my uncle is working on them."

Stanie did a three point turn in the middle of the road and returned to where they had dropped Tiger off only seconds earlier. He was nowhere to be seen; all three lads got out of the car and looked around the deserted station.

"Maybe he realised there was no train and took a taxi," suggested OB.

"Are you a fucking simpleton? Do me a favour and act your age for once and not your shoe size," snapped Stanie. "Do you think his taxi was Dr Who's fucking TARDIS? We'd have seen him leave; there is only one way in and out of the station approach!"

Stanie decided that now was a safe time to express his concerns about what was happening.

"Look lads something is not right here, whatever that was it wasn't our Tiger. No matter what it said about drug deals and mysterious passengers the Tiger we knew would never have treated his family this way, we all saw his Mum and sister at the funeral; if he'd been alive he'd have got a message to them somehow."

Stanie raced through his narrative, he explained all his concerns about Tiger's story, everything he'd been bottling up while Tiger had been with them but now he was like a broken dam gushing forth with his opinion on what he thought Tiger was. OB was the first to speak after he had finished.

"You've been watching too many horror movies mate," he said looking confused at Stanie.

"Hold on mate, he might be right, something is wrong," confessed Jay. "When we were walking across Belmont Bridge towards Tiger I thought I'd heard Christ Church clock strike Midnight. I looked back at the church and I could have sworn the clock was back in the steeple lit up like a beacon, but when I double checked it wasn't there, I just assumed it was the beer playing tricks on me."

Stanie was relieved that he wasn't alone with his misgivings.

"Now I'm not so sure," Jay admitted.

For the second time that evening the hairs on all three lads' necks were stood on end. They were brought back to reality by the ringing of the mobile phone. OB was that startled he dropped the phone on the floor like it was a hot potato. The three of them huddled around the phone and watched the screen light up each time it rang, in the still of the night the trill of the ring seemed almost deafening. It had been ringing for well over five minutes; none of them could summon up the courage to actually answer it, when for the second time in a matter of moments they all received a collective shock when they heard Tiger's voice again.

"Is no one going to answer the fucking thing, I know you lot aren't used to them but they don't answer themselves!"

He bent down and turned it off then handed it to Stanie.

"Here you go you keep it Stephen I can trust you, OB's a fucking simpleton," Tiger said almost mimicking what Stanie had called OB moments earlier.

He'd appeared as if from nowhere and he wasn't alone this time, there was a man dressed head to foot in black who Tiger introduce as Stan, a friend from London. What was most striking about him was the fact he was wearing a pair of designer sunglasses despite it being the middle of the night. He was well over 6 foot and built like the side of a brick shithouse, as the saying goes. The sort of guy you didn't mess with, if he told you it was Christmas in the middle of July you didn't argue you just started singing Jingle Bells. Tiger explained that Stan had heard about the maintenance work and the fact there were no trains between Manchester and London and had driven up to take him back to London.

"That's what true friends are like ain't it lads, do anything for you," he said looking at Stanie. "Now off you go lads, after all you've got a big cup game in the morning."

This time after their goodbyes Tiger stood at the entrance to the station and watched as the three friends got in the BMW and drove off. As they drove back to Heaton Norris Stanie tried to work on the other two again to bring them round to his way of thinking, however even Jay had changed his mind.

"I'm not sure about the clock, it must have been the beer," he said.

After being parked for over an hour on the lads' street, Stanie admitted defeat and agreed with them that he'd pick them up at 10am. A few minutes later he was parked up outside his house and was locking the car when he stopped in his tracks.

How did Tiger know about their cup game!

He went straight to bed when he got in but knew it would be hard to get to sleep, so much was playing on his mind. When he did eventually manage to drop off he had his recurring dream except this time Tiger was warning him to 'be careful because the wolf is watching.'

The team they were playing their cup game against was called "South Park"; they had been a great team in their day, although they were never quite the same when they lost the services of the Murphy Brothers. Now these days the team was definitely on the slide. As the Heaton Norris boys looked at their opponents a few minutes before kick-off their manager was giving them his team talk.

"We can beat this lot, they've only got two players who can hurt us," he was telling them, "the ginger lad who looks like Catweasel and the fat lad in midfield; don't be mislead by his size, he is very deceptive, he is actually slower than he looks, but be warned on his day he can turn on a sixpence."

Jamie interrupted the team talk while looking at his oversized opponent on the other side of the pitch.

"That fat bastard couldn't turn on a tap nowadays"

The rest of his team-mates couldn't stop laughing and their manager didn't resume his team talk, he decided it would be better to leave the boys in a jovial mood. OB was still sniggering to himself as the game kicked off. Stanie from his position of right back looked towards his big daft centre forward and thought 'how could he be laughing at a time like this?' A few hours ago they'd been talking to a dead man.

The South Park pitch had a slight incline on one side, known to their players as 'the hill'. Now the fat mid fielder knew the pitch like the back of his hand. He would always play on the opposite side to the hill, one half on the left the other on the right. His team-mates had jokingly blamed him for making the hill steeper with his weight on the opposite side of the hill. Joking aside he certainly knew how to play the hill, he would hit the ball over the fullback going towards the incline. His opponent would assume the ball was going out of play but his own winger would know the slope would keep it in play. With Stanie pre-occupied with the previous night's events he was not only got caught out a couple of times like most opponents but on five separate occasions. If it had not been for his own lightning turn of pace, when he realised he'd been duped yet again by the ploy, they could have been five nil down by half time.

At half time Jay told Stanie they would lose the game if he didn't concentrate on the matter in hand.

"We will think about Tiger when the game's over," he said at the break.

The fact that Jay was aware of why he was off his game seemed to have a calming affect on Stanie and from the start of the second half he began to play his normal game. Towards the end of the game something very strange happened. Stanie picked up the ball in his own half and went on the most amazing run of his life. The first adversary to come towards him was the fat midfielder; Stanie quickly made a fool of him by putting the ball through his legs. When the next two opponents came he simply pushed the ball around them and used his speed to leave the two eating his dust. The ball seemed to be stuck to his boot as he danced his way past most of the opposition leaving them kicking fresh air. He was now thinking to himself how he would gloat in the pub about being the best player the team had. Although he did have a nice turn of pace and a good footballing brain, even he would have to admit he was no Maradona, but today It seemed like he was wearing a pair of magic boots. When he arrived by the corner flag he played the ball through the fullback's legs and when another defender slid in for a tackle he flicked the ball over his head and volleyed it into the penalty area to where OB was waiting.

It was as if as well as receiving the ball from Stanie he also took possession of the magic boots. With his back to the goal, in one move he controlled the ball with his left knee, flicked it up in the air, and while it was in the air with his right foot executed the most perfect bicycle kick ever seen in the Stockport and Cheadle Sunday league. The ball flew into the back of the net and OB fell backwards hitting his head on the ground with a sickening thud. Amateur football pitches are hardly the best maintained pieces of turf around and the penalty area was barren of grass, and usually at this time of year it would be a muddy mess, however during the recent dry spell the ground had dried into what looked like brown concrete. The sound of OB's head hitting the rock hard surface was audible across the whole pitch and despite him scoring a goal worthy of a spot on the 'goal of the month' on Match of the Day nobody was concerned about it. Everyone ran over to OB expecting to find him unconscious at best, or at the least lying in a pool of blood close to death.

"What you lot looking at then?" was all he said as he lay on the floor looking up at the circle of concerned faces.

And with that he jumped to his feet and seemed unaffected by his smash on his head, there didn't even look to be a bruise or lump let alone any blood.

"Look son it might be best if you go to hospital and get your head checked out, just to be on the safe side;" Suggested the ref. "You've probably lost half your brain cells."

"In that case that only leaves him with two," quipped Jay.

The joke seemed to lift everyone and after OB reluctantly agreed to be substituted the game resumed. When the final whistle was blown there were scenes of jubilation as all the players lifted OB onto their shoulders and carried him back to the changing rooms. During the celebrations, for one fleeting moment Stanie though he saw Tiger walking away from the pitch.

"You okay mate?" Pete the team captain asked OB once they were in the changing room. "That goal was out of this world"

Stanie had a sinking feeling in his stomach that Pete was right. The goal had been orchestrated in another world by something not human. Stanie knew that at the very least OB should be concussed right now instead of basking in the glory of his wonder goal. Was this a sign he wondered that Tiger or the thing that was in his body could kill at any time, even in the middle of a football pitch? As he left the changing room and walked back to the car he had a crushing feeling, he could hardly breath but it wasn't from the energy he had expended during the game. The feeling came from the knowledge that his and his friends' lives were in danger and only he could see it. From now on he would keep his own council, he would go to London, do as he was asked and pray to God that he came back with his life.

He didn't go to the pub with the rest of the team to celebrate their victory. He told OB and Jay that he wanted to be fresh for the drive in the morning. The truth was, on the drive back home after the game he'd remembered what Tiger's sister had said at the funeral; 'If only I could have seen him one more time to tell him how much I loved him.' A voice in the back of his mind was telling him he may not come through the next few days and that something more important than his own life was at stake. He wanted to spend the next few hours putting his own house in order and not leave anything unsaid. As soon as he got home he thanked his Mum and Dad for everything they'd done for him and although he didn't always show it he loved them both very much. He then called his sisters and brothers and told them the same thing.

His eldest sister had called her Mum later that night when Stanie had left the house and asked,

"Is everything okay with our Steve, is he ill or moving abroad? He called me this afternoon and told me how much he loved me and the kids."

"He has been acting really strange," she replied. "He said exactly the same to me and your Dad and he hasn't said that since he was a kid."

She then went on to explain to her daughter about the car he'd turned up in the other night and how he'd told her he was going to deliver it to London.

"I thought he was dying or joining the Foreign Legion or something," his sister said. They both laughed and the conversation drifted off to a typical mother and daughter conversation, one that lasted for hours but nothing in particular was talked about.

Stanie had left the house because there was one more thing he needed to do before he went to London. Now as he stood outside Tiger's house he wasn't so sure it was the right thing to do. As he stood with his finger poised on the doorbell he remembered the Tiger they'd met the night before and what lay ahead and then pressed the bell.

"How nice to see you Stephen," said Mrs Carlton as she answered the door. "How lovely to see you, how are you?" she continued. "You don't need to answer that question; you know what day it is don't you?"

By the rings around Tiger's Mum eye's it was obvious she'd been crying. She'd done a lot of that over the last twelve months and on the odd occasions Stanie had seen her since the funeral she had looked bad but today she looked like she did at the funeral itself. He explained that he knew it was the anniversary of the funeral and that he'd called round to see if they were all right.

"How lovely of you dear," she said with another tear welling up in her eye, "you were always a good boy, definitely a calming influence on our Terence."

He felt guilty then when he had to admit there was another reason for his visit, that he wanted a private word with Sharon. He needn't have worried, as his confession seemed to cheer her up. She smiled as she showed him into the front room and called for Sharon. Sharon came in a few seconds later and even though she was in jeans and a sweatshirt two sizes too big for her and it looked like she'd done her own fair share of crying with her mother, she looked beautiful.

"Hi Steve great to see you, I believe you wanted me," she said.

God only knew how much he wanted her! She was four years his junior and until the accident if he was honest he hadn't taken much notice of her. She was his best mate's kid sister and there was an unwritten rule that you didn't go there. However since the funeral, while he'd tried to avoid Mrs Carlton, as her pain was at times too much to bear he'd seen a lot of Sharon. They both missed Tiger desperately and found comfort in each other's company. He'd told Jay about his growing feelings for her but Jay had told him.

"Don't go there mate, she'd too young for you and even if she wasn't she's way out of your league. Yes she's definitely first division where you my little midget are strictly non league."

After he came back to reality he looked at her standing there in front of him as beautiful as ever, looking a little confused, and he decided it was now or never.

"Sharon I love you," he said tentatively. "I think I always have but since..."

Before he could finish his sentence Sharon had run across the room and collapsed into his arms, and as she gazed into his eyes she slowly kissed him. It was a slow and passionate kiss that seemed to last for ages. When their lips eventually parted she said,

"At last! I can't believe it's taken you so long." Stanie looked at her amazed.

"I've loved you since I was thirteen," she confessed to him. "Mum always told me to have faith, that one day you'd eventually notice me!"

Stanie couldn't believe this was happening. He'd found the love of his life, was he going to lose her just as quickly?

"I have to go away tomorrow," he told her. "Delivering a car to London, but as soon as I come back I'll take you out on a proper date."

"I've waited this long," she teased him, "I'm sure I can wait a few more days but only if I can tell my Mum, she could do with some good news today of all days."

Sharon kissed him once more then left him to tell her Mum their news. She returned moments later with her Mother. Mrs Carlton had a smile on her face, something Stanie hadn't seen since before the accident.

"You're very slow on the uptake young man," she said as she kissed him on the cheek, "this girl has been in love with you for years."

He spent the next few hours with Sharon at her home making plans for their date and the future. At midnight as he was making his final goodbyes on the doorstep he told her,

"I love you and I'll call you as soon as I get back. If anything did ever happen to me I could die a happy man knowing you loved me."

"Don't be so morbid, there has been enough of that around here to last a lifetime," she told him.

With that he left her standing at the door waving; he blew her one final kiss, then he turned the corner. Stanie had never in his life felt so happy and sad at the same time, and as he walked back home the tears started to trickle down his face in despondency and frustration, But most of all he cried like any broken-hearted lover would at the final separation of a loved one.

CHAPTER SEVEN

The New Beginning

I don't know how long I was under the water, it could have been minutes, hours, days or even years. I remember the water level coming up to my mouth and nose and I felt a choking sensation, I couldn't breathe. The next thing everything went black, my body must have gone into some sort of hibernation and had shut down. Don't ask me how I was able to breathe I can't explain it but, there again I can't explain why I'm still alive now. As they say, God works in mysterious ways. Perhaps I was on the bottom of the sea that long that the oar I was chained to could have rotted away releasing my body and sending it back to the surface. I have no answer to what happened, I just recall coming round on a beach, that turned out to be Cyprus, and looking into a familiar set of eyes belonging to a middle-aged man.

"Father is that really you?" he said.

I couldn't believe what I was seeing, had I died and gone to heaven or was this really my boy, my very own Nathaniel grown up into a man? He assured me I was alive and this was really him, I was back home on Cyprus. We held each other for what seemed like an age and when I finally let go of him I could see there was a young boy of about 10 with him who seemed quite confused as to what was going on. I pointed to the boy and asked if he was my grandson.

"Well in a way he is, he's the son of Amos from Jerusalem, he has come to live with us. It's a long story and I will tell you after you've had some rest. And you could do with some new clothes, you look like you've been wearing these for years."

When we arrived back at our home I washed and shaved and Nathaniel cut my hair, I was given new clothes and then shown to my room.

"You must rest now Father, and I have a lot of things to do," Nathaniel said.

I lay on my bed but couldn't sleep, you could say the penny finally dropped; I realised I was brought back from the dead for a purpose, but why? My mission now was to find out.

After a few hours Nathaniel came for me, and he took me downstairs where a feast had been prepared for me. He introduced me to the occupants of the room.

"This is Tabitha, daughter of your friends Jacob and Durcas and that young man is Beor, her son. This lovely lady is Ruth, the wife of Amos and that strong young man next to her is Matthew her son, you met him on the beach today, and this is the most beautiful girl in the world, Matthew's sister Olda," Nathaniel said smiling.

Before he could speak again Olda shouted,

"I'm three how old are you?"

"Good question," I said.

"This is the man John wrote about in his letters. I would like to introduce you all to my Father, Lazarus," Nathaniel interjected.

There was a look of total disbelief on their faces and now came the most unenviable task for Nathaniel, he had to tell me what had happened to my sisters. The year was now 66AD and I had been away for twenty-nine years and had not aged a day. Cetura had died nine years ago and up until a few weeks ago both my sisters were alive and well. There had been a Jewish uprising against Roman Rule in Jerusalem. The Christian community were instructed not to support the rebellion and had moved out to Pella, the other side of the Jordan River, but my sisters refused to leave. Martha took the women and children to stay with friends in Bethesda and Mary decided to stay and look after the menfolk. It seems Jacob, Edom and Tabitha's husband Cham and my sister were all killed defending the shop, either from Jewish looters or from Roman looters when the uprising abated. The womenfolk came back to the city only to find a total destruction of the shop and everyone they loved dead. This was just too much for my sister and the Doctor said she had suffered a heart attack after the burial of her loved ones. Even though Martha was very weak she decided she would visit her nephew, Nathaniel, against her Doctor's advice and she took the arduous journey but, unfortunately her heart gave way again just before reaching Paphos. Nathaniel took her body up to the old sheep farm in the hills and buried her with his parents. He also told me that john was still alive and had set up home in Ephesus. When Nathaniel had finished telling me everything I then told my own extraordinary story.

The next day we held a service in the magnificent little church that Nathaniel and the Islanders had completed, it was a thanksgiving for the lives of our loved ones.

After over a year of getting to know my new family I told Nathaniel I would like to stay here forever but, I think God has plans for me so I will go to Ephesus to see John for instructions as to what to do next. Nathaniel understood but said he would be coming with me this time. I did try to stop him but he was now a grown man and I had to respect his decision. Nathaniel had already formulated a plan. Naas his friend and co-worker would look after the business and would see that Tabitha and Ruth would get half the profit, they could also have the house as it was made for children - he had extended it when he got married twelve years ago but, tragically his wife had died in childbirth a year after they were married. He had not re-married because he felt a light had gone out in his heart when both her and his child had died. I felt so sorry for him but, I was also grateful that he had known real true love.

Before I said farewell to the island yet again, Nathaniel and I made a sad pilgrimage up to the sheep farm. There were five graves side by side; his parents, Cetura, his wife Zelphe, and he told me he had buried the boy child in her arms as she would have wanted that, he lamented. He had christened the child Lazarus after me and now in the final grave was my own sweet Martha. Both Nathaniel and I said a tearful prayer for our loved ones and I told Martha to look after my grandson and to give him a kiss for me. So, after just over thirty years I set sail for Ephesus yet again. I have been back to Cyprus many times over the years and spent many happy times there but, none as happy as the year I spent with my son and the girls and their children. I also made one very painful journey to take my son back home to bury him; I don't care how old your child is we are not conditioned as parents to bury our children. It's hard losing one's own parents and even harder to lose your life- long partner but, it is almost too much to bear to bury your child and my heart goes out to anyone who has had to do that. So, with a very heavy heart that day I put my son into the ground next to his loved ones on the old sheep farm and if I was to go back there today there would still be a tear in my eye.

Directly on our arrival at Ephesus Harbour we were taken to John and there in front of me was a man about fifty.

"I'm looking for that young fool John," I said with a smile.

"Well, well, well if it's not the infamous Lazarus, I thought you were dead again, but you've not changed at all. I don't know what you've been taking but I could do with some of it myself," John said smiling profusely.

What surprised me the most was that he was totally unfazed by my lack of ageing; it was as though he had seen it before. I looked him up and down and said,

"You've not changed a bit, your sense of humour is still terrible."

The people that were standing around John were shocked at what they saw as my lack of respect for a founder member of the church of Christ but, to me it was just good old John my friend. We both laughed and hugged each other. I then introduced him to my son and he took us both into an anteroom where there was a large table in the middle with a map-come-model of the known world, with crosses indicating where churches had been built. I told him my story and when I had finished he didn't comment directly about it, he told me he had seen many things including the end of the world.

He also said that the devil had been to see him to try to convert him to the dark ways.

"He will try to seduce as many important people as he can to the dark way. I will be gone soon but I think you my old friend will have to walk this road alone until its completion, when the bad deeds of this world outnumber the good. That will be the end and I think the devil will try to hurry this process along. Like he entered the wolf to attack you, he will enter people of power and influence others to commit evil. You must use the spear on them to take the beast out and send him back to where he belongs."

He then asked for the spear and I gave it to him, it was glowing red and I had never seen anything like that before. He took hold of it and walked around the map. When he reached Rome it turned white, he then did the circuit once again and the same thing happened.

"It's Rome, you must go to," he said. "Rome, that's where you will find him, I think you should go at once, there is no time to lose."

So on the first available vessel going to Rome Nathaniel and I booked a passage. John wished us God speed and said he would see me again as he had much to tell me before he eventually went to his maker.

It just so happened that the Sea Shark, the vessel we were travelling on, was owned and captained by a friend of John's, a Roman named Lysias, who had used the boat for transporting slaves around the Roman world, before turning to Christianity. Now rather than a cargo of human misery he would take linen from Ephesus to Rome to be exchanged for pottery that he then took to Byzantium, where horses were then the cargo to be taken to Caesarea for the Roman military. They would pay in bitumen and gold. He would then take that to Paphos to exchange for copper then return back to Ephesus to start all over again.

"It keeps me out of trouble, and that my friend is where you are heading. You see after the fire there was chaos everywhere. The Christians had to go underground, because they are being blamed for everything. Don't tell anyone who you don't know that you are a Christian if you want to survive to your next birthday," Lysias warned us.

When we docked Lysias introduced us to Seleucus who took us to the Roman Christians' new headquarters in the catacombs. He told the people 'This is the man John told us about in his letters, Lazarus.' A man who had been on his knees praying turned to me and said

"You have been sent by God, you're the only man who can help me."

His name was Antonius, he was a high born Roman convert. He then poured out his problem for me to solve. His son's wife had been raped by Nero's private secretary, Ephas. When the young man, Marcus, found out a fight took place resulting in Ephas being mortally wounded.

"When Nero finds out it will not only be my son who will be put to the sword, he will blame all Christians and that's why I have been here praying for a miracle and one has been sent to me, you," Antonius said hopefully.

We went directly to his house and I was taken to the dying man's room. The Doctor was just leaving.

"It's no good going in there unless you are the undertaker," he said.

I told Nathaniel to stay outside and let no one enter and I went in. I went over to the corpse and put the spear onto the wound, but it was no good. I tried everything for over an hour but the spirit had gone.

"Why bring me this close only to fail Lord? Please help me to help your people," I prayed.

The next thing I knew I was lying down looking at my hands that weren't mine anymore and I screamed with shock. Nathaniel ran in.

"Where is my father, what have you done with him Roman?" he said to me.

I answered in my own voice, "It's me, now quick shut the door at once."

Nathaniel hesitated for a few seconds than looked deep into my eyes and seemed to recognize something in me. Although he was somewhat confused he did as requested, turned and shut the door. He than came back to the bedside and I explained what I thought had happened. It seems that along with all the other gifts I could now enter a body like the devil. I told Nathaniel to tell no one the truth, just to tell them I have cured him and he has taken me to Nero's palace to thank me. I knew now what to do and how to do it.

The first time in a new body is very strange, rather like driving a new car and finding the previous owner's belongings are still there. I knew the directions to the palace because I still possessed Ephas's memory and I had no trouble getting past the soldiers, I even nodded to one or two. I also had no trouble getting past Nero's German bodyguards and into his private quarters. Instinctively I knew the figure in front of me was that of Nero. Although I must say I was a little shocked by his appearance for he was nothing like the image I had seen of him on Roman coins and the like. He was small and somewhat overweight for his size. No doubt his overblown appearance was brought about by his corpulent lifestyle. His face and arms were full of specks and freckles. He had a very fat neck with thin dirty yellow hair. As he began to speak his eyes started to blink like he was short sighted.

"Where have you been? We have big trouble and I need you," Nero said.

"Don't worry your greatness all your troubles are over, get rid of everyone I need to speak to you in private," I said.

When everyone was out I locked the door. "Look what I've got for you, it's the magic spear they have all been talking about," I said.

The look of excitement soon changed to shock as I cut his throat, and then to horror when he realised he was dying. He just lay there gagging in his own blood, and then I heard a voice from behind me,

"I see, you thought that fat fool was me. You have been a bad boy, you've got the blood of a human being on your soul now."

I turned to find the beast dressed as one of Nero's Praetorian guards.

"I thought you were on the seabed for eternity. I see you have learnt one or two new tricks since we last met, it's surprising what you can look like when you take the trouble to dress but I wouldn't have put that body on, it's crawling with infestation. I think he would have copulated with a pig if nothing else was available. Talking about pigs that bitch of yours couldn't get enough rutting before she died, but let's not talk about the past. I see by your face the mention of her still causes you pain and that, my dear old friend, I do not wish to do anymore. So as the saying goes 'Let sleeping dog's lie'.

No dear boy I do not wish to destroy you, I want you to live to witness the end of the world when I beat your Master."

As he was talking to me his gaze never once left the spear. It was obvious that his words were just bravado, he was afraid of the spear. He shouted for the guards without his eyes leaving the spear. The door started to splinter and I had to act now before it was too late so I threw the spear head at him, he tried to avoid it but it acted like a guided missile and went straight into his side. I had just retrieved the relic when the door broke open.

"Kill him" were the last words the devil said before leaving the body.

They were on me before I could react; four of them were holding me, when their officer came so close to me I could smell the garlic on his breath.

"Now what's a nice man like you want to go and do a thing like that? Now we are all out of work," and as he said this he drew his short sword and plunged it into my gut.

I felt a red hot burning sensation and the last thing I heard him say was, "Throw the bastard off the balcony and then find anything of value you can carry, call it severance pay."

I remember flying through the air and landing with an almighty smash. I lay there not wanting to move, the pain was so bad, but somehow I got to my feet. I was now looking down on Ephas's broken body and my pain was gone.

I went back to the catacombs and told them what Ephas had done and they would have no more trouble with Nero. Nathaniel winked at me and I said to him,

"Do you fancy a trip to Byzantium to get some horses?"

So we said our goodbyes and went back to the harbour. Lysias and his crew were still loading the pottery.

"How do you fancy taking on two new crew members?" I asked him. "It seems our business here in Rome has come to an abrupt end," I laughed.

So we set off to report back to John the long way round and even managed to pay a short visit to Paphos to see our family.

CHAPTER EIGHT

A Trip to London

They arrived at their destination the next day, half an hour before the agreed meeting time. The trip had been uneventful apart from hitting a bit of traffic at Birmingham. However, the journey was made monotonous by OB's incessant vocal replays of the goal he had scored. Stanie accepted a long time ago that OB would always remain at the mental age of twelve. In fact if OB had been Jackie Paper from the song 'Puff the Magic Dragon', Puff would never have gone to the place called Honalee, he would still be living in Heaton Norris in a cave on the Red Rocks.

They all alighted from the car to stretch their legs. When Stanie turned around there was a white limousine about fifteen yards behind them, he could have sworn it wasn't there when he parked up moments before. The electric window automatically came down then Tiger's voice shouted from inside,

"Come on boys, get in!"

When they were inside, Tiger gave each of them an envelope containing three thousand pounds, a map to locate the apartment and also a sketch of the spear head they were looking for. He then handed Stanie a pass card to enter the underground car park at the building and a key to the stairway leading up to the apartment. Finally he gave him a crowbar and a black magnetic box. He told them the guy who owned the place would be at a meeting this afternoon at Downing Street. He would have to pass through a metal scanner, which had now been installed in all government buildings after the Brighton bombing a few years earlier, consequently he would not be able to take the spear with him and therefore it should be in his home. They were told to enter by the car park then take the stairs, not the lift, to the third floor and to break in using the crowbar. They would then have sixty seconds to locate the alarm and attach the black magnetic box to the right hand side of it, within fifteen seconds a four digit number would be displayed on the small screen on the box which they were to enter into the alarm. He told them he would phone them on their mobile to arrange a pickup point for the relic. They then said their goodbyes and got out of the limo.

As they were walking back to their own car Stanie stopped and gave the keys to Jamie, he told him to open the car and that he would be back in a minute, he needed to have a quick word with Tiger. The window of the limo began to open again and Tiger's voice said,

"Did you want me or was it my little sister that you were after Stephen?"

The word sister made him shudder. He opened the door and got in. He seemed to receive some courage from somewhere because he was no longer afraid, just annoyed. The thing inside Tiger said,

"Did you enjoy the goal by the way? If you want me to, I could have you playing for Manchester City's first team and let's face it they could do with my help at the moment. I could make them the best team in the world, there is nothing beyond me."

Stanie said with his new-found bravado, "I think there is something you can't do. It's impossible for you to go to that guy's apartment and get the spear."

Within a second, the interior of the car went completely black and Tiger's head seemed to jerk back at an angle, his eyes went red and now a different voice emanated from him. It whispered in a malevolent way,

"I am legions, I am many, and I can do anything."

Stanie knew he had pushed the right buttons and with his new found inner strength he said, "Okay, okay, wind your neck back in, I will bring you the spear but after that will you let everything return to normal?"

The thing then said back in the voice of Tiger again, "Nothing will ever be normal again. You will do what I say because you have played your life's trump card, no one can help you now. The game is over when I say it's over. Now go along little boy and bring me back what I demand before something nasty happens to my sister."

It was just after three when they arrived at the apartment block, they drove into the underground car park using the pass card to lift the barrier. The place was empty apart from one car, coincidentally a green BMW. They parked near to what they believed to be the door to the stairway, and as he was looking at the other car Jay said jokingly,

"You should think about getting rid of this car, they are becoming too common."

Stanie just smiled but inwardly he thought he had no intention of keeping it knowing now where it had truly come from. He tried the key in the door to the stairway, it opened. They all went up the stairs to the third floor, and when they reached the door to Lazarus' apartment they took a quick look round to see if there was anybody about. They then assured themselves that they would not be disturbed so OB proceeded to force open the door with the crowbar. The door splintered and the lock gave way. The circuit around the door was broken and the alarm was activated. They quickly enter the apartment and located the alarm box. They found it on the wall to the left of the front door, the black magnetic box was attached to the side and as they were told, four numbers came up on the panel at the front of the box. The numbers were quickly entered on to the alarm's keypad and it de-activated.

Now for the hard part, trying to locate the spear. Stanie and Jay began to look for the relic but to no avail. OB had his own agenda, he was looking round the place for things to steal; he'd already taken a gold Rolex watch off the bedside cabinet and was now trying on a lightly tanned leather jacket. It was waist length and at the bottom left hand side an extra pocket had been sown into the lining. Inside was a leather pouch containing the spear head. When Stanie looked into the bedroom and saw OB trying on the leather jacket and looking into the mirror, he went into a rage, he was fuming. He shouted at him,

"When you have finished having your fashion show you big daft useless lump, can you possibly try to remember why we are here?"

OB just tossed the leather pouch at Stanie and winked then said, "Not so big and daft after all eh midget?"

It was precisely ten to four when they left the apartment. OB was hungry again so they decided to find somewhere to eat. Halfway through the meal the mobile went off; Tiger's voice was on the other end. He told

Stanie where to meet him, it was a loading bay at the back of a row of shops not to far away from where they were having the meal. The meeting would be at seven. After the conversation, Stanie lost his appetite, he just watched OB wolf down his own meal then finish his too.

They all decided to go to the meeting point early. The loading bay entrance was between a bank and discount supermarket that specialized in taking old buildings and, with little renovation, used them for their own purposes. You could still see it had originally been a cinema. Halfway down was a set of stairs in an alcove leading to a fire door, in the days when it was a picture house the door would probably have been used as a fire exit. Stanie drove down the passageway and turned the car around in the loading bay at the back of the shops. He was now parked at the very top of the passageway looking down towards the road. Just before seven, both he and OB got out of the vehicle. He gave the spear head to Jay who had now moved over into the driver's seat, and said he would indicate when he wanted him to drive forward. He thought to himself that he wanted to be assured of one or two things, before he handed over the spear. A voice in the back of his mind was telling him not to give the spear to anyone other than Tiger. As he walked down the passageway leading to the road it began to rain quite hard. Both lads jumped into the alcove in front of the fire door of the supermarket.

The rain stopped as suddenly as it had started and then the white limo appeared. As Jay sat behind the wheel of the BMW, he thought a few more deals like this with Tiger and he would be able to buy one of these beauties for himself. Then, his attention was drawn to the white limo, and he watched as Stanie and OB approached the vehicle. Two large men got out of the limo; they were big but not as big as the monster they had met at Stockport station the other night. He wondered what was going on, it looked like the little midget was arguing the toss with the two men. That little guy really does have chip on his shoulder about being small, he always said one day his big mouth would get them into trouble. As he leant forward to take a closer look through the windscreen, he thought to himself this could be the day his prediction came true.

Then he heard a noise and saw a flash of light; or did he see a flash of light and then the noise? - he didn't know, but he was sure about one thing, the bastards had just shot Stanie. As Stanie staggered back into the alcove, he felt a burning sensation in his side. He then fell on the stairs clutching his side; OB went into the alcove after him. The two guys slowly walked after them like two cocky bloodhounds knowing the fox was cornered and they had all day to kill it. In one quick movement, Jay put the BMW in gear, slammed his foot on the accelerator and shot down the passageway. He missed OB's heels by a fraction as they were slightly stuck out of the alcove, and a second later there was a sickening sound of metal hitting skin and bone full on. The heavies weren't that heavy compared to the BMW; they were both knocked into the air and thrown behind the car. Jay managed to stop the car just before it hit the limo.

As he ran over to see how his friend was, he observed the carnage he had caused. By the position of one of the men he could tell without checking that the man was dead and even if the other was still alive he wouldn't be shooting anyone for a very long time. When he entered the alcove, Stanie was lying on the stairs like Nelson on the deck of the victory. Stanie had OB's shirt pressed against his side to stem the blood flow. He bent down and slowly removed the shirt and said,

"It's only a graze you old woman, unless you are a haemophiliac your blood will congeal and stop the bleeding. Anyway, what the fuck did you say to them to make them want to shoot you? I sometimes wonder whether you could cause an argument in an empty house."

"I didn't ask them to shoot me, I just told them that I was only giving the spear to Tiger - but thanks for your concern by the way, and as for your professional advice Dr Legg, I would appreciate a second opinion from someone who has actually been to medical school," said Stanie.

"Everyone wants to go private these days. Look I've watched all that medical stuff on TV, it's just a graze," Jamie said as reassuringly as he could.

"I've seen all the Airport films, but I couldn't land a bleeding 747, now will you please take me to fucking hospital quick before I bleed to death," Stanie said pleading with them.

OB came from the passageway, he had been to the car to get another shirt from his bag. He told the lads that they wouldn't be going anywhere as the front of the car was knackered. Stanie sighed,

"Here we go, another bloody expert, three weeks on a YTS scheme in a garage does not make you qualified to give out MOT certificates."

Despite the situation they all laughed. OB and Jay helped Stanie into the back of the limo; OB had elected himself the driver. After only a few short yards he stopped to talk to two girls for a moment. Jamie opened the glass partition after the girls had gone and asked OB what the hell he was doing, did he not realize that there

was a dead body back there, if they were caught he could
be going to prison for a very long time. OB just told him
that he was asking the girls for directions to the hospital
and then added,

"If you are going to prison for the rest of your life and
midget is going to die then I will need someone to talk to,
so I got their phone numbers." Jay and Stanie just looked
at each other and wondered whether the big lump was
joking or not, it was hard to tell.

By the time they arrived at the hospital they had
formulated a plan. Stanie would give a false name and say
he was shot by a mugger, if the gun wound wasn't serious
then he could nip out of the hospital, take a taxi to the
train station and head back to Stockport. They would
leave the mobile with him then contact him later to see
how he was getting on. In the meanwhile, they would
take the limo somewhere secluded and torch it. OB would
then hotwire a car so they could get back to Stockport.

They parked in a Doctors' parking space, and OB ran
inside to get a wheelchair. They pushed Stanie inside to
the casualty department and told the nearest nurse that
Stanie had been shot. When the nurse turned her back to
get help the two young men disappeared. Stanie's injuries
were not life threatening but they were far more serious
than Jay had made out. He had lost a lot of blood and
would need an operation. While the medics were undress-
ing him to prepare for surgery, his Manchester City
season ticket fell out of the back pocket of his jeans, and
it had not gone unnoticed by one of the nurses. After his
operation, it was reported to the police that a young man
had been brought into hospital with a gun shot wound.
He had been registered as Peter Kelly from Oldham but
in his belongings was a season ticket for Manchester City

in the name of Stephen Stanton. The report was nothing special it was just hospital policy to report to the police all information regarding gun related injuries.

Around about the same time as Stanie was being wheeled into a recovery room just outside the ICU ward, the other two lads were halfway home to Stockport in a stolen black mini. They had successfully destroyed the limo. Jay said to OB,

"Drive the mini to the Bonks then we can set it alight, we can then walk back to Heaton Norris by the fishpond track, the best thing we can then do is have a good night's sleep and ring Stanie in the morning to see how he is doing."

About an hour later in his hospital room, Stanie received a visitor who woke him from his sleep, and said, "You have been a very bad boy, now tell me what you have done with the spear?"

Stanie was still groggy from the operation. He now found himself looking at Tiger, not knowing if he was real or imaginary but he answered all the same.

"The spear's not yours; it's going back to its rightful owner."

The beast inside Tiger went mad, it plunged its hand into Stanie's chest and tore out his heart, and then pushed the still beating organ in front of his eyes. Stanie knew that this was not possible; it was just an illusion for he would be dead now otherwise. From the other side of the room came a bright light, and out of the light came his grandma.

"It's okay Stephen, no one is going to hurt you anymore. I am going to take you to somewhere nice now, so now lets say a good act of contrition."

They both started,

"Oh my God, I am so heartfully sorry I have offended thee and with the help of thy grace I will not sin again."

The beast stood frozen as the sacrament was being said, unable to interfere with something more powerful that itself. At the end it burst out in indignation and said, "No one can help you, you are going to die my little midget."

Stanie just smiled and said, "Let's get two things straight, if I am going to die. One I am not a midget I'm five foot six, and two, even if I were a midget I would definitely not be your midget."

At five minutes to midnight on that Monday night, Stephen Stanton died at a happy man for two reasons. He was loved by the best looking girl in Stockport, Sharon Carlton, and he was going to a far better place with the Gran he loved with all his heart who had died and left him when he was nine- years old. This time she would never leave him.

CHAPTER NINE

Losing Nathaniel

For ten years Nathaniel and I worked closely with John in Ephesus. He told us he had received visions from the Lord regarding the end of the world and many other things, including the sinking of the pirate vessel I was incarcerated on. That is why he was not startled by my lack of ageing when we once again met. I was told to keep a written record of my life with the Master as he was doing, as well as Matthew and Mark. Years later I did meet a young physician named Luke and dictated my account of what I had witnessed.

Then came a very black day in my life, April 7th in the year of Our Lord 78AD. The week before, John and I had gone up into the hills to stay at the house John had built for the Master's mother. He showed me the site where Mary had ascended into heaven. April 7th will always be a sad day for me; it always reminds me of my loss. About two in the afternoon, one of Quintos' servants came up from the city to tell me that Nathaniel had been murdered. It seemed that early that day my son had stopped two drunken Roman soldiers who were violating a young woman, but when he broke up the assault the two soldiers turned their anger towards him beating him to death. In retrospect it would have been the way he would have wanted to go, helping someone else. When I heard the news I flew into a rage, never have I experienced so much built up anger inside me. God forgive me but I ignored my Master's teachings on turning the other cheek, I took the servant's horse and went directly back to the city not listening to John's pleas to calm down. On the way down to Ephesus I felt so cold, I do not know to this day if it was the chill of a bitter cold April day or an internal coldness I was feeling.

I passed through the city gate, then went down Curetes Street to the library and dismounted when I saw a servant girl from the house of Quintos. She told me Quintos had gone to the procurator to have the soldiers arrested but the Roman military's argument was this was a lawful killing of a troublesome Greek. Deep down they knew this was not the case, but like in today's society, they were closing ranks. To find the soldiers guilty would be to find Rome guilty. In a week or so the soldiers would be sent to some miserable place on the outpost of the Empire where they would probably die of some disease or at the hand of some barbarian. That news sent the rage in me to boiling point.

"Where are they?" I demanded the girl to answer.

From the look in my eyes she knew I could not be put off. She told me the soldiers in question were in a down market brothel near the public latrines. When I reached the brothel I was met by the brothel keeper and his bodyguard. I asked them,

"What room are the Romans in? The soldiers who killed the Greek?" They didn't answer. "It would be a good idea for you to tell me or you will not live to see tomorrow," I added.

The little fat brothel keeper started perspiring profusely, he made a signal to his bodyguard and the big man went for his weapon. I spotted his motion out of the corner of my eye; I picked up a stool quickly and caught him full on the side of his head knocking the big man unconscious, I then turned towards the fat man. He made an apology for his servant's aggression trying to look innocent; I pushed the man to the floor and held the blade of his bodyguard's sword to his throat.

"Listen to me very carefully fat boy; you have one more chance to avoid meeting the devil today. What room are the soldiers in?" I said quietly, but firmly.

The man was convinced that if he did not tell me he would die so he had no alternative than to pass me the key to the soldiers' room. I tied up the brothel keeper and his bodyguard and made my way to the Romans' room. The door to their room was not locked and I slipped inside. Directly in front of me were four naked people, two men and two young women. They were too preoccupied in their actions to notice me. I took one of their swords which was lying on the floor and put it behind my back. The noise must have disturbed them and they turned towards me.

"Are you responsible for unburdening the world of yet another festering Greek?" I said nonchalantly.

"Yes we are and if you want to buy us a drink it will have to wait, can't you see we are engaged in a little relaxation at the moment?" said a bald fat soldier.

He pushed the girl to one side and leant under the bed and retrieved a pot of what I assume to be urine and threw it in my direction. Their apprehension of the situation turned to amusement when I turned to walk towards the door, but the room went deadly silent when I locked it.

"Do not stay anonymous my friend, who are you?" the befuddled bald soldier said.

"My name is Lazarus and I am the man's father, and now you must be made accountable for your actions," I said firmly.

The second man was the bigger of the two and looked like a battle-hardened warrior; he was greying at the sides with a scar above his left eye. He moved swiftly to the weapons in the corner of the room. As he jumped off the bed to my good fortune he slipped on the liquid from the disregarded missile sent at me a few moments earlier, and fell forward hitting his head on the wall. In one movement, without thinking I moved towards him and pushed my blade into the exposed part of his neck. I did not flinch at his eradication from this world; I just turned to the shocked occupants of the beds. The bald soldier was now pleading for his life while churning out the age-old excuse that he was just doing his job. Without engaging in any further dialogue with the man I lunged forward plunging the blade directly into his stomach. This stopped the man mid sentence, the girls began to scream and in that instance blackness left me. This was replaced with an overwhelming feeling of guilt, not for the soldiers, - by this time, the bald one was clutching his stomach and blood was running down the side of his mouth, - no not for killing as over the centuries I have sent many a man to meet his maker, I felt no guilt for that, my guilt was because I had ignored my Master's teaching about turning the other cheek. I killed those men not out of necessity but out of rage which was wrong. They were wicked men I know, but I should not have done what I did, as two wrongs do not make a right. I threw down the sword and left the brothel by the back entrance and made my way to the house of Quintos.

I confessed to him what I had done; he understood but told me I would have to leave Ephesus by the first available vessel. He told me he would take Nathaniel's body to John for burial. I would not hear of it, Nathaniel's body would be going back to Paphus for internment. I was then taken to Nathaniel; his body had already been wrapped in a burial cloth. Quintos could not dissuade me in my actions. I had to act fast so I begged him to see John and asked him to give me absolution. With a heavy heart I helped put the body of my son on the back of a donkey and headed for the harbour.

I turned into the Arcadiana, the harbour street, and I could see there was a back log of traffic heading towards the harbour. I knew now that the Romans had found the bodies and were searching people at the harbour entrance, so I turned down the side of the gymnasium where there is a back passageway. I unwrapped my son, kissed him and then I took over his body. I was instantly filled with an overwhelming feeling of depression, what with the fading memories of Nathaniel coupled with my sadness at losing him. I soon regained my composure, let the donkey go free and I walked to the harbour.

I assumed the Romans were searching for me because the two young prostitutes from the brothel were there with the soldiers, they were looking at everyone. This did not worry me as I was in the guise of Nathaniel. When it was my turn to go past, one of the girls looked me in the eyes and I am sure was about to say something. I was not Nathaniel's biological father and I was not a Greek, so there was no resemblance between Nathaniel and

I, however, she did see something in me. Whether she changed her mind or something changed it for her, perhaps the real reason was she did not want to help the Romans, to this day I do not know the answer. Anyway I was allowed to enter the harbour and was then able to book my passage to Cyprus.

I landed at the other side of the island from Paphus, which suited my purpose much better; Nathaniel and I were not that well known this side of the island so I traveled overland to the sheep farm bypassing Paphus. I prepared a place next to his wife and child. I must have sat there almost all the next day not wanting to leave his body, knowing when I did it would be a long time until I saw him again. When I eventually did leave his body, I kissed my son for the last time and buried him. I just felt so alone I just could not go on. I walked further up into the hills and found a cave; I went into a self serving hibernation. I can't tell you how long I was in an inactive state but when I did go down into Paphus to break the news about Nathaniel, the family informed me that they also had news of their own. It seemed that Vesuvius had erupted in Italy killing thousands of people in Herculaneum and Pompeii and totally entombed the latter. Whether it was a coincidence or another burden I must carry I do know, but every time I came out of my self-exile it seemed another disaster had happened. I know it's selfish of me but sometimes I feel I can't go on, I feel that way now. But don't worry reader I will not be going anywhere at the moment because if I do not locate the spear soon we will all be having a long rest.

Finally I end this chapter with a personal message for the people of Cyprus who believe they have the bones of

Lazarus. I am afraid you do not have them in your possession for they are a necessity I can not dispense with at the moment, but do not despair for you have a far greater treasure in your charge, you have the bones of a far superior man, my one and only son Nathaniel. So take good care of them my dear friends for you have the final remains of a truly chivalrous humanitarian.

CHAPTER TEN

What Isabella wants, Isabella gets

Alexander Longsden-Smythe, or plain Alex Smythe, graduated with honours from Cambridge University fifteen years ago. He joined a merchant bank in the heart of the City of London. Everyone who met him knew that he was going to the top one day but what took most of them by surprise was the short amount of time it took him to get there. Alex became the golden boy when he caught the eye of Isabella Longsden. She made it clear that she wanted him and what Isabella wanted she always got, and so two years after they met they married. The following year Isabella gave birth to a son, Oliver. No one could deny Alex had talent but it doesn't harm your prospects when your boss is also your father-in-law.

After seven years of marriage something altered in Isabella's demeanour, she became moody and would lose her temper at the slightest thing. Oliver was in school all day and when Alex was at work she became very bored, almost with life itself, so they jointly decided to try for another baby. The total anticipation of the birth of the baby appeared to pull her out of her melancholy a little but when she gave birth to another boy she slipped right back into deep depression almost immediately after

Ashley's christening. Alex knows now that he should have made the observation sooner at how depressed Isabella was becoming but he was too preoccupied with business. He was in the middle of taking a huge risk with the bank's money, it entailed sailing pretty close to the wind but why did he take these gambles? The primary reason was the money but he was filled with adrenalin when he came out on top, and that was the case on this occasion. His father-in-law was delighted; he showed Alex how to divide the pie to their advantage. After a little tax avoidance by a very creative accountant, Alex's allocation was over a million pounds, this would secure theirs and the boys' financial future but Isabella had other ideas for the money.

She decided she wanted to buy a house in a rural setting. "The fresh air would be good for the boys and they could learn to horse ride, it would make us so much closer. It would be great for the boys to grow up in that environment," she told Alex.

When he pulled up in the drive of a Georgian mansion in rural Oxfordshire he could feel something was not right. The estate agent said it was in need of updating and the vendor was flexible about the price but that did not matter, Alex had no intentions of buying this house at any price. He was getting bad vibes from it, it was as if an inner voice was telling him not to purchase the house. Unfortunately Isabella fell in love with the place, and what Isabella wants, Isabella gets.

Two months later, contracts were exchanged and a total renovation was underway. Whilst the renovations were taking place, the builders discovered a secret underground chamber; it seemed like the sort of place that clandestine activities of black magic had taken place.

Alex wanted to have the contractors brick it up at once but Isabella thought it would be fun to restore it to its former glory, they could then show it to family and friends and use it as a talking point.

"How many people do you know who have a secret room in their house, it would be great to flaunt it," she said excitedly.

Work did eventually take place on restoration of the room because what Isabella wants...

The nearer to completion the more obsessed she became with the room and black magic, this was detrimental to the rest of the house and the family. She persuaded Alex that Oliver would be better off at boarding school; Ashley in the meantime spent more and more time with his nanny. Instead of helping her, Alex started to stay at his in-laws to be nearer to work. At the weekends, all Isabella wanted to do was to travel the country going to book fairs trying to find books on the occult. One bookstall holder told her of a French man who had a bookshop that specialized in the occult; the address he gave her was in Dover. The following weekend, Alex and the boys went south with her.

They met the French man, named Raul Henry, he was tall with short neatly cut black hair with a swarthy epidermis. He was very well dressed and very good looking, he was oozing with garlic charm. Almost immediately, Isabella became obsessed with him. She invited him to stay the weekend at the house so that he could examine the secret room. The following Saturday, he arrived just before noon. His car was full of books; he had also brought a puppy for the boys. Now any womanizer will tell you that the best way to seduce a woman is to befriend her children first.

"What a really nice man Raul is, I said we were thinking of getting the boys a dog," she said to Alex later.

"Exactly we were thinking, we should not let some French prat make our minds up for us," Alex said annoyed.

"Are you jealous of him my darling?" Isabella asked half jokingly.

"Have I cause to be?" Alex responded.

She did not reply, she just laughed and carried on preparing lunch but inwardly she was fantasizing about what it would be like to have sex with Raul, she loved her husband with all her heart but she no longer desired him. A crack in her life had emerged almost overnight, now whether the fault was always in her personality and was just waiting to break out at any time or this man had brought about an internal earthquake that had put this rupture in her world she didn't know, she did however know that if she took one more step forward she would fall head first into a void she could not return from. A voice inside her head told her to stop this dangerous game she was playing but she couldn't, Isabella wanted to go on and what Isabella wants...

Over the next few months she fell completely under the control of Raul. He convinced her to invite over several French Satanist to re-enact a ritual in the room. In return she assured Alex it was just a harmless masquerade and it would be fun. The children were sent to stay with their grandparents before the French arrived. When Alex was introduced to the leader, a man named Antoine De-Burgh, he laughed to himself thinking that if he was ever to make a film about vampires he knew who he would cast in the star role.

That all happened three months ago, now Alex was in the back of a rented Ford with three French Satanists he barely knew heading north up the M1 with instructions from De-Burgh to retrieve a spear head and to kill those who had it in their possession. He had witnessed three terrible scenes that night that still haunted him so much that he could scarcely go back into his memory to replay the actions because they were so distressing.

Firstly he had seen a young girl ritually murdered in the secret room at his home. Watching this brutal act, he was still in a state of shock when all at once an entity appeared to emerge from her body. It was hideous, like a type of deformed lizard. Larger than a man it stood upright on its two back legs and started to converse with De-Burgh in what Alex believed to be Latin. Alex's legs went weak and he felt like he was going to be sick but what happened next was even worse. Isabella was fornicating with Raul Henry; her eyes were full of glee and excitement watching the demon. Alex knew his wife was too far gone to save, he now believed in the devil and consequently accepted that there was a God and he had offended him, for weeks earlier he and his wife had sold their souls to Satan. At the time he thought it was just harmless bullshit but he now knew it was a binding contract. Alex had the overwhelming feeling that he was going to die so he began to think about his family and about how much he had upset them by changing his name to Longsden-Smythe when he married. On reflection he now realized it was his father-in-law's doing. He contemplated on John Paul Longsden and it dawned on him that he had been used right from the start; all the questionable deals that had taken place at the bank were all authorized by Alex. Should any of them had gone amiss it would have been left for Alex to carry the can on his own however, when it came to dividing the ill-gotten gains Longsden would always take the lions share. The Longsden family had certainly used him. John Paul had persuaded him to sell his ethical business soul and his wife had seduced him into selling his immortal soul to the devil. He knew what he had to do. He was going to try to pull off the most complicated deal of his life; he was going to attempt to win back his immortal soul.

As he sat back in the car waiting for the opportunity to act he started to think about a girl he had met at school, Helen Henshaw. Helen was blonde whereas Isabella was dark; both women were beautiful but completely different. He wondered what his life would have been like if he had married Helen instead. He was still dating Helen when he met his wife, Isabella, but she made it clear to Alex that it would be good for his career if he dated her instead. And we know all too well that what Isabella wants, Isabella gets...

CHAPTER ELEVEN

A History Lesson

I sit here now thinking about what to tell you and what to leave out, feeling like the best man at a wedding looking at all the cards and messages from well-wishers knowing that I can't read them all out for fear of boring everyone. Allow me to tell you one or two facts about your history, hopefully without being too monotonous, for you see the information you have attained from your history books has not always been the truth. In most cases it has been written by the victors and anything from a little spin to a complete fabrication has been inserted. You see if someone puts a falsehood in print then everyone believes it. Take the other day; I was having a drink with an acquaintance at my club when I couldn't help overhearing a man talking to his companion. It seemed to me that he wanted the entire room to hear.

"Christianity is a load of bullshit, Jesus didn't die on the cross, he went to live in France and he had children with Mary Magdalene."

I think he was referring to a book published a few years earlier but he was getting his facts a little mixed up. He pontificated on, saying,

"He was visited by all the apostles and even his mother's sister went to see him." Again, like I said, because it's in print it has to be true.

I just couldn't help myself, I had to interrupt.

"Did his mother visit him?"

The man was in his late forties. He was well dressed probably a high powered company director or something, someone who liked the sound of his own voice and would stick to the age old principle of answering a question right away so that he didn't sound unintelligent, and what he didn't know he made up.

"No she didn't."

"So all the apostles and even his aunt visited him yet his own mother stayed in Ephesus, I think you would have to agree with me that any self respecting mother would have walked on her hands and knees to visit the son that she presumed was dead. What you are saying makes no sense, I don't know what book you have been reading but I wouldn't put to much credence into something that has made a fundamental mistake like that."

When I finished I turned back to my companion. I think for the first time in his life the man was speechless. I don't know what facts were in this book, if any, for I haven't read it - but don't you see that even if the evidence was overwhelming that Jesus Christ was not the Son of God or someone was claiming to have found his body, then that evidence would have been planted in the past by the devil, for he is trying to end this world and is trying to undermine your faith just like he did with Judas, and he is a very clever manipulator. Although I have to give my nemesis some credit because the cleverest thing he has done is to convince the majority of you that he doesn't exist. You see there is a gate between this world and the next and every so often demons sneak through causing havoc in history while trying to impress their Master; it is at those times when the evidence would have been planted. This time though, I think he is here himself.

The last time we met was in 1944 when he was helping the Nazis with their nuclear testing. I stopped him on that occasion and will tell you more about that later but first I would like to tell you about one or two people I have met over the years.

Emperor Hadrian (76AD - 138AD)

Publius Aelius Hadrianus, to give him his full name, was a good man in spite of what my fellow Jews may have thought, although he was responsible for knocking down Jerusalem after suppressing yet another Jewish uprising. He then established the Roman city of Aelia Capitolina in its place banning all Jews from entering. He was not being anti-semitic, he was just trying to keep the peace. That is what he did in Britain when he built the famous seventy- three mile wall to keep out the savages from the far north. Some say it should never have been taken down, - only joking, over the years I have met some very good Scottish friends. He brought stability and peace to the Empire so yes, he was a good man.

Constantine The Great (280AD - 337AD)

Now the only thing great about this man was his mother. He had been credited with bringing Christianity to the Roman Empire, but the credit for that should have gone to his mother and I will go into detail later.

Attila The Hun (406AD - 453AD)

Historians haVe asked the question of why Attila stopped at the gates of Rome when he could have ransacked the city. I will tell you why, because I stopped him. It started with him invading Gaul, he was defeated by the combined forces of the Romans and Visigoths so he turned towards Italy ransacking and pillaging everything in his way until he reached Rome. The city was at his mercy, he camped outside the city walls ready to attack the next day when an envoy was sent from the city by Pope Leo I. How do I know? Because I was the envoy. I reached Attila's line and asked to be taken to him. The first thing I noticed about the Huns was not only did they look like animals with all their fur but they also smelt like them.

Attila was feasting when I was taken before him. Because of my gift of tongues I could converse easily with him. I explained that Pope Leo had sent me with gifts and a blessing from the one true God. He thanked me for the offerings and said he had a lot to do in the morning and needed his bed.

"I will see you on the morrow minus your head," he said while yawning.

I thought I must have misheard him but how very wrong I was for the next thing I knew I was being manhandled by two barbarians and taken outside. I was pushed brutally to the ground; I was confused at what was happening at first until I felt some kind of blade hitting the back of my neck severing my head. It was surreal; I could see my headless body still twitching and Attila's men laughing. This was the first time in my life when I have to say I literally lost my head. I lay there with my head to one side and my body to the other until I was alone.

I always like the theatre and knew it was time for me to perform my theatrics. I crawled over and retrieved my head and made my way back to Attila as he was sleeping. I crept past his guards and into his tent keeping my head under my arm. I went over to Attila and woke him from his sleep.

"I couldn't wait till the morning, I would like to go back to the city to my bed as I have a lot to do tomorrow, so I need to know if you will be heeding Pope Leo's request and not attacking Rome."

At first I think Attila thought he was dreaming but when he realised he wasn't, the man who was terrifying the world soiled himself. It was time for part two of the theatrics, I affixed my head back onto my shoulders and the wound in my neck began to heal itself in front of Attila's eyes. He just sat upright in his own excrement not moving a muscle. I then said with a hint of amusement,

"Now I have got my head together I can think more clearly and can take my time to assimilate your answer."

Attila just sat open-mouthed. "I take it from your lack of response that you will take up the Pope's kind instructions and go from whence you came."

Against the advice of his generals, he turned his army away from the city and he died completely insane the following year. A horrible individual.

Louis IX (1214AD - 1270AD)
The only French ruler to be declared a saint, although many convinced themselves they were. He made running the country look easy, he improved the tax system by distributing help to the poor, and he truly was a saint.

Edward I (1239AD - 1307AD)
What makes me laugh about the English is that they were so outraged when the Nazis made the Jews wear the yellow stars so that they could be easily identified yet it

was their own King Edward I who started the evil practice. A truly wicked man.

ISobella (1451AD - 1504AD)

A very evil woman who browbeat her inadequate husband Ferdinand II. She was best known for her support of Christopher Columbus but should be remembered for the Spanish Inquisition she established when an innocent person was sent to a distasteful death. A very evil woman who you would not want as a mother-in-law.

Napoleon Bonaparte (1769AD - 1821AD)

The 'little corporal' started out with the right intentions but like so many leaders, he started to believe his own propaganda. In the end he made the mistake of caring for himself more than France. He was no Alexander the Great although he may have thought he was.

Simon Bolivar (1783AD - 1830AD)

Simon served under Napoleon but became disillusioned with him and went back to South America. He freed Venezuela, Columbia, Panama, Ecuador, Peru and Bolivia from the control of the Spanish. A man who started and finished with the right intensions, a man I am proud to have called a friend. A magnificent general.

Abraham Lincoln (1809AD - 1865AD)

An oasis of sanity in a desert of madness. From 1861 to 1865, America's darkest time, many demons slipped through the gates from the underworld to cause devastation on both sides of the conflict. I was just too late from removing one from John Wilkes-Booth on April 15th

1865 and had to watch yet another good man go before his time was due.

Mohandas Karamchand Gandhi
(1869AD - 1948AD)

Gandhi led the freedom strUggle against the British on a non-violent policy. A great man who not only was concerned about his own people but was an ardent supporter of the Muslims. It's ironic that his concern for others should result in his assassination.

John F. Kennedy (1917AD - 1963AD)

The Kennedy family's intentions may not have been that forthright regarding the office but when John took on the role he developed into a good president. He had his human frailties and at times found it hard to control his own animal instincts but as a leader he was trying to do the right thing. Why else was he eliminated? That also begs the question as to who killed him, was it the Soviets, the Cubans, the Mafia or even the Americans themselves? No, it was the beast in the guise of Lee Harvey-Oswald. When the devil departed Oswald, he was aware of what he had done but also knew he was not responsible for his actions hence him saying, "I am just the patsy."

These are just a few people I have known throughout the ages. Next I would like to tell you about three incidents in my life. One successful and two not so! They involved three main people and I would like to dedicate a chapter to each to them. Empress Helena, mother of Constatius I; King Arthur of Britain, the most noble Roman of them all; and Gregory Efimovich Rasputin. But first I must explain how I was inaccurate about the date of my Master's birth.

CHAPTER TWELVE

The Loft

They were about twenty minutes from reaching the outskirts of Stockport at the very precise time their friend died in a London hospital. OB woke up Jamie, who was sleeping and said,

"For the past hour there have been four brand new Fords following us, each car had four people inside. Do you think it's the police?"

For the next fifteen minutes Jamie watched as the cars alternated to the lead position. If the motorway had been full of traffic they may well have got away with their manoeuvres but not at this time of night. They didn't even fool OB and he wouldn't have been given a policeman's job in Toy Town, but even he could see a tail that was blatantly obvious.

"Well spotted OB," Jamie said and patted OB on the back.

The big simple lad just smiled, if he had possessed a tail he would have wagged it. Then Jamie starting barking out his commands.

"Now don't take the first turning off, leave at the Lancashire Hill roundabout," OB did as requested and sure enough the four cars followed.

Jamie said, "Right Steve McQueen let's take these boys on a wild goose chase. Turn down Belmont Way and do a left on to the A6 then a right down George's Road. Take it nice and easy until you turn off George's Road then drive like a bat out of hell to the Bonks, they won't realize it's a dead end until the last minute. It will be pitch black by the fishing pond; they will break their necks when they start to follow."

The lads had doubled back on foot to the A6 while the occupants of the car were still trying to negotiate the path by the fishing pond.

OB and Jamie were now back on their own street. Jamie told OB he would see him first thing in the morning and he watched as OB went into his own house just four doors away. When Jamie went into his own house he realized OB could have stayed the night as his mum was away visiting her sister in Middlewich. He washed and went to his bed at the back of the house. He couldn't sleep; he just lay there thinking what they were going to do.

About an hour later he heard a noise in the back garden; he went to the window and looked down. There were four men climbing over his back gate. He ran through to his mother's bedroom and looked into the street; he couldn't believe it, parked outside were the four cars from the chase. He knew now that these were not police; they had to be friends of the heavies. How had they found them? Maybe Stanie was right all along, it was supernatural. He had no time to think, but both he and OB were in very serious trouble.

Before they attempted anything from outside, Jamie had dressed, taken the spear and run downstairs into the kitchen. He opened the cupboard door under the sink; he knew what he was looking for he just hoped it was still there. He was in luck, 'Thanks mum' he said to himself and picked up the spare washing line. As he went back to the bottom of the stairs and he heard a knock on the front door,

"Police, open up," a voice said, the voice had a hint of a French accent.

"Interpol in Heaton Norris, I don't think so somehow," Jamie whispered to himself, he still had his sense of humour even though he didn't have an audience. He took the washing line and tied it to both interior doors at the bottom of the stairs; he walked back up the stairs and fastened the line to his mother's bedroom door, then went into his bedroom and knotted it around a rock the size of a football. His father and he had found the rock fifteen years ago; it had a seashell fossil hidden in it. His dad explained to him that a million years ago it had been on the sea bed. He always though his dad was the cleverest man in world, however five years later he wasn't clever enough to get out of the way of a bus when he was walking home drunk from the pub. Jamie felt bitter towards his dad for leaving him when he loved him so much, he was only twelve, and he should have been out with his friends not stopping, his mother from getting drunk all the time.

The men were now attempting to break in the doors, front and back. He took a set of loft ladders that were always under his bed. All the lofts in the street were connected, he used to climb up there to get to OB's house, and when they had been on the rob in the bad old days they would hide things up there. He put the ladders against the wall, climbed them and opened the trap door in the ceiling. He then went back to his bedroom and secured the washing line around his bed post, leaving just enough line for it to drop out of the window.

The assailants were now in the house. He needed to act fast. He opened the window and looked down; one guy was still in the garden smoking. 'Good' he thought, 'my mum doesn't like smoking in the house', the humour was still coming even at a time like this. The witty temperament he had developed was when his dad had died, people kept coming up to him and asking if he was alright. How could he answer that? Of course he wasn't alright, he would never be alright again, his dad was dead and his mother was a drunk so he started to be funny and crack jokes at every opportunity. It stopped people from asking him if he was okay.

He then threw the rock down with the line. It hit the man right on top of his crown, and he collapsed without a murmur in a heap in the garden. 'That sucker will have some headache when he wakes up, if he ever does', he thought. He ran back to the ladders and scaled up them into the loft. He had just managed to lift the loft ladders up through the hatch and close it when the interior doors at the bottom of the stairs began to break. He slowly and silently moved along the central beam of the loft to OB's house to warn him.

He opened the hatch and couldn't believe his eyes; a man had his hand over OB's mother's mouth while with the other hand he was stabbing her in the stomach. Jamie could just make out the dead body of OB's dad on the landing. He slowly replaced the trap door. What was he to do? His best friend and his family were being murdered; reluctantly he realised there was only one thing to do, save himself. He took a very slow pace along the beam to the end house. There was an old man who lived there on his own, and he just hoped that the thugs had been fooled by the rope out of the window trick.

When he eventually reached the end house he opened the hatch. He hung down before jumping the rest of the way. He went downstairs and opened the door; he took a chance and ran round the side of the house. He poked his head round the corner to see if he had been noticed, only to see a very distressing sight. The big daft, gentle giant OB, dressed only in his boxer shorts, was being punched and kicked by three men, who eventually forced him into the back of one of the cars. What could Jamie do? Nothing, he felt sorry for his best friend but ultimately he was glad it wasn't him. He thought to himself, 'What would OB have done in my position?' He knew the answer, like the US 7th cavalry he would have run in there all guns blazing. If he could have told OB one last thing it would have been, with his childlike qualities he possessed, that this world would never be as good as him.

He was just about to turn around and go when he felt the ice cold feeling of a gun barrel in his neck. "Don't move or say anything or you are a dead man my friend."

CHAPTER THIRTEEN

Making Time

The monk, mathematician and astronomer Dionysius Exiguus has been given the dubious credit for setting the Christian calendar wrong, it is now I have to make my confession, I was more responsible than "little Dennis," the name by which I knew the monk.

The Pope sent me to work with Dionysius in 1267 in the Roman Calendar, the year you have come to know as 524AD, and we were given a year to set it up. The Christian Calendar would come into implementation on January 1st 1268RC or Anno Domini 1. Dennis with his knowledge of the planets and the constellation of the stars had made a chart of the heavens over Bethlehem going back through the ages, and came up with the answer that Our Lord was born some time between 736RC and 738RC. The dates are not entirely consistent with the accounts in the Gospel that Mary and Joseph had gone from Nazareth to Bethlehem because of a Roman Census being taken. The date the Romans took their Census of the empire was 745RC or 3AD, but two years earlier a test case was taken and Palestine was picked as the guinea pig. The year was 743 in the Roman calendar, so I overruled Dionysius and settled on this date as the first year of Our Lord 1AD. Now are you with me so far? If you found my explanation complicated can you imagine how difficult it was for Dionysius and I.

Anyway we went with that date and we still use it today. Although a few years later a Bishop from the South of France pointed out to the Holy Father that if this date is correct then King Herod the Great, who slaughtered the holy innocents while Mary and Joseph and the infant Jesus escaped to Egypt, died in the year 4BC according to our ambiguous calendar which made it four years before the Lord's birth. That's why I don't like the French, they always like to point out a mistake as long as it's not theirs!.

Needless to say we received a Papal kick up the rear but the date still stood. I just could not understand how I got the dates wrong.

About fourteen hundred years later I was working for the King of Spain when several airtight pot jars filled with Latin manuscripts were unearthed. One told how a great census had taken place in Spain in 738RC (or 5BC) but because most of the Roman Empire had made a mess of their attempts of the Census the thing was abandoned and re-done in the year 745RC (or 3AD), so a Census took place in 738 in the Roman world but because they made such a mess it was ripped out of the pages of history. Like I say the victors write history at the time. Of course they don't make errors and when they do, they don't want to tell us about it. So that explains why Mary and Joseph visited Bethlehem in 738RC.

I also found out years later that Chinese astronomers recorded in their annals about an exploding star or super nova in the spring of 5BC. This must have been the star the Magi observed from the East. So you see Dionysius was right after all, Jesus of Nazareth was born in the year 5BC. Consequently making the Christian calendar five years out, all because of my fault and the failed Census. What is there to say? I may be nearly two thousand years old but I am still only human and we all make mistakes. Anyway I was approximately right and what's five years between friends.

CHAPTER FOURTEEN

Consecrated Ground

The man holding the gun to Jay's neck was Alexander Longsden-Smythe, who said quietly in Jay's ear,

"Listen to me very carefully; I am not going to hurt you. I think you are already aware that there are people after you, they will cause you a lot of misery before they kill you. Now listen to me I am deadly serious, something more important is happening here than that. There is another individual who is after you and this one is not human, believe it or not son you are being pursued by the devil. He's after the spear you took and if you have it in your possession you must take it to consecrated ground."

Alex could see the young man was confused so he said it again very slowly,

"Get to a church as soon as possible, that is the only place you will be safe. Now go, get out of here, I will see what I can do for your friend. Go!"

For a few seconds Jay couldn't move, it was as if he was paralyzed. He managed to move his right leg slowly and then ran through the pub car park opposite the houses and across the road; he just ran and ran as if the hounds of hell were after him because apparently they were.

Alex doubled back down the alley and then ran towards the railway embankment to discharge his weapon into the bushes. The other men came running towards him. Alex just said,

"I saw the other lad go in there."

"You fool, shooting your gun off like that will wake up everyone around here, we will have to leave before the police get here," De-Burgh said angrily.

'That was my intention, frog' Alex thought to himself. He was informed by De-Burgh that his wife had proved more useful than him, she had found them a safe house just a few miles away, they would take the other boy there and question him.

They returned to their cars and turned onto the A6 towards Macclesfield. Isabella had a friend from school who she had kept in touch with, she now lived in a restored farmhouse just outside Macclesfield and she was in Spain for the winter. Isabella remembered that she always kept a set of keys in the greenhouse in case of emergencies, so OB was taken there.

As Jay was running he thought to himself that Stanie was right about all the supernatural stuff. He had now run through the park and down into Stockport town centre through the shopping precinct. He ran up the other side of the hill towards Offerton. It then dawned on him that he should have been looking for a church and by coincidence, and not design he now found himself not that far away from the church where his father's requiem mass had been held.

He ran down to the church and as he had expected, the doors were locked. He ran around to the priest's house and began to bang on the door.

"Father let me in, help me, the devil is chasing me."

The commotion woke the priest and he opened the upstairs window. "Do you know what time it is?" he shouted down.

Jay looked up and said,

"I've not come here to answer questions at this time of night." He couldn't help himself with the witty remark, if a joke was set up he had to hit for six no matter what the time or place was. It didn't even matter if it was funny or not it just came out automatically. "I need your help Father, the devil is after me!"

The priest had no intention of letting anyone in at this hour, especially a drug gazed yob. He was just about to close the window and phone the police when he noticed something familiar about the boy. He had big sad eyes like a puppy, and he had seen those eyes before.

"You buried my dad, Father, about ten years ago. My name is Jamie Bredbury and my dad was Peter Bredbury, he was an altar boy of yours."

Father Furpay remembered Peter's boy, the sad little twelve-year-old who stood there all through the service not crying but having the saddest eyes he had ever seen, like the weight of the world was resting on his tiny shoulders. The priest went down the stairs and let Jamie in. He could not calm the poor boy down, he kept wanting to go into the church and eventually the priest relented and took him through to the church. Jamie told the priest his unbelievable story; he seemed to be relieved that the burden of the terrible tale had been shared with the priest.

Father Furpay had put a blanket over Jamie, who was now sleeping peacefully, and he contemplated what to do with him. He knew one thing about the story, the boy truly believed it and whether it was true or not he owed it to Jamie's father to help him. He had also made an oath with God to help those in need and he did believe in the devil. He was professionally obliged to help him however. He didn't really believe that the devil was chasing this lad, although he did decide to check out some of Jamie's story.

He left the boy sleeping, clutching the spear head which was obviously a very valuable antique. He took his car and went to Jamie's home; there were police everywhere. He asked one of the policemen what had gone on and when the policeman saw he was a man of the cloth he decided to tell him what had happened, and he confirmed parts of Jamie's story. He informed Father Furpay that a man and woman had been killed and a woman and two young men had been abducted from the two houses. Father Furpay was just about to tell the policeman that he had one of the boys at his church when something almost physically stopped him, he tried to speak but couldn't. An inner voice was telling him to be quiet and not to say a word but to go back to the church because his life was in danger here. For some illogical reason, he complied with the inner voice and went back to his car. It was a good thing that he didn't say anything because there was a man standing near to the policeman listening to the conversation. He was one of the French Satanist's left behind to keep an eye on the scene and report back to De-Burgh what was going on.

When Father Furpay arrived back at the church Jamie was still sleeping. He looked at him and thought that if half of what he said was true then this poor young man had seen more heartbreak in his short life than most people see in a lifetime. He knelt in a pew near to the sleeping boy and began to pray for guidance.

As dawn broke the light shone through the stained glass windows of the church. Father Furpay had never seen the church looking more beautiful and holy. The light gave him inspiration, and he knew now what he needed to do. He would try to contact the original owner of the spear; he would get the address from Jamie when he woke up. Perhaps if the spear was back with its rightful owner the young man would feel at ease.

OB had been tortured for hours by De-Burgh and his men. Alex had noticed how much they enjoyed it, even his wife. The spectacle sickened him to his very soul, that's if he still had one. The poor young man had told them nothing because the unfortunate lad knew nothing, most of what had happened since Saturday night had gone completely over his head apart from one thing, the goal he scored on Sunday, that had gone over his head and into the back of the onion bag.

CHAPTER FIFTEEN

In Hoc Signo Vinces

In 312AD, I was in the guise of a dead Roman General named Janus; I was working with the Co-Emperor Constantine who was ruling the empire with Emperor Licinius. You notice I said with and not for, as no man on earth has commanded me since the Master although many a King and Ruler may have thought they did. I would go to where the spear sent me and if needs be would fight for the right side, especially when the opposition contained a demon in their ranks as was the case in 312AD.

The self proclaimed Emperor Maxentius' army had surrounded Constantine's army about four miles north of Rome. We were outnumbered two to one and slowly but surely we were losing this battle, when a message came to me from Constantine,

"You must keep them at bay until nightfall."

I assumed he wanted me to hold them back until dark, so that with the cover of darkness he and a small band of cohorts would try to save their ineffectual hides by reaching Licinius. It was just then that I noticed Maxentius about two hundred yards away from me, smashing through our columns like they were made of paper.

I knew then for sure that a demon was inside him so, like the English Bowmen of Henry V a few centuries later - who would hold two fingers up to the French before the commencement of battle, indicating that they still had their ultimate weapon - I produced my own secret weapon, the spear of Jesus Christ that was hanging around my neck. I took it off and held it above my head, then roared at Maxentius. When he saw the spear head he went white in the face and his eyes turned red, as he began to slowly fall back.

I sent a runner back with a message for Constantine that I would take a third of the men and push Maxentius' army back towards the Milvian Bridge; with a Centurion and his men I would hold the bridge until he came. I would send the rest of the men back to him to help him mop up what remains of Maxentius' army.

The plan was working well; Maxentius' army was snatching defeat out of the jaws of victory. Eventually we managed to push them to the other side of the bridge. I kept just one hundred men and two officers, like I said I would, and then sent the remainder back to the Emperor. The one thing I did know was that Maxentius or the thing inside him would be nowhere to be seen because he could not dare to come into contact with the spear. So he was somewhere at the back of his lines martialling his Generals to overwhelm the occupants of the bridge. In doing this he could reclaim the spear and destroy it for his Master. What the demon didn't take into account was the Roman short sword and the men who carried them, but most importantly the position we were in, it would only take a few men to contain the bridge. It was not wide enough for a large charge so my fellow officers, Horatio and Markus, and I held off attack after attack.

Every so often a spear bombardment was launched; we had advance warning when the spears were coming because the attackers of the bridge fell back, and so we locked our shields together over our heads and in front of us to form a defensive position called a turtle. On the odd occasion a spear would break through wounding one of my men, but both ourselves and our assailants knew we could hold this position all day and night.

That was when the deadlock was broken; the demon initiated a spear barrage to be sent over when we were engaged in combat with his men. Far from being our downfall it became his. The shower of spears came over as we managed to form a turtle at the last minute, but our opponents were not that fortunate and were pulverized by their own men.

Now any good soldier needs to believe in something, when he loses that he forfeits the battle. I once asked an Irish soldier at the Battle of Waterloo why he was fighting for the English. He said,

"I hate the English with a vengeance but I would die for the British Crown."

You see that was the case with all these soldiers, they were not fighting for Constantine or Maxentius; they believed they were fighting for Rome. The one thing Rome did not do was to kill her own men in battle, so they retired from the conflict never to attempt to take the bridge again.

About one hour later they came forward to the bridge with no weapons and with Maxentius and his generals in shackles. I sent Markus back with a message that we had taken Maxentius' army. Constantine and his men could not believe their eyes; a hundred men had taken three-quarters of Maxentius' army prisoner. When

Constantine realised it was true that he had won, his face was full of jubilation. He made his way to the manacled Maxentius, and before I could say anything he ran him through with his sword. When the man lay dying the demon left his body and came out in the open. It seemed only I could see him, he had a twisted distorted body full of scales and sores, a lizard type creature standing upright on his two back legs. He just smiled at me and bowed, then ran across the ground on all fours and entered the carcass of a dead horse. No one paid any consideration when the white horse got up and ran away; maybe they thought it was a wounded animal running away to die. The men's attention was drawn to Constantine who was running down the line of shackled generals, killing them like they were sheep in a slaughterhouse. The men were not cheering; they just stood there in total silence. The one thing about a soldier, he knows how battle was won and who won it. It certainly was not Constantine and they knew it, he was acting like the recipient of a surprise party, opening all the gifts when in reality he was more like a gatecrasher.

When he finished the entire killing he looked to his men for approval. When no one was forthcoming he realised the gravity of the situation; he felt like a jackal at the kill that decided to dine before the lion. He knew he had to win them back so he told them to kill and loot the vanquished army of Maxentius.

That is when I made my intervention. I told him I had given my word, the word of a Roman General which cannot be broken, that as part of the terms of surrender I would give them their lives. Constantine went red in the face and came towards me with this sword still drawn; this is when Horatio acted, whether fearing for my safety or deliberately trying to orchestrate a military coup against a corrupt Emperor, I don't know. He banged on his shield, at the same time shouting "Jan-us Jan-us."

Then his men did the same. The gamble really paid off when the rest of the troops joined in, and by the time Constantine had made the short journey to me the vanquished army of Maxentius were joining in with the shouting,

"Jan-us, Jan-us, Jan-us."

I held my hands up to stop them. Constantine was anything but an idiot and could see that if he didn't act fast he could lose it all, he came up to me and dropped the sword at my feet, then kissed me on both sides of my cheeks and said,

"You are not only a great General, you are a great man. Tonight there will be a banquet in your honour." The men cheered.

That night at the end of the feast, Constantine told me to go away and have a good sleep, then in the morning meet him for breakfast and should I ask for anything it would be granted. I couldn't make up my mind whether he was being genuine or not, but at about three in the morning I got my answer.

I was in a sound sleep when something woke me. I started to rise but some heavy weight bore down on me, it seemed a pillow was being held over my face. The next thing I knew my throat was cut. The pillow fell from my face just before I lost consciousness, and I was able to see my assassins. I can't put into words how disappointed I felt when I recognised one of my assailants to be Markus, the man who had fought so gallantly by my side on the bridge. I tell you, to be let down by someone you like takes a long time to forgive and even longer to forget.

I do not know what inducement Constantine offered Markus to betray me. In the short time I had known him I really began to like and trust him. He was a man I would have died for. I grant you not that much of a big deal for someone who couldn't stay dead but it's the thought that counts. I just can't make out my fellow man, are the majority of you just shit bags waiting for the opportunity to be corrupted? Was the married woman faithful for forty years because she was honest or because no one took time to seduce her? I did take some comfort that Horatio was not part of the attack.

The next morning I went to breakfast with Constantine and his mother as arranged, and obviously he was surprised to see me. I told them I'd had a dream last night that my throat was being cut and I had woken up this morning with a very sore throat. Constantine seemed uncomfortable; he was playing nervously with his neck. Helena, his mother said,

"It is funny you should be talking about dreams, I have just been telling my son about the one I had before the battle. I saw a vision in the sky of a shining cross bearing the words 'In Hoc Signo Vinces' which means 'by this sign you will conquer'."

We both agreed it was the work of the Christ so I knew what I wanted from Constantine; permission to go to Aelia Captalina, the Roman name for Jerusalem, to search for Golgotha the place where he was crucified, and reclaim him back for Christ. Empress Helena was so excited she pleaded to go with me. I said if the Emperor's mother was going with me I would need a bodyguard, I knew just the men, Horatio and his men. This would do two things, it would keep Horatio out of the way of reprisals and promote both him and his men to the rank of Praetorian guards, which would double their pay and take them out of the front line for the lifetime of Empress Helena. What became of Markus I do not know, I assume Constantine had him killed for lying about my demise. He must have been befuddled when he died but like the saying goes 'you reap what you sow.'

The most important thing, we found Golgotha and the tomb of my Master. Eventually in the year 326AD, the Church of the Holy Sepulchre was built over the two sites. Christianity became the official religion of the Roman Empire. In the year 313AD, the edict of Milan was signed returning property back to the Christians. Once Constantine realised I had no political desire he left me alone. That cannot be said for his Co-Emperor poor Licinius who was eliminated and Constantine became the sole ruler of the empire.

After his mother's death he re-wrote the history of the battle of the Milvian Bridge, claiming that before the battle he saw a vision in the sky of a shining cross bearing the words 'In Hoc Signo Vinces'. There was no mention of a general called Janus, just an account of how almost single-handedly he averted defeat while being outnumbered two to one. Like I said before, he was the victor so he could write history.

Constantine may not have been a good man or Emperor but as for the creation of pure fiction William Shakespeare, Charles Dickens and modern day authors like Stephen King would have had a run for their money. You may ask why I did not stop the murdering Constantine. It is because I believed I achieved my purpose bringing Christianity to the Roman world. I also heeded my Master's words, "Render to Caesar what is Caesar's and to God what is God's."

Just one more detail before I finish this chapter. Maxentius' body was never found on the battlefield. The rumour circulated at the time that Maxentius was seen riding away from Milvian Bridge on the back of a white horse. Shortly afterwards his entire family disappeared and everyone assumed that Constantine had had them liquidated. I don't know what really happened to him, but I do know that when a demon is taken out of a mortal the individual gets a second chance to live their life the right way. Did Maxentius take the opportunity he had been given or did he just fall back into the saddle?

CHAPTER SIXTEEN

MC and Anybody's Piece

At 9am in the CID's office of a police station not to far away from the hospital where Stanie had died the night before, DS Sue Hogan sat at her desk reviewing reports that had been brought to her from incidents that had taken place last night. One report was about a dead body found in an alleyway along with another seriously injured man and a green BMW. The seriously injured man was now in an intensive care unit and was hanging onto his life. Sue then came across another report that had just come in. The report ascertained that a young man had been shot and had been taken to the same hospital as the seriously injured man from the previous report. The report then got interesting. It stated that the young man had registered himself as Peter Kelly but in his possession was a season ticket for Manchester City Football Club and a credit card in the name of Stephen Stanton. She then went back to the previous report. In the first report it was said that inside the glove compartment of the BMW was a logbook made out to a Stephen Stanton. 'These two incidents were related', she thought.

Sue looked up to a glass partition and into the office of her boss DI Mike Connor. He wasn't there. She thought to herself that he was probably out buying another egg and bacon sandwich, and she wondered how many more bacon sandwiches it would take to see him off, the fat bastard. She hated him with a vengeance; she often wondered how she would keep a straight face at his funeral, that's if she bothered to take the time to go. She looked around the open office and realised that she didn't like any of her colleagues; in fact if they were all to go on a day out and the coach crashed, the only thing that would upset her would be the fact that Mike Connor wasn't driving it.

She was twenty-five, tall, slim and very attractive with long dark hair. She worked out twice a week at a gym near her home. She was young with a very healthy sexual appetite and she had no intentions of settling down at the moment as she wanted fun while she was still young. Her mother had married young and grown old before her time, and Sue was determined that wasn't going to happen to her. In the past two years she had been romantically involved with three people from her own station. If she were a man she would be known as a 'jack the lad' but to her male chauvinistic colleagues thought of her as a slag. She and Mike Connor had a nickname bestowed upon them by the others which was 'MC and anybody's piece'; it was supposed to sound like an old TV police show called 'Dempsey and Makepeace'. Anybody's piece was a reference to her, they were trying to imply that she was easy meat. The name and rumours stuck and everyone tried it on with her as though she was desperate, even fat Connor tried his luck with her which almost made her physically heave. She hated all the men at her station and was rapidly becoming a man-hater; that was when she started her fling with Gaynor from the station's canteen. She didn't know Gaynor was a lesbian but they just seemed to click. She asked her out on a girls' night out with some friends and that was when it dawned on Sue that Gaynor was gay, after a few drinks one thing let to another.

As she was daydreaming Mike Connor came in, eating a bacon sandwich, surprisingly. The man was a walking heart attack just waiting to happen. Sue ran into his office excitedly and said,

"I've come up with some very interesting developments on the stiff and the BMW, the logbook in the car..."

He interrupted, "Hang on, get your knickers untwisted and slow down. What stiff and what BMW?"

He hadn't looked at the night brief reports, he had obviously just come in at eight and gone for his first breakfast sandwich of the day, his second would be at about ten-thirty. She sat down and told him about last night's developments regarding Stephen Stanton, when she had finished he said,

"Come on, don't just sit there let's go and see this guy, we'll find out what he's got to say for himself whoever he is."

When they arrived at the hospital they informed the receptionist that they had come to interview a patient in the name of Peter Kelly. Instead of being taken to the young man's hospital room they were taken to the hospital's Head of Administration, John Barrow. They told him they had come to talk to Peter Kelly or Stephen Stanton,

"We think he could be responsible for the death of an individual last night."

"He was almost responsible for another death here this morning," Mr Barrow said.

Connor interrupted, he made a habit of doing that, "You dummies, you haven't let him escape have you?"

Mr Barrow said angrily, "Let me make one thing clear to you, we are not a secure unit in a prison we are a hospital. Now if you would be so kind as to not interrupt when I am speaking, it is very ill-mannered."

Sue couldn't help but smile, it was nice to see the fat man put firmly in his place.

"In answer to your enquiry about the young man in question, he has not escaped, he is dead Mr. Connor."

Connor interrupted again, not learning his lesson, "I thought the injuries were not life threatening?"

Mr Barrow just looked at Connor from over his glasses. "If I may continue, the injuries sustained from the gun wound were not the cause of death; this is where it gets interesting. An autopsy was performed first thing this morning and when the boy was opened up, the pathologist nearly suffered a cardiac arrest. The heart in the boy's chest was not connected. The pathologist swears that there was no evidence of surgical scars around the chest, the only marks on the boy's body were on the right side as a result of the operation on the gunshot wound."

Connor interrupted again, "Is that possible?"

In the nanoseconds it had taken for the words to leave his mouth he instantly knew what a stupid thing he had just said! Of course it wasn't possible; it had just been a knee-jerk reaction to make a verbalization of his thoughts before he'd thought them through rationally. As his face began to go red with embarrassment he wished he could repossess the remark before it could be taken in by the other in the room.

Mr. Barrow looked at him with a knowing look as if he could read his thoughts and he realised the Detective hadn't meant to speak his thoughts out loud. Maybe he didn't, or he was tired with his constant interruptions but he erupted,

"Of course it's not possible you moron, that is why I have instigated an internal investigation." Connor was totally embarrassed by his stupid remark, but Sue was ecstatic at his stupidity.

In the car on the way to the loading bay at the back of the shops where the incident had taken place, Sue asked Connor what he made of it all.

"It's quite simple really. If you were to check with the forensic team's report you would find three types of blood, two would be from the French men and one would be the dead kid's. It's just a drug deal gone wrong. The French men shot the kid then whoever was with the kid ran them over and took off in their car,"

Connor said with a mouthful of sausage which he had got from the hospital canteen. Sue waited until he had finished, not wanting to interrupt as it was rude. "No I didn't mean that, I meant the guy's heart not being connected to anything, with no marks on the body and the doctor ruling out your theory that he could have been born like that."

Connor went red in the face then said, "Oh you're so fucking funny aren't you, none of this better get back to the station. You are such a clever bitch but very naive. It's a well known fact that all doctors are drug addicts, he was probably on a trip brought about by some drug or another, that's what happens when you have the keys to the sweet shop."

Sue just hoped that when Connor had his heart attack, and make no mistake he would have one, she hoped that the doctor who attended him was on drugs and would kill him - which wouldn't just do the world a favour by getting rid of a useless prat like him, but would also be doing the pig population of the UK a favour by stopping them from becoming extinct with him single handedly trying to eat them all.

CHAPTER SEVENTEEN

King Arthur
(Quondam Rexque Futurus)

Yes, King Arthur really did live, however it is his death that has caused most speculation. Was he mortally wounded at the battle of Camlan by his nephew Mordred? Was he killed in an ambush by Maelgwn, the King of Gwynedd? Perhaps it was a Saxon axe that was responsible for his demise or per chance he did not die, but was he taken aboard a barge containing women who looked like angels all dressed in white, that headed towards the Isle of Avalon never to return? I can tell you that Arthur did pass from this world, the noblest Roman of them all died of a broken heart. Why is there no written documents confirming this? Well like I keep telling you, history is written by the victors but when the conquerors are the Saxons, hell bent on destroying everything they came across - for example, on finding Roman villas in mid-winter with central heating, flushing toilets and a heated bath houses, they would smash them up then live in a shack with their animals, wash in a stream and defecate in a field - would imbeciles like that take the time to keep a written account? I think not. So I will tell you the real story of the one and future King (Quondam Rexque Futurus).

Arthur, or his Roman name Arthurian, was born in the year of our Lord 487AD. Although Britain was no longer under Roman occupation it was still a trading partner with the Roman world. Arthur was born in Britain but was as Roman as any occupant of the empire. His great grandfather, a Roman general, on retirement took up the option to take free land to settle on; the land was north of Aquae Arnemetiae (Buxton). The land contained a small salt mine, although the Romans didn't know that at the time it was given anyway. Maybe Arthur's great grandfather had a Roman surveyor in his back pocket, I don't know, needless to say the family became very afflu- ent. Arthur's grandfather, father and Arthur himself were sent to a Roman military school in Constantinople. It was there that he received the news that his family estate had been plundered by Saxons, and all his family members slain apart from his sister Morgause who had married Maelgwn King of Gwynedd, fours years earlier. Britain had become a very lawless place to live after the Romans went home; slowly it started to divide into small king- doms or large estates with private armies. One land owner, neighbouring to Arthur's family's estate, had decided on a cheaper option for their protection. They employed Saxons and this worked out fine until they had a bad year and couldn't find the money to pay them, then the Saxons just turned on them killing them all. But they didn't stop there, they invited a Saxon war band to come over telling them the land was full of rich estates that were easy to take, this was when Arthur's family's estate was attacked. Arthur decided to go back to Britain and avenge his family.

I was working at the school teaching military history; although Arthur was my star pupil I still felt he was not ready to command an army. I tried without success to dissuade him in his quest but when I couldn't, myself and several of his fellow cadets decided to go with him. They included Lancelot, Yuain, Lione, Turquine, Beaumains, Lucan, Palomides, Safer, Segwarides, Ector, Giriflet, Dagonet, Dinadan, Marhaus, Sagramore, Pellinore, Balin, Bor, Balan, Taliessin and Bard. I may have said that these young men were not ready but any one of them was a match for ten Saxons, these men and more became the Knights of the Round Table.

We landed at Dubris (Dover) in 515AD because the people there were still living the Roman way. Our plan was simple; we had to unite the kingdoms to fight off the invaders. We went to Durovernum (Canterbury), Duro-brivae (Rochester), Londinium (London), Verulamium (St Albans), Caesaromagus (Chelmsford) and all the other major towns in the south east, recruiting as we went. While Arthur and his knights trained the recruits in the Roman military warfare, I went north on my own to persuade the true people indigenous to this land, the Celts and their leader Merlin. Arthur had given me instructions to offer them anything and accept any conditions they demanded because the Celts were integral to our plan. They were to come at the Saxon's from the north and the Roman Britons from the south and Maelgwn, Arthur's brother-in-law, from the west. That left only one route for the Saxon's to escape, the east. We were going to push the Saxon's into the North Sea and back from whence they came. Merlin agreed, he liked the Saxons less than the Roman Britons but it was his terms that took me a little by surprise. He asked about our leader and I told him that

Arthur was born in this country and loved her; he was a good man who hated the Saxons.

"Does he have a wife?" Merlin asked.

I told him he had no time for women; he was here to avenge his family and to save this country.

"Then he must make time because my terms are that he marries my oldest daughter."

Well I thought to myself Arthur had told me to accept any of their demands so I agreed and gave my word that our leader would accept. I just couldn't wait to see her, I thought she must be a right old cart horse to make her father want to marry her off to a man he had never met. I could not have been more wrong. Merlin may have been her father but she took after her mother completely, her mother had been a Roman slave of Greek extraction. She had pale brown eyes, high cheekbones, softly rounded lips and a long slender neck that matched her long slender olive body. Her long black hair looked like it had just been styled and would have been considered the very best at any twentieth-century hair fashion show. She was the classic Greek goddess who looked somewhat out of place in fourth-century Britain. Yes, if Helen of Troy was half as good looking then one can almost condone Paris in his inexcusable actions.

The plan worked, Arthur's Roman style army smashed any large band of opponents he encountered. Maelgwn's army stopped them from running west and Merlin ambushed any Saxon trying to escape to the north, eventually we had then penned in the ex-Roman city of Lindum (Lincoln). Arthur had won the war, now was the time to try to win the peace. You should bear in mind that all of Arthur's family apart from one had been murdered by the Saxons. I for one would have understood if he had wanted to kill every last one of them, but no, not Arthur, he wanted peace more than vengeance, that was the nature of the man but also the type of man the devil would like to see on his knees. He offered them safe conduct back to where they had come from or they could settle here and would be allotted small parcels of land to farm as long as they took an oath to Britain. Some Saxon's remained but most returned to their homeland. Arthur was elected high King of Britain by all the other kings, most importantly the Celts saw him as their King as well. Arthur had truly united the kingdom.

Now came the difficult part for me, I had to tell him that to attain our objective I had agreed that he would marry Merlin's daughter.

"No," he said, he was emphatic about his answer, "When I want a wife, I will go out and find one that I love."

He agreed however to meet her. When his eyes met the beautiful brown eyes of Gwenivere, it was love at first sight, or just induced endorphins in the brain. I have often wondered whether my wife would have still loved me when the endorphins had started to fade, after all I had only known her for a few weeks. I know for my part that I will love her until eternity and beyond. I think that was the case with Arthur.

The marriage took place not long after their meeting, and as you know from legend, everyone did not live happily ever after, and I think the infatuation with Gwenivere started for Lancelot at the wedding. He was Arthur's best friend and the most handsome man I had ever perceived, apart from when I look in the mirror that is. He just could not keep his eyes off her. I could see trouble beginning so I introduced Gwenivere's sister to him, she was just as beautiful as Gwenivere and her name was Isolt. Sometimes what you can't have makes you want it more but the good man inside Lancelot realised it was wrong to desire another man's wife, especially his best friend's. The times when I have heard the excuse 'We couldn't help ourselves'; well that's rubbish, we can because God had given us free will that is what distinguishes us from the animals, we do have the ability to fight the hunger, the lustfulness and the endorphins. I think at that brief time during the wedding feast, Lancelot fought with his own animal demons inside and won but another type of demon was watching and waiting for an opportunity to change all that.

Eventually Lancelot did fall in love with Isolt and they married, soon afterwards Isolt gave birth to a son whom they named Galahad. But there was still no heir for Arthur so both he and Gwenivere doted on their nephew.

Everything in the kingdom was running smoothly, a new tax system was implemented whereby five percent of the landowner's income went to maintain the army and to rebuild and upkeep the Roman roads so the soldiers could get from place to place as soon as a Saxon incursion was being initiated. The only black cloud on the horizon was that Merlin was dying and that was the reason that he wanted his daughters married.

"When Merlin dies, will we still have the Celts' support?" Arthur asked me one day.

It was obvious at that point that Merlin was dying as the poor old man could not hide it any longer.

"We will just have to make sure that he doesn't die, after all he is a sorcerer, he gave you that magic sword, Excalibur, did he not? And we all know sorcerers can live forever," I said whimsically.

Arthur looked totally bemused. I had a plan for when Merlin passed away, I would take over in his place. I told them I would take Merlin to someone in the east of the empire that I knew could cure him. Gwenivere did not want him to go but I managed to persuade her that it was the only action we could take; to do nothing would result in his death. Reluctantly she consented.

Merlin was made as comfortable as possible when we said our goodbyes and by the time we got to Dover, he was dead. I took on the guise of Merlin and when I returned to Arthur I gave him a letter from myself explaining that I would be going back to my old life as a professor because he did not need me anymore. I also suggested that his father-in-law should take my place at the Round Table.

Then a catastrophe hit Lancelot that would eventually bring down Camelot, Isolt died in childbirth. Lancelot and Galahad were inconsolable. As each day passed the more embittered Lancelot grew with the world. Over the years he had developed an all consuming love for Isolt that was stronger than life itself. One day Lancelot turned on Galahad and when Arthur defended the boy he turned on the high King of Britain with his sword, that was a crime against the crown and he was condemned by his fellow knights. Arthur, the man and the King, did not take offence for he saw no aggression in Lancelot's actions just a sad grieving old friend. Arthur told him to take some time away from Camelot and that he and Gwenivere would look after Galahad. Lancelot went deep into the west of Britain where they still practiced the old religion. He went in pursuit of a sorcerer who could converse with the dead. Some individuals who practiced the black arts could communicate with the other world but I would never advise anyone to go down that road.

As much as I would like to speak to someone on the other side I would not take that route because it goes against God and it leaves you open to be possessed by demons, and that is what came to pass with Lancelot.

When he returned to Arthur's court he was not alone, he had brought a demon with him. Although I did not know at the time, when I look back Lancelot was never the same with me after his reappearance. Everyone was happy to see him especially Gwenivere, she had been very concerned about him. Arthur had been married for nearly twenty years and there was an obvious infertility on someone's part because Gwenivere had not produced an heir to the kingdom. The court may have worried about succession but not Arthur, he had made up his mind to bestow the honour to Lancelot's family and make Galahad his heir. While he was thinking about that, Lancelot was bestowing dishonour on Arthur. Everyone in the court knew that Lancelot and Gwenivere were having an adulterous affair, apart from poor Arthur. If anyone did not deserve that fate it was him, he would have died for her without a second thought.

I had only found out about a week before; I went to see her as her father and told her in no uncertain terms that it must stop at once. She told me that she knew it was wrong and didn't want to hurt Arthur but she could not help herself, I didn't know what to do for the best. Then one day not long after, things came to a head. Arthur was presiding over his weekly court; two neighbouring landowners were in a dispute over straying animals being slaughtered on the other's land. The debate turned into an all out argument and when Arthur intervened between the two men one of the men turned on Arthur with indignation in his voice and said,

"How are you supposed to see a solution to our dilemma when you can't see that your best friend is having an affair with your wife?"

The court went completely silent but by the way Arthur acted you would have thought he had not heard the remark, he just made his pronouncement on the matter in front of him that animals should be branded and no man should kill an animal that was not identified as his own. When the court was dismissed, he asked me if the rumours about his wife were true and I confirmed that they were. He just looked at me with contempt and said furiously,

"Lazarus would have told me, no matter how difficult and heavy the chalice he would not have failed me."

Arthur would not be able to comprehend my innermost embarrassment. He turned away from me and walked slowly towards Gwenivere's quarters, I went after him and begged him to stop. The door to the room was bolted and without thinking he just kicked it in. There they both were, naked on the bed. Lancelot looked up and smiled. Arthur's normal calmness went up in smoke, it was like watching a volcano erupting; he went for Lancelot and I just managed to knock the sword out of his hand and we wrestled to the floor. During the struggle Arthur had pulled off the spear head from around my neck. Lancelot came towards us still gloating, then Arthur broke away from me and rolled over and before Lancelot could react the spear had entered his unprotected testicles and up into the lower part of his stomach. The pain that his love rival was feeling was only matched by the pain the demon was feeling in having to leave his host. Lancelot screamed and fell backwards like he was mortally wounded, Gwenivere shrieked and this brought

Arthur back to his senses. I then watched in total amazement as the demon departed from Lancelot's body. The creature was like the one I had observed at the Battle of the Milvian Bridge, slimy and ugly if anything perhaps even more distasteful on the eye. I was really astonished that I didn't realize he was possessed; this one had kept itself completely hidden from me. He smiled and shrugged his shoulders, the equivalent of saying, 'The game's up so what'; it then jumped out of the window. Arthur wept as he believed he had killed his best friend but he was taken aback when Lancelot stood up apparently unharmed, and Lancelot immediately began to beg for forgiveness. However that was not the case with Gwenivere, she was not looking for absolution but vindication for her actions. She believed she was not to blame, she thought she was too young when she married, she admitted that she only married for the sake of her father and that she never really loved him. Every statement she made was like a red hot poker being driven into Arthur's heart. He told me later that he had never experienced so much pain, if only she had asked for forgiveness. The biggest mistake that Judas Iscariot made was not betraying my Master but not asking for forgiveness, because it would have been granted. I think Gwenivere needed to forgive herself first.

Arthur divorced Gwenivere when the majority of his knights said that Lancelot and Gwenivere should pay for their adulterous affair with their lives. It was treason and the only penalty was death. Arthur would not hear of it, he told Lancelot to take Gwenivere to his homeland and marry her. On the day of their departure the land was hit by a terrible storm, the wind and rain was blown into Arthur's face which was a good thing as it hid his tears.

He placed his right hand on Lancelot's left arm in a tight grip like a Roman military salute. This was no tribute far from it, as he pulled him forward his face was like stone, as he whispered into his ear so no one could overhear,

"Look after her and keep her safe, there is no person nicer outside my family I have met in this world. Do everything in your power to make her happy and don't ever hurt her because if you do no army on earth or in heaven will protect you, mark my words well my very best friend, I will kill you."

Make no mistake readers, Arthur would have done it or died in the attempt. Those words chilled Lancelot to the bone; it wasn't the forewarning of being killed but the words 'my very best friend'. Lancelot left the court of King Arthur with his head hung in shame and a tear in his eye, never to return.

Arthur stood there, the wind blowing in his face and tears running down his cheeks watching the love of his life leave. He said sadly, "Should I have told her how much I loved her and how much I needed her? I don't think it would have helped, it's not the words one says it's the person who says them that makes the difference and she does not listen to me anymore." So if you love someone set them free.

They may well have married and had children and lived happily ever after for the rest of their lives but what probably happened was, like with most people second time around, they would have put on a united front telling everyone how happy they were when deep down they really didn't trust each other, for if someone has cheated before, the shadow of doubt always remains hanging by the door. If they did decide to have children it would have been to justify their relationship. The gift of life is a wonderful thing but even that does not vindicate breaking the heart of someone who loves you. Life has a funny way of coming right back and hitting you right in the face when you least expect it, and remember no matter how often you put it to the back of your mind the burden of guilt just gets heavier with time.

I do find it hard to have any sympathy for Gwenivere for, like Helen of Troy who was ultimately responsible for destroying a wonderful city, she was the reason for the downfall of Britain. Today there would have been no England, Scotland and Wales, only a truly United Britain. I think Gwenivere would have cried when she learned of Arthur's death because as much as she tried to convince herself she really did love him she could not live with him and the guilt at the same time. Did she think of him on her deathbed? Who knows? What I do know is that Arthur, with his very last breath, called out her name.

Arthur did keep his word and named Galahad as his heir. Far from uniting the kingdom, the decision caused a civil war because his own blood nephew, Mordred, thought he deserved the crown. Arthur had no stomach for battle; since Gwenivere left him he was hollow with no feeling, inside a part of him was already dead. Arthur met Mordred at the battle of Camlan and killed him with a spear thrust, only to be wounded in return. The injury in my opinion was not life threatening but Arthur did not respond to any treatment I gave him. Unbeknown to me he had taken the spear head before the battle commenced, a true sign I think he wanted to die. It was only after his death I found a note in his belongings to the whereabouts of the relic. Along with the note, I found a half written letter from Arthur to his ex-wife, it read;

As I slowly descend into the land of Somnus and the worries of the day slip away, any anxiety of what the future may have in store subsides for a few short hours; my mind drifts off to a warm sunny afternoon in the past. I then think of happier times, but most of all I think of you my love.

So you see he did love Gwenivere right up until the end. Arthur was not a Christian but his actions mirrored my Masters. He still loved in the face of rejection, Britain's King of Kings carried a torch for Gweniwere from the first moment he set eyes on her. In the last twenty years the flame may not have shone as bright, but it never extinguished. He couldn't care if Gwenivere didn't think of him anymore, let alone love him. He just hoped that she was happy wherever she was.

As Arthur's life faded away I baptised him into the Church of Jesus Christ, and In spite of encouragement from me, he died near Glastonbury.

Was Gwenivere to blame for Arthur's demise? Yes, most definitely, she could not have been more responsible if she had plunged a dagger into him herself, in fact that would have been less painful and over instantaneously. I think the real problem was the fact that they couldn't have children, with lots of children she would have been happy and contented and she would never have taken a bite of the apple that the demon offered.

After Arthur's death, the Anglo Saxons took over and you know the rest. There is one thing though; his body never decomposed in the cave where I left him so perhaps the legend is true that when Britain is on her last legs Arthur will come back and save her. Well maybe with just a little help from me, who knows?

CHAPTER EIGHTEEN

The Sanctuary

Jamie awoke in the church. He was lying on a pew, and two rows in front of him was Father Furpay who was knelt down praying. Jamie said nothing, he just lay there. He asked himself why this had happened to him, he wasn't that bad a guy. Okay, he had left his best friend to be murdered or worse but he could not have helped or he would have got himself killed. He had done good things in the past though; he had helped people but not told anyone about it.

He replayed an episode over in his mind like he was watching the incident for the very first time; he had gone to a singles club held in a hotel on the A6, a real pick-up joint. The place was filled wall to wall with two species, foxes and poor little birds with broken wings, both the male and female gender. Now, he was definitely a fox. In an hour he had left Tiger and OB propping up the bar as he had tried it on with two vixens, to no avail. Then he spotted her, a very attractive little bird quite definitely the worse for drink. Not paralytic but heading that way, he knew all the signs from the years of watching his mother. He knew for sure that she was quite definitely a bird with a broken wing, and before you could say wham, bam, thank you mam, he had said his goodbyes to Tiger and OB and was in a taxi taking the blonde home.

They ended up outside a pretty substantial detached house in Hazel Grove; the old bird had money although she wasn't that old, probably about thirty. She had a great body; he could tell she looked after herself. She turned out to be thirty-four and had just recently lost her husband. Jamie had thought he could string her along for months and he could get lots of sex and money in return. They went inside and a babysitter came to meet them at the door to the lounge, she was about eighteen and a real stunner with a very tight ass. He smiled at her and she winked back unbeknown to the blonde. Jamie had to keep his mind on business, he wasn't going to make a play for the doll on the promise of 'Will she won't she', all his hopes were riding on the filly with the broken wing. The babysitter was paid and she left.

As soon as she had gone they wasted no time, they went directly to the bedroom. If he had to say it himself he gave a great performance. When the blonde feel asleep, he decided to get up and have a good look around to see if there was anything worth taking, as he could have just made it a one-off performance. He was just about to start his search when he heard crying coming from downstairs. When he went down to investigate he found a little boy of about eight, wearing blue pyjamas and a pair of slippers that were about six sizes too big for him. He was holding a picture of a man which was taken at Christmas time; it was obviously the boy's father. There were tears running down his little cheeks. Even thinking about it brought a lump to Jamie's throat. The boy just said,

"You should not be in that bed, that's my dad's bed."

Jamie was overwhelmed with the sadness of the scene. He just hugged the boy and began to cry himself, he let out all his repressed feelings. He told the little lad, whose name was Johnny, how he had lost his dad when he was not much older than him. He then set about telling him all the things that he wished someone had taken the time to tell him when his father had passed away. How his dad would be watching every good thing he did in life, and how he would always be beside him and would never leave him. In years to come when he was very old he would eventually die and go to heaven and the first person he would see would be his dad.

He picked up the lad and took him back to bed; he sat on the boy's bed talking to him until he went back off to sleep. Just before the lad had fallen into the land of nod he had said something to Jamie that brought a tear to his eye. He told him that if he was really tired he could sleep in his dad's bed because he said he didn't think his dad would have minded because he had cheered him up. Jamie thanked him for the kind gesture but told him he was right the first time, he should not have been in his dad's bed; he would never have been that good. He went back to the blonde's bedroom and started to dress. She woke up and said,

"Going now you have had what you came for?"

Jamie told her not to use that old chestnut.

"I have just spent an hour comforting your son. I got up to use the bathroom when I heard crying from downstairs, it was your son holding a picture of his dad and he was breaking his heart because I was in his Dad's bed."

He told her she was a good looking woman who would still have been good looking in ten years but her son would not be a boy anymore. He told her to stop feeling sorry for herself, to stop the drinking and clubbing and most definitely stop bringing low life men like him home.

"You could have been robbed."

He finally told her that her son had never asked to be born and that he had already lost one parent so don't let him lose the other; she should have made the boy her number one priority. He kissed her on the forehead and left. She called him afterwards and thanked him; she had said that he would make a great father someday. As he lay in the pew he thought there was not much chance of that, he would be lucky to see the next twenty-four hours let alone get married and have a family.

All the time Jamie had been awake thinking, the priest had been making plans on how he would go about contacting the original owner of the spear. He didn't think he could persuade Jamie to drive with him to London, in his state of mind he didn't think he could get him out of the church let alone to London. He turned to look at the young man only to find him awake looking back at him. He asked him if he would like some breakfast and Jamie replied that he would only eat in the church, if he couldn't do that then he would not eat at all. Father Furpay told Jamie that the vestry was also consecrated ground so the boy relented and ate breakfast in the vestry. In there was a changing room for the altar boys, a washroom and a toilet. It seemed to the priest that the lad had claimed the age-old religious right of sanctuary.

After they had finished breakfast, Father Furpay told Jamie about his idea of contacting the rightful owner of the spear. The lad thought for a while then agreed that it would be a good plan.

"The man may well be able to help," he said, "there is always some expert or holy man in every film that can beat the devil, just maybe you and him could save the day."

The priest was not totally convinced by the lad's unbelievable story but just maybe there was some truth no matter how unrealistic it sounded, and an inner voice was telling him to accept the young man's story as fact.

Father Furpay always said mass at nine o'clock each morning unless a requiem mass was being held later that day for some departed soul. Before the mass, Father Furpay heard Jamie's confession and gave him absolution. Jamie went to the mass and took communion for the first time in many years. Only about twenty of his parishioners attended mass midweek but not all at the same time. When Father Furpay had remembered to count there was always only twelve, quite befitting really. On the odd occasion when a regular missed like last Thursday, Mrs. Bennett was not very well and Mrs. Freeman was visiting her son, two others would turn up who had not been for weeks. It was like an unknown hand was keeping the number to twelve. When the people had left the mass the priest thought to himself as he locked the door that incidentally there was only eleven at the mass, but there was Jamie to make up the equilibrium.

Father Furpay took the note with the address on that Jamie had given him into his office in the house; he then made a phone call to the Bishop's office. The top man's personal assistant was Father Phil O'Malley, a great friend of Father Furpay's, they went way back. He didn't tell him the full story just that he needed the name and number of a priest whose church was the nearest to the

London address he had. Father Phil told him that it would take a bit of time to locate but it could be done.

"What's it all about then Jim?" Father Phil asked.

Father Furpay just said that he could not tell him because it related to the seal of confession.

"Oh," said Father Phil intrigued, "so you still adhere to that sacrament? The Bishop will be pleased. He thought you were becoming a bit of a renegade, someone had sent him a copy of one of your recent newsletters castigating the church on giving murdering south American dictators confession and absolution only for the despots to go from the church and kill again, fairly strong stuff Jim."

"Well, you know something; I have never had to put my principles to the test. We don't seem to get a lot of South American dictators in Stockport," Father Furpay said.

They both laughed. Father Phil said he would ring back later. When he did eventually ring back he apologised for taking over an hour.

"Those cockneys aren't as well organized as us northerners," Father Phil said.

"You were born in Kent," replied Father Furpay.

Father Phil just laughed and continued, "You are so pragmatic, anyway you are not going to believe this. The church is called St Mary's and the priest in question is south American, his name is Father Diego Mendez and I have it on good authority that he has never been a dictator, nor is he thinking of overthrowing anywhere in South America to become one in the near future."

Both of the priests laughed. As Father Phil gave out the number he said, "What's it all about Alfie?"

Father Furpay just said that if he told him he would have to kill him, and again they both laughed. Father Phil arranged to meet him for lunch the following week. Father Phil ended with,

"I will get to the bottom of this next week, after all I am number two in this firm and I want to know if our men are defecting to MI5 because your answers are very Bond-like, James. Anyway you go and play secret agent, I have a bishop to keep in line. See you next week 007."

Father Furpay phoned Father Diego Mendez directly after putting the phone down on his friend. He explained who he was; again he did not tell the full story. He told him it was very important to contact the man at the address he had just given him. Father Diego said he was really busy today and could he not just ring direct enquiries on the phone. Father Furpay said,

"I don't think this man would talk to just anyone over the phone, for you to be able to get in contact with him shows that I have links with the church. I think he would then be ready to listen to my story." Something made him say, "It could be a matter of life and death. I will give you the phone number of my bishop's office, check it is right and then phone, they will verify that I am who I say I am. In turn you can convince him I am with the church."

Rather reluctantly he did as requested. When he phoned, he ended up talking to Father Phil O'Malley. Father Phil told him he had known Father Furpay for over twenty years and in all that time he had never asked him for a favour until now. So Father Diego did as requested, he cancelled all of his appointments and went to the address he had been given.

CHAPTER NINETEEN

Gregory Efimovich Rasputin

No figure in history in my opinion has been more maligned than Gregory Efimovich Rasputin. They started gossiping about him when he was alive, they said that he had unholy powers over Tsar Nicholas and was the lover of the Russian Queen and her four daughters, and even after he was killed the rumours did not stop. It was said that as a young man he was always in trouble, in his home village of Prokovskoe in Siberia, for stealing, drunkenness and womanising. He was no more than a rake with an endless sexual appetite, it was all total spin, just total character assassination put together by the St Petersburg Secret Police to justify what had been done to him, in a vain attempt to passively control the Russian population. 80% was made up of poor peasant stock that thought Rasputin was one of them, 'A man of the people'.

Now let's face it they may not have fooled the Russian peasantry but they did hoodwink the rest of you. Like I keep telling you history can go through a slight modification before being written down, or even a total alteration. The history book tells you what the author wants you to believe. A picture is a simulation of what they want you to see. For example, a few years ago during the miners' strike the front pages of all the newspapers showed the miners assaulting the police when in reality the miners were retaliating to the police's unprovoked attack, but your Government orchestrated the complete misrepresentation of the incident, not allowing you to see the full picture. So once again it is left to me to tell the authentic story.

The year was 1902. I was making the journey from Siberia to St Petersburg, complying with the spear; when the relic turned white I knew I had to follow it. If I veered from the path it wanted to go the spear would go cold and return to its original colour, it was obvious to me now that the destination was St Petersburg. I could feel a chill setting in, not the coldness from a frost on a winter's day but an overwhelming chill of evil emerging out and penetrating one's soul. I tightened the belt of my fur coat and preceded onwards. A wind started to blow and I could feel the first ice flakes of snow falling onto my face and eyes and I knew we were in for yet another snow storm.

I was just reaching the outskirts of the city when my attention was drawn to a large mound of fur half covered in snow. At first I thought it was a dead animal's carcass then I observed a pair of black leather boots. I quickly ran towards the bundle of fur. It was a man, a mountain of a man with long black hair and a beard but unfortunately he was dead, he had only recently passed away. I ached with frustration, and if I had been less than an hour earlier I could have saved the unfortunate man. All at once I sensed a movement from the spear head; I fumbled when taking it from around my neck because the relic was now red hot. I then understood that this man's body was here for a purpose. When I took on the role of the Monk, I felt like he was communicating with me from beyond the grave, imparting his memory and instructions to me. I absorbed them into my mind. His name was Rasputin, he was a skopsty monk from a monastery at Verkhoturye, and he was going to St Petersburg at the request of a set of Russian Orthodox priests so I carried on with his journey and went directly to the Church where Rasputin had received his invitation. I was treated very well and at dinner that night the priests wanted to know about my trip to the Holy Land and if it was true that I could perform healings. Well, with the help of the spear I supported the myth regarding Rasputin's healing powers.

It was not long before I came to the attention of the Russian Royal Family. The reason I came to their attention was need. Nicholas and Alex were not bad people they were just a couple in love with one another, and they also doted on their immediate family. They lost sight of the outside world and could not see the suffering of the Russian people. To be fair to them the Government and some members of the Imperial Family concealed the facts from them so they could make personal fortunes on the back of their poor subjects. You may ask what I did to help; well their son Alexis was a haemophiliac and was on the verge of dying from his inherited condition so I was sent for. The Tsar was against the idea of me treating the boy, I could see it in his eyes but I could also see and feel his desperation. The doctors had already informed him to prepare for the worst, and for the second time in his relationship he was keeping a secret from his wife. He started to recall the time he brought Alex a puppy for the first birthday she had shared with him. He had taken a picture from her room, a family photograph taken in her home country of Hesse and by

Rhine, on her lap was a small black puppy. Nichols thought his young wife was a little homesick; the puppy could take away her melancholy so he set about finding an identical puppy. The idea was to put it into a box and gift wrap it then put it with the rest of her presents. He kept making excuses where he was going so that she wouldn't find out he was looking for the puppy. On one such occasion his manservant informed him that yet another puppy, had been found for his inspection. He told the Tsar that this one was identical to the one in the photograph. The animal was being kept in the summer-house in the garden. The Tsar started to make excuses to his wife when she began to cry,

"Have you got another woman? I would like to know, you have been telling me lies for weeks. You told me last week you were going to see the Grand Duke Nicholaievich and not ten minutes later I saw him in this very palace."

Nichols remembered how he ran towards Alex to put his arms around her and said,

"To my shame I have slept with many women before I met you, but I swear on my unborn children I have never so much as looked at another woman since we have been together. If you want I will make an oath with God that if anything happened to you I will not share that intimate sexual act with anyone again." He then took her by the hand to the summerhouse to show her the dog and promised her he would never keep a secret from her again.

Now here he was looking at me with contempt, breaking his promise and heart at the same time. He told me to do what I had to do, as far as he was concerned this was the last throw of the dice. In his heart he believed it was hopeless but he also knew it was giving his wife hope and relief from the pain. It may only be a short respite but any, no matter how short, would be welcome. She had been in torment for days, ever since the Tsarevich had fallen and cut his leg. Like most young boys of his age he would try to get up to mischief whenever he could, they told the servants to watch over him all the time. In just one unguarded moment, just one small lapse on their part, Alexis had slipped away out of their sight and began to climb a tree like most young boys would and like most boys at one time or another he fell and grazed his leg. But unlike most young boys he was the heir to the Russian empire and also he was a haemophiliac. If accidents like this happened, the Royal doctors would inject him with a mixture of drugs that would act as a congealing agent to stop the bleeding but on this occasion it did not work. The disease was inherited from his great-grandmother, Queen Victoria, so a doctor was sent from the English Royal Household. This was to no avail so consequently the boy was dying, desperate times called for desperate measures and I entered the equation. When I came into the room the doctors protested to the Tsar who just simply said very quietly to them,

"If you can guarantee to cure my son, I will send him away, if not be silent."

The doctors reluctantly stepped aside. There was a collective gasp when I started to remove the bandages from the boy's leg, and the blood began to flow more freely. There was a total look of dismay on their faces when I took the spear head from around my neck and placed it on the wound. Almost instantaneously the bleeding stopped and when I removed the relic you could visibly see the wound healing itself. The Empress ran to me and said,

"Father, ask of me what you will and I will give it to you."

I simply said, "Mother, your son is restored to you, throw off your veil of sadness and shed no more tears, your son is well. That cannot be said for mother Russia, I can hear her crying every day for her children are dying in your land, and her tears are no less painful than yours. If you wish to thank me, help your fellow mother by helping her people."

Over the next few months I got to know the Royal couple very well, in particular Alex, or to give her full name, Alexandra. She was a deep thinking and very meticulous woman. She went about ensuring no food was wasted in the Royal household when so many people were starving, any surplus food was taken to the food distribution centres she had set up at her own expense with a few close friends around the city. No one, apart from her close friends and the business men she had persuaded to help sponsor her ventures, knew she was totally responsible for the welfare centres.

I had talked to her and the Tsar about King Louis IX of France who had implemented a tax system many years ago in his homeland. He would tax the rich more while distributing help to the poor. These measures were slowly being introduced in Russia, and if it had not been for the assassination of Archduke Franz Ferdinand of Habsburg culminating in the outbreak of the First World War, I do not think there would have been a Russian revolution. For my part in the Empress' venture I was to recruit money people to her crusade. I also had to find old build-ings we could attain at a peppercorn rent so that we could change them into distribution points. I had attended a very strange meeting one night at a local inn with one potential benefactor. During our discussion a young woman came up to me and put her arms around my neck, she then proceeded to sit on my lap. I cannot deny I prefer the company of a beautiful woman to a man; I talked to her for a short while then gently removed her from my knee. No sooner had I done that when another girl took her place. With my own looks I could understand but in the guise of this big, ugly brute of a man Rasputin something was definitely amiss. Unbeknown to me photographs were being taken, so you see that is where the myth of Rasputin the drunken womaniser was born.

On the way back to my apartment after this peculiar meeting I was attacked and killed by six men. What made this so called robbery more unusual what that as I lay dying from a blade wound the men were about to leave when one of the assailants said,

"What about his money?"

It was more of an afterthought, not like the primary reason for the attack; I take it the money was taken to make it look like a robbery that went wrong. When I had recovered from my death I tried to find out who wanted me dead so I made a prediction to Nicholas and Alexandra. I told them,

"If I am killed by common assassins and especially by my brothers, the Russian peasants, you Tsar of Russia have nothing to fear for your children will reign for hundreds of years in Russia. If it was your relations who have wrought my death then no one in your family, that is to say one of your children or relations, will remain alive for two years. They will be killed by the Russian people."

I hoped this would dissuade any members of the Imperial Family from getting involved in any attempts on my life. If it was found out by the peasant stock that it was a relation of the Tsar that tried to kill me there would be an outcry against the family.

This brings me to Prince Felix Yussupov and Grand Duke Dimitri Pavlovich. Historians agree that these two may have been foolish but they were not cowards, if they had been cowards they would have just paid assassins to do the blood work. I beg to differ, these two were not honourable men. Prince Felix was a transvestite with the morals of an alley cat while Grand Duke Dimitri was a drunken womaniser with no morals at all, they were just two murderers ultimately responsible for the Russian revolution when they completed their evil deed.

I shall now tell you why they did the killing themselves, for three times they paid assassins to kill me and each time they had succeeded; if I had been your average man I would have been dead. When they saw that I was still alive they assumed they had been defrauded out of their money, but they could hardly take the killers' to court for breach of contract; this is why one cold night in December they decided to complete the task themselves. Some months earlier I had been befriended by Prince Felix. He told me a few days before that night that he would like to talk about donating money to the Empress' project so I was invited to the Palace that mid-December night. He told me he could not meet me in public for he believed I was being set up by someone. Hence all the photographs in the local newspapers with young women in drinking houses. He thought it would be wise that we held the meeting away from prying eyes.

At the time I did not know that he was behind the attempts on my life but I must say I was not surprised that the Grand Duke was one of the assassins. I had always known he had never liked me; he didn't like my closeness to the Royal couple. Anyway on December 16th 1916, I went to Prince Felix's Palace unaware this would be my last night in Rasputin's body. When I arrived I was given a glass of Madeira and a plate of cakes that had already been laced with cyanide. Not long after drinking and eating I began to feel that Rasputin's body was unwell. I was experiencing dizziness and I had the overwhelming feeling of not being able to breathe, then finally I could feel the body expire - then just peace and blackness. I do not know how long I was in that state, but when I awoke from my enforced absence I realized the Prince had poisoned me. In front of me I could see Felix and Dimitri with another man, whom I later found out was the conservative Duma Deputy. They were all laughing, and Prince Felix said,

"My father would always say if a job's worth doing, it's worth doing yourself. Quite funny really when he didn't even shave himself."

They all began to laugh but not for long, their merriment soon changed to fear when I began to speak in a quiet whisper.

"Unfortunately gentlemen, you did not do the job yourselves, you used poison. Do you not believe your own propaganda Dimitri? You said I was sent by the devil, if so, did you think I would be that easy to kill?"

The Grand Duke began to cry with fear. Prince Felix ran to his desk to retrieve a pistol from the top draw, and with shaking hands he shot me once in the heart. I fell back against the sofa mortally wounded; when

Rasputin's body had passed away once again a doctor was sent for. When the physician confirmed that I was dead the conspirators began to relax once more. Their relief was only short-lived when I was resurrected yet again. They all looked at me with expressions on their faces like they did not know me at all; it was as if I was a creature from another planet. As you can well imagine I was really enjoying their discomfort. I then started to have some fun and came up with a jovial little rhyme that went like this,

"Gentlemen you are acting as though we have not met, you cannot tell me that I am that easy to forget."

Then all hell broke out. Maybe out of fear on their part, maybe one of them started shooting and the others just joined in from panic but all the party began to shoot at me. Although I was standing a few metres away I was only hit twice, and neither wound was fatal. The room was full of smoke and the smell of cordite; it was also full of holes. When the smoke began to lift they found me lying on the floor bleeding and unable to move.

"Quick let's get away from here, he really is the devil," said the Grand Duke.

Prince Felix would have done so if this had not been his home, but then his fear lifted slightly when he could see I was immobile, and he said to the others,

"Quick whilst he's in this state we must tie him up."

He then fetched a roll of carpet which I was wrapped up in, a chain was tied around the middle and by this time my wounds had healed. I was shouting a warning to them that I would see them die. I was carried out and thrown into the Moika Canal. My body was seen the next day from a bridge over the River Neva. I was frozen like a block under the river's ice. Eventually I was fished out of the river, and a large crowd had gathered at the riverbank to watch Rasputin's body being pulled out. This left me in an impossible predicament. I could hardly resurrect Rasputin's body with so many people there to witness the event so I had to hold up my hands and realise I had failed in my quest to avert the Russian revolution. In amongst the throng of people that day was a demon in the guise of man, his red eyes were blazing and I detected a slight smirk on his face, so I assumed he knew what I was trying to achieve. Also, like me, he had realised I had failed in my mission hence the little smile.

Years later I came to meet the demon whose human name was none other than Stalin. Also like I predicted the Romanov were removed from the Russian throne only months after Rasputin's demise and like I also said, Nicholas and Alexandra along with all the immediate family were murdered in cold blood by the Russian people. What became of Grand Duke Dimitri and Prince Felix? Shortly after my removal from the river they were both charged and found culpable of Rasputin's murder. The Tsar was reluctant to execute or imprison his own relations so they were both exiled. This only infuriated the Russian people and I think was one of the major causes of the revolution, ironically the exile saved their lives.

Before leaving, Felix managed to remove some valuables from one of his Palaces; this included two Rembrandts which he later sold to the National Gallery in Washington DC. This and the money he received from an out of court settlement with MGM Movie Studio for what was libellous depiction of him in the 1930's film about the Russian revolution, enabled his wife and himself to have a reasonable lifestyle in America.

But like I warned him on that oh so cold night in old Russia in December 1916, I would see him die. I met up with him again in 1967, I informed him who I was and told him that his evil action that night caused the lives of many innocent Russians. Then I went about telling him word for word what was said that night. I could still tell he did not believe me so I took the paper knife from his desk, proceeded to cut the palm of my hand and then held it up for him to watch the cut heal itself. He instantly put both hands on to his chest and said,

"Rasputin is it really you?"

In reply I said, "No actually, the name's Lazarus but that's a long story and you my Prince just do not have the time," and like I said I would, I watched him die of a heart attack.

CHAPTER TWENTY

1914-1918: Willie McBride

I suppose I cannot sit here in Europe and not tell you what really happened in what was called The First World War. It started with the assassination of Arch duke Franz Ferdinand, the heir to the Austrian empire. It was just an excuse for the old die-hard militarists from the European countries with territorial ambitions, who had long since said goodbye to their youth. More than likely, these privileged individuals had squandered their young lives in the drinking houses and brothels all over Europe when they were not playing soldiers in fancy colourful uniforms on magnificent horses. Now they wanted to play warrior yet again, maybe in somewhat less vivid but still elaborate uniforms. Although this time, there would be no strenuous horse-riding, they would let the young men have all the fun. They would do all the hard work sipping fine French wine in safe warm chateaux doing the real arduous task of working out their percentages while many young men would be blown to kingdom come while running over a short distance of ground, as if they were just lead soldiers in a child's game. They just sat back and observed these young men, the cream of Europe, fritter away their youth, not in drinking establishments and whore-houses but in fields of mud, blood and death.

Their only respite from the hell was to sit, eat and try to sleep in ditches often knee deep in water, infested by rats the size of cats that had grown to these enormous magnitudes from over-indulgence in the rich pickings of the cadavers in no man's land. They just sat there wait-ing to have some more fun by running head first into the jaws of death while the General's staff did all the hard work a couple of miles away. I would like to tell you the truth about the evil conditions that both sides inflicted on their own men, who in 1914 had gone so willingly to war. Why? Because they were bloodthirsty morons? No, they were hoodwinked by their own leaders, to rally more volunteers. They deliberately circulated stories around the United Kingdom that the German devils where going into Belgian and French villages killing innocent men, women and children. Their secret agents told people that they were raping the women and young girls. These tales and more like them were being told up and down the country, in every public house and work-ing man's club, I even saw a cartoon in a newspaper depicting a big fat evil looking German soldier with a baby on the end of his bayonet. So, like I said before, if it is in print we believe it. The British and French govern-ments were in fact brainwashing the youth to go out and kill for them. Is that not what these present day govern-ment officials are accusing some fundamental Islamic states of doing now? Before the west criticize today, should they not look into their own past and say that we were wrong and now we have learnt by our mistakes?

The British government's devious and deliberate plan in 1914 was so successful that it was implemented into

Australia, New Zealand and Canada. That was also deemed to be a success. This is how a young man - no, boy for he was only fifteen, big and strong for his age, but alas still only a boy, -joined up. Let's call him Willie McBride for he was born in Manchester but from Scottish parents, he had taken the birth certificate of a dead brother and had travelled to Scotland to join a highland regiment. Like I said, McBride was not his real name but we will use that for fear of distressing his descendants. He was from a large family, he had seven brothers, four of whom managed to return from the killing fields of France and no doubt went on to have families of their own, who may well be living all over the world who may not wish to know what really happened to their great uncle. For in my opinion, he was murdered by the British army. Many a man was taken out by the British and French and shot at dawn but what I think was very interesting, is that not so many Germans were shot by their own side. Perhaps their men were too occupied in their evil deeds in raping women and killing babies, if we were to believe the British propaganda.

Anyway, let's go back to poor Willie. I came across this brave young man when I was in the guise of a Scottish officer named Allan Cunningham. I will not tell you the exact regiment for it is of no consequence in my tale, more importantly it may well lead to McBride's real identity and I do not wish that to happen. It was 1918 and by that time I had been on all sides several times trying to locate the demons that had entered unprotected men. It was an impossible job, for no sooner had I sent one demon back to hell when another one would pop up to cause mayhem. For you see, war is a great playground for the unclean spirits from the underworld, the opportunities for them are so vast. As you can well imagine, there are so many men who have lost the guardianship of their angel. My sad story of Willie McBride doesn't appertain to a demon directly; it is about man's inhumanity to man or in this case, to a boy. Young McBride had been serving with the Scots for two years, which still would have made him only seventeen. He did stand out in the ranks with the Manchester inflection in his voice but also because he was brave. One non-commissioned officer did not like him; he thought an Englishman had no right to be in a highland regiment. Never a day went by when he didn't pick on him; many times I had to reprimand him for going too far. This very boy was now on trial for his life for cowardly actions in the face of the enemy, yet four months before he had gone back into no man's land to rescue his sergeant. William McNeil, or big Billy as he was known to his men, the very same sergeant who had picked on McBride so unmercifully. Big Billy had been hit in the leg while retreating from another ill advised attempt thought up by the inebriated imbeciles from the General's staff. As Billy lay there very still, he was thinking that he would never see his wife, Annie, and his three children, Alistair - twelve, Cameron - eight and his wee baby girl, Katrina, although she was not that small now, she would be four soon. In his mind she would always be his wee baby lassie. Billy lay there face down in the stinking mud knowing if he made a move with his leg injured he would be too slow to reach his own lines and would be an easy target for a German sniper. He reflected that if the Generals on both sides were made to do these futile charges, at best gaining a few miserable feet and at worst losing a few thousand in a morning's work before breakfast, this bloody mess would have been over after a few weeks.

He turned his head slowly to the right and saw the outstretched left hand of a dead officer. He noticed the third finger had a gold wedding band on it. He then followed the bloodstained arm up to the shoulder to see the pips. He knew the man had once held the rank of Captain - perhaps that was wrong, he would always hold the rank of captain; however he would take it to his grave. He moved his eyes to look at the dead man's face but he did not recognize him. He had the face of a boy with blood-matted blonde hair pushed against the side of his head. He had no whiskers and looked as if he had yet to start shaving. How could they make a boy like that an officer? He could now clearly see the cause of this young man's demise, the back of his head was missing. He felt so sorry for his young bride as she would never see her sweetheart again. He hoped this madness would end before it was Alistair's turn to sign up. He began to pray, 'Please God, let me go back to Scotland one more time. Let me see my wife again, let me hold her and kiss her, and tell her how much I love her. Let me say goodbye to my children, let me see their faces just one last time, then you can bring me back up to this place and I will gladly die'. His prayers were then answered.

While grown men stood back, up popped the brave young McBride. He jumped up from the protection of the British lines; then ran back into hell to rescue the soul of big Billy and proceeded to carry him back to safety. When they were inside the trenches, the medics started to attend to Billy's leg wound. Not only had the leg been hit several times by machine gun fire, it was also broken. This could have happened when he fell on it. Even though he was in great pain, he needed an answer to his question and said,

"Why Willie, why did you do it? You could have got yourself killed. Why did you do it for a mean bastard like me?"

McBride just smiled like a Cheshire cat, "I like you sergeant, if you did but know it, you are the man who made me the soldier and man I am today. Without you I would be nothing. With all this noise and killing going on I would have been petrified just waiting for my turn to die, but I have never been afraid of going over the top after what you told me. You remember Sarge? The very first time I had to go over the top I was scared shitless and you said, 'Don't worry wee boy, your time is due when it's due, it's written in the big book the day you were born. So you could die now or be sat at home one Sunday morning and choke on a wee piece of bacon'. That was it, word for word, I will never forget it till the day I die. So you see, today was not the day that you and me were suppose to die."

Billy just looked at him. He didn't remember saying those throwaway remarks on the eve of the battle, to be honest he did not recall talking to the boy that day at all. He realised McBride was just a wee boy who had taken every word he had said literally, like his own son would have done. He looked at the boy closely and could see clearly that he was not much older than Alistair. How could he have been so mean to such a nice wee boy? It could only be this place which brought out the demon in him? McNeil knew he had been given another chance to put things right. He also knew he had been given another son to protect so he pulled the boy's head down towards the stretcher he was now lying on and kissed him on cheek, like he would have done to his own sons and said,

"Now keep your head down, no more heroics. This regiment would not be the same without you my little Manchester mate."

McBride's face had flushed red because of the sergeant's kiss but inwardly it felt good to be liked by your hero. As Billy was being carried to the field hospital, McBride shouted after him,

"Hurry up back Sarge, the place won't be the same without you shouting at me."

Billy McNeil was transferred later from the field hospital to a real hospital behind the lines with nurses and clean sheets, and the most important thing of all, good food. Three days later, he received his first visitor, young McBride, who had just started a ten-day leave from the front that would come around once in a while. At the beginning of the war it was done on a frequent basis but at the Battle of the Somme which lasted from July to November 1916, the British and their allies lost a total of 794,000 men. The high command had ordered the biggest bombardment of the Germans ever seen. On the first day, 1,437 British guns sent over one and a half million shells. This was supposed to totally demolish the German defensive position; however, it did not go as planned. Perhaps the enemy forces were dug into their trenches too well or the artillery officers had somehow miscalculated the range, for when the British left the trenches it was cold-blooded murder. They walked across no man's land with the pipes playing and were just knocked down like helpless ducks on a fairground side show. On the first day 19,000 men were killed and over 35,000 wounded. The Commander-in-Chief, General Douglas Haig, came up with a great strategy so as not to be disturbed by the complete carnage and shambles of the wholething. He never visited the front lines so he would not have to register the suffering of his young soldiers that had been induced by his own incompetence. Rather like a child at night petrified of the boogie man, he would put his head under the bed sheets believing what you can't see won't harm you.

So in real terms, what did the Battle of the Somme achieve? Absolutely nothing, for what land they obtained was eventually acquired back by the Germans later. But what did the battle mean to the ordinary soldier? It was a significant loss in regular furlough from the front, with so many casualties they did not have the same manpower or ability to apply the rotation plan so as a result soldiers like McBride rarely got a chance to get away from the front. Even so, this boy spent every day of his leave visiting McNeil, the man who had bullied him. On one visit, Billy told the boy,

"I was wrong to say you weren't a Scot for you are as brave and have a bigger heart than William Wallace himself."

McBride responded with, "Who is William Wallace? Did he get killed before I joined the regiment?"

Billy just laughed, "No you wee daft lad, he was the bravest Scot of all time, and he could not be bribed by Scottish Lords or an English King. He would rather die than betray the Scottish common people. Before they killed him, they tortured him but he still would not give in. He died spitting at the English."

The day before McBride was due to go back to the front, Sergeant McNeil received the news that he had been praying for. He was to be sent back home to recuperate from the broken leg. He instantly felt guilty, when he told McBride that he would be going home to

Scotland he was so happy he could not contain himself, he blurted the news right out. The boy smiled and pretended to be happy but Billy could see through the smile. He realized that he had been insensitive coming right out with it. He sympathized with the boy, how would he have felt it someone had told him they were going to heaven while he was going back to hell? He tried to cheer the lad up.

"Don't worry, I will be back before you know I have gone. Can I bring you anything back or can I do anything for you while I am over there?"

McBride thought for a little and said, "You can... no, I can't ask you to do that."

Big Billy said, "You can ask me anything and I will do it. I would cut off my right arm for you if you asked me to for I owe my life to you Willie McBride. You and you alone, are the reason I will be going back to see my family again. Perhaps I should thank God as well, for out there in no man's land I prayed for his assistance to help me get out of there and he sent one of his angels to rescue me. This angel didn't have wings though for he was born in Manchester."

For the second time in a matter of days, Billy made the boy blush. The red-faced boy asked Billy if he could go and see his mother and tell her that he was going to receive a medal for bravery and that he was fine. Billy agreed to do just that. On the final day of his leave, McBride came as usual to the sergeant's bedside; he had two things to give to him. One was a letter to his mother and the second was his St Christopher medal to ensure that Billy got home safely to Scotland. This time, it was the sergeant that was turning red with tears. As he took the medal, he thought to himself that this is the most gallant boy in the history of the world, not only did he save his life but he now gave him his own St Christopher to make sure he got home safely. Before the boy left the hospital for the last time, Sergeant Billy McNeil hugged McBride tightly and said,

"I could not be more proud of you even if you were my own son. Now keep your head down. I'm not asking you to do it, I'm ordering you to do it Private McBride and correct me if I'm wrong, but to my knowledge you have never disobeyed an order yet."

They separated that day, one man went back home to Blighty while the other went back to hell. After three months away, McNeil returned to the trenches. The first person he went to see was McBride. He gave him a tin containing a Dundee cake his wife had baked for him; also, the children had sent sweets and chocolates for the boy who had saved their father's life. They had heard the story so many times they could recite it word for word, even wee Katrina. Billy also had a letter from McBride's mother and a pair of gloves that she had made especially for him; Billy told McBride how very proud his mother was of him. After staying an hour with McBride and the boys, the sergeant concluded that Logan's tea was still the worst drink he had ever tasted in his life,

"The medicine I had to take in hospital was more like tea than that witches' brew," he said, and leaving the lads laughing, he went to report to Commanding Officer Bunker.

I was inside with Major McCumsky when McNeil burst in and said, "Colonel Cunningham, I need to talk to you about Willie McBride."

"It'll have to wait," I said, "The Major and I are discussing tomorrow's big offensive."

McNeil interrupted me again to say, "I want Willie out of this madness, he's only a boy."

"I want every man and boy out of this carnage," I said.

"No you don't understand, Willie's not old enough. He joined up when he was only fifteen."

McNeil then went about telling the story word for word of how he had found out the boy's real age. He told me what took place in the hospital and how Willie had asked him to go and see his mother. So, when the plaster was taken off his leg and he could walk with the aid of a stick, he and his wife took a trip down to Manchester to meet with the mother of Willie. She was fifty years old but looked so much older, which was not surprising when she told him about her life. She had been made a widow when her husband was killed at work. She received more money from donations collected by his workmates than she did from the compensation from the company. Money was tight so she had to take a job working nights while her eldest son, Andrew, was left to look after the younger children. This went on until Andrew managed to secure full time work. It was difficult but with the help of Andrew, she managed to bring up seven boys including Willie. She fed them, clothed them, held them and nursed them through illness. She was given no help from the state but when the time came that the government needed her boys, they just took them away. He could see this poor woman was heartbroken, for she had already lost one of her sons in France. Now the last boy had been called up; Davey, who had just turned eighteen. Mrs McNeil said in a throwaway remark,

"So is he your youngest then?"

"Oh no," said Mrs. McBride, "Willie is my youngest, he's my baby."

She told them that when she had found out what Willie had done, she thought it was too late. She was afraid that if she told someone what Willie had done, he could have got into serious trouble. She said he was headstrong and always considered himself as a Scot. It seemed she kept all the boys' birth certificates in a tin box in the top draw of the sideboard in the front room, in there must have been that birth certificate of her son who had died at the age of two just before Willie was born. He was called William so when the new baby arrived, he was christened Willie in memory of his brother. Willie still had nine months before he came of age to serve.

A big offensive was being planned for the morning so I went directly to headquarters to report the matter. I could take one boy out of this hell on earth for nine months at least. When I informed my Commanding Officer he said,

"This is terrible, quite unsatisfactory. We don't want this leaking out to the press that the British army has been using under-age boys, that will never do. Go back at once and get the sergeant and the boy to sign the Official Secrets Act. Tell them no action will be taken against the boy."

I just sat back down infuriated and shaking with frustration. I told the oversized imbecile,

"Do you understand what I am saying? We have a boy in our ranks of insufficient age who has already been to hell and back on many occasions and all you can say is you won't take any action against the child? You just want to cover the whole thing up so the army can come out of this mess without egg on its face. I suppose you want him to die tomorrow so the army can safely stay unblemished."

"Of course not, but you must admit it would get us off a sticky wicket," the fat commanding officer said uncaringly.

God forgive me but I could not contain myself any longer. I went up to him and hit him so hard that I knocked out his two front teeth and said, "You fat unpitying bastard."

With tears in his eyes, the commanding officer screamed while spitting blood, "You are finished Cunningham, I will have you shot for this."

"Why don't you crawl up your fat arse and die, there's definitely enough fucking room up there. I'm going back to my men; they will need me for this next push that you and your half wit friends on the General's staff have planned for dawn."

The corporal who had been typing away while my assault on the commanding officer had taken place, walked up to him to give him some assistance. The bleeding commanding officer said, "You witnessed that, didn't you Murphy?"

"Witnessed what sir? I was concentrating on the letters of condolences for the officer casualties of our last offensive. Remember sir, you told me to give it my full attention, you needed that crap out of the way before it started mounting up again."

The commanding officer pushed away the help that Murphy half-heartedly offered. The corporal was now standing behind his commanding officer smiling profusely, and then he started to mouth the words 'well done' in my direction.

I left the office and started to go back to my men but I was arrested by the Provost Martial before leaving the British HQ. I was taken by military police to the cells to await a certain court martial. Once again, I had let my Master down by not turning the other cheek. I should have gone back to the front and stopped the boy from going over the top in the morning. If anything happened to that boy it would be my fault.

An English Colonel, named Carlton Ashton-Jones, was sent to command my regiments. He met with my officers to discuss the attack on the German lines. At the end of the meeting, he asked where I had observed the offensive from. Major McCumsky and his fellow officers looked dumbfounded; they just didn't understand the question. Then, the penny dropped with one junior officer.

"Oh," he said, "he perceives the action from the very front sir; he leads us all out and then takes out the regiment football and kicks it at the Germans. Don't ask me how but he brings the bloody thing back with him for he is always the last man back in the trenches. You could say sir, he is the W.C.Grace of no man's land, first in last out."

The rest broke into spontaneous laughter so he dismissed the entire officers apart from McCumsky. He wasn't sure if he had been the recipient of a joke; if that young runt was trying to make a fool out of him he would definitely regret the day, Ashton-Jones thought to himself. When they had all left the bunker, he said,

"Is it true about Cunningham leading the attacks?"

McCumsky confirmed that Colonel Cunningham was always at the front. He emphasized the word Colonel for he felt the Englishman had shown a lack of respect by not using his correct rank when referring to him moments earlier. Ashton-Jones said,

"Well, no wonder the man's under arrest, he must have been going off his head for some time."

McCumsky said annoyingly, "You told me he had been unavoidably held up on regimental business."

The Englishman was annoyed with himself; for he didn't wish to inform the men until after this morning's actions. He stammered, almost having a subservient tone in his voice,

"Well, he has in a way, he's been detained by the Provost Martial."

Major McCumsky was visibly disturbed,

"Well, I would not whisper that too loudly around here for he is held in great esteem by these men. The admiration is stronger that any I have witnessed between an officer and his men and we have had some fine Scottish officers in this man's regiment." Again he emphasized a word, this time it was Scottish. "They believe him to be indestructible, you heard the way that young Callum talking about him, it's like they are worshipping a hero. There are so many stories circulating about him, one was that he was seen being blown to kingdom come by a mortar yet two hours later he came back to our lines clutching the bloody football. He's more than a colonel, he's the reason these men keep going. I hate to think what the men would do if they knew you had their colonel under arrest. One thing is for certain, you would find it hard to induce them to go over the top this morning."

Ashton-Jones said anxiously, "Be very careful about what you say and how you say it, for that sounds very like you have a touch of insurrection in your tone."

Major McCumsky just smiled and said, "You don't seem to appreciate the way things work around here. These men are all killers, the British army trained them to kill. They know they only have a three-to-one chance of coming back this morning. It only takes a small spark to start a bush fire in Australia that could lay to waste half the country if not stopped. I also think you should remember that these men's ancestors would not have thought twice before putting a claymore between your shoulder blades, to them you are just another English Sassenach. Put yourself in their shoes, you can only die once whether it is by a German bullet or an English one. These men need to know they are dying for the right cause. They do not believe in the succession of your English King for he doesn't bear the name of a Stuart, he is a German is he not? None of these men give a toss for your British Empire; they go out and die for their colonel."

After he had finished, he walked right up to the Englishman, so close he could smell his sweat. He smiled for he knew that the English man was shitting himself. He looked directly into Ashton-Jones' eyes and could see they were full of fear. So he went on to finish off his speech in a condescending manner by saying,

"Now don't fret sir, you will not have to get that nice new uniform dirty."

How did he know the uniform was new? Call it instinct or intuition but he knew this man had only just been put into the rank of CO. They were really scraping the barrel with this ineffectual creature. He also knew another thing, today was the day he was going to die. Call it a soldier's intuition, he had seen it before, a fellow officer had given him letters to send back home and sure enough he'd bought a bullet. This was the reason he was giving this useless shit every last piece of his frustration. But it was all just wasted on Ashton-Jones for he was not a real man, let alone a soldier. No, young McBride was more of a man than this thing in a coronal's uniform so he gave up with him and said,

"You just sit in here sir and have another cup of tea, you don't really want to be going outside, I think it's starting to rain. I will take the men out for a stroll this morning and with a bit of luck for you, I may not come back."

McCumsky saluted and left before the colonel could reprimand him about his insubordinate manner, which was a relief because he could see the man was on the edge. Ashton-Jones was beginning to feel more afraid of the Scots than the Germans. He thought to himself, 'What kind of bucket full of worms has HQ given me here?' He had heard the Scots were mad fighters, but he thought it was just a saying not an actual description of their insanity. Now, with his first hand knowledge of one senior officer knocking out the front teeth of his CO, he himself had now been the recipient of a verbal assault of another of these Caledonian cavemen.

After he had regained his composure he went to the phone to ring the Provost Martial's office, he told them he needed a detachment of military police. When the MP's arrived, they were placed up and down the trenches to look out for any signs of disquiet amongst the men. When one lad from the Scottish ranks shouted out,

"Hey, we didn't need to fear today lads, the red tops are coming with us," an enormous MP sergeant went to approach him to either hit him or arrest him. However, he had second thoughts when four mean looking Scots stood in front of the lad.

The MP just smiled and said, "Like that joke, very funny indeed jock," trying not to show any signs of fear and hoping above hope that these men would go over the top when the whistles sounded, otherwise it may well be a safer alternative for him and his men to go over than to stay here with this lot.

While that little incident was taking place with the NCO of the MP's, some far more important development was taking place further up the trenches with more far-reaching consequences. Sergeant McNeil had been trying to convince young Willie not to go on the attack. All Willie would say was,

"If you and the lads are going then so am I and anyway what will happen will happen, I am just as safe out there as in here."

McNeil had been hoping the colonel would come back at any moment to say he had secured Willie's discharge. What a tragedy it would be if the colonel returned only to find that young McBride had been killed climbing out of the trenches. So McNeil ordered Willie to stay out of the action, but on reflection he knew that as soon as they had gone over the top the lad would follow. He turned around quickly and hit the boy knocking him unconscious, then with the help of one of his corporals, a man named Jock Murray, tied the boy's hands and feet together.

Now all this was being observed by the biggest rat that had ever been in the trenches. This one had not grown fat on eating human remains in no man's land, no, this one had gained his weight problem in drinking and eating in the French taverns in the town behind the lines. For this rat was of the human variety in a military police uniform. He had watched the whole incident take place from a distance and had put two and two together, but did not come up with four. He completely fabricated a story saying that he actually saw the young soldier screaming that he would not go over the top; he said he was acting in a cowardly manner and had to be restrained by a sergeant and a corporal. He did not however comment on what he had also witnessed. Just before the whistle sounded and the brave Scots went up and over the top, the sergeant had knelt by the boy, kissed his forehead and ruffled his hair kind-heartedly, then saluted him. No, not the type of thing you would do to a coward, but that part of the incident the dirty rat did not understand and anyway, it did not fit in well with his tale so he left it out when he reported the incident to his NCO. This was a Godsend to the sergeant of MP's for he needed an excuse to leave this place of death and get back to the real world. He also didn't fancy being there when those mad Scots came back minus comrades and with more reason to turn cantankerous. He reported to Ashton-Jones that there had been no unrest, he added that the men were brave and did their duty, they went without a semblance of perturbation, like lambs... then he stopped himself mid-sentence and changed his choice of words to, 'like brave Scottish lions', but both the coronal and his Batman knew what he was really going to say, something along the lines of lambs to the slaughter which would not have been an appropriate thing to say even though sadly it was true. Then, almost as an afterthought, he said,

"Oh, we did come across one coward who would not go over the top so we arrested him."

He almost made it sound like him and his men were the deciding factor as to why Scots went over without a fuss, when in reality, for a few seconds after the whistle went, he was petrified, for the Scots didn't move. Then a voice had said,

"Oh fuck it, for Bannockburn and Colonel Cunningham."

It was Major McCumsky who believed he was going to die but went just the same. Although the NCO of the MP's didn't know who the voice belonged to, he was none the less grateful for it. The NCO said,

"So, I'll be taking the man directly back to HQ."

The look on Ashton-Jones' face was one of complete horror, it was almost saying, 'Don't leave me alone with these mad Scots', so thinking on his feet he said, trying to sound calm,

"No, you can wait until this action is successfully completed and I will come back with you to make my report first hand to the General."

So they both took up position in the trenches using the observation telescopes. They watched the catastrophic fiasco unfold before their very eyes. When the first senior officer arrived back from the carnage, a Captain Lomas, they took him back with Willie to HQ. On the way back in the car, the Captain told of the unsuccessful attempt on the German lines and how Major McCumsky had ordered the retreat before being killed. He said he had never seen anything like it.

"They seemed to know the exact point on their line where we were about to hit so they had reinforced that position. Where normally they would have had one machine gun, they had three, it was murder. Bloody murder!"

So Ashton-Jones took his findings to his new CO as the old one was at the dental hospital. This man was again English but he had more upstairs than his predecessor. When the new CO was summing up his verbal report, the words he used shocked the colonel for he believed he was above criticism. The CO said,

"So, you in essence, tell me that you left the advance to be led by an officer who was totally insubordinate and in your own words 'off his head'? For your sake, I hope you have not put anything down on paper yet for if you have, you young fool, you will be in line for a court martial. If you knew the man was unfit for action, you should have taken the advance yourself, for is it not your regiment at the moment? I tell you this, it will not be any longer if I have my way you incompetent imbecile. Now go and write up your report and have it on my desk within the hour, I want to see what you have to say about the dead Major McCumsky, for he can no longer defend himself and people may well believe you are using a dead man as a scapegoat."

Ashton-Jones left an office for the second time in his life totally despondent, he vividly remembers the first time. It was when he was at boarding school at the age of about twelve, he had gone to the head teacher's office to report seeing four boys going out of the school grounds which was prohibited. Only to his surprise, rather than receive gratitude, he was caned for telling tales. He thought on that occasion it was an injustice, for like on this occasion, he could not see what immoral wrong he had done.

Back in the military prison compound, I was standing waiting at my cell door for the news of the attack. It was not that I wanted the British to win, I had no preference who came out as the victors of this war, I just wanted this madness to end so no more mothers would be crying over losing their sons, no more young wives would be without the companionship of their husbands and no more children would have to grow up in this world without the special love of their father. I received a shock as in walked Willie McBride with an MP on either side of him. He looked as though he had taken a beating. I said,

"What's going on, what have you done to him?"

One of the MP's said, "We have done nothing to him, he is just another coward who didn't want to go over the top this morning, only this one didn't want to hit his CO, it was his NCO that hit him."

He seemed to be implying that both Willie and I were cowards so I answered, "I have been into no man's land many times with that boy at my side, I have never seen him so much as flinch as he ran towards the German line. I can tell you he is no coward. Now as for you lot, you have always been conspicuous by your absences. You look to me like the type of man who would wet himself having to spend a night in the trenches, let alone go into no man's land."

The MP just looked at me and said, "Now if you were not an officer you would get a kicking for that remark."

"I am a disgraced officer, so don't let that stop you," I replied, "but you won't come in here on your own will you fat boy because you know what would happen to you."

The corporal of the MP's came up to my cell door and looked at me. He knew instantly I wasn't joking so he said, "Not today, sir."

I ran at the door and hit it so hard with my shoulder that it made an almighty bang. The corporal jumped back in shock and lost his footing and ended up on the floor.

"You absolutely shit yourself then didn't you big man?" I started to laugh so did the other MP. "You're an absolute disgrace of a man, one rap on a door and you're on your arse. What in God's name would you be like when you heard the explosion of a shell a few feet away? One thing I know for certain, you wouldn't keep on running forward like that boy would. I think your mate there would have had to change your pants like a baby and by the look of him, I don't think he is averse to taking men's pants off. You two are not fit to lace up that lad's boots you spineless pair of bastards."

I was deliberately trying to provoke the men so that they would come into my cell and I could make good my escape, but I had over estimated these men. I just thought they were bullies but they were no more than a pair of trapped and frightened rabbits caught in the headlights of a car. Even suggesting that one was a homosexual wouldn't have got these two to come into my cell. They would have only ventured in with an army and even then they would have been at the back. I knew then that I would have to come up with another idea of getting out of here. After they had gone, I asked Willie what had happened. The lad seemed to be in some kind of shock, all he would say is,

"I'm not saying a word until I talk to Sergeant McNeil." Something had gone badly wrong; I needed to get out of the cell to find out what.

I waited until twenty minutes after the guards changed over; I got completely undressed and got into bed. I then left the body of the colonel. I looked at him from the outside for the first time in almost a year, I had forgotten what he looked like for when I shaved his face in the morning, it was my reflection that I saw. I dressed myself quickly in Cunningham's uniform, it was a perfect fit. I looked again at the body of the colonel, he didn't look dead just asleep. I then started to bang on the door and shout,

"Quick! There is something wrong with the colonel, send for a doctor at once."

The guard looked past me into the cell to see the dead Cunningham on the bed. He told the other MP to ring for the MO. He then looked back at me; he knew that the cells should only contain one prisoner at a time so he said to me,

"Who are you then?"

I put on my very best English upper-crust accent and said,

"I am Colonel Cunningham's defending officer, I am a barrister by profession but while this war is on I wear a British colonel's uniform so when you address me you insolent ingrate, you do not say 'Who are you then' you say, 'who are you then, sir or colonel'. Now open the door at once you fool and fetch that doctor now."

It worked, I got the guard so confused that he did just that. By the time the MO had arrived, I had made it look like I had tried to revive the colonel. The doctor examined the body and when he had finished I said impatiently,

"Well, what did he die of? This lot have not poisoned him with this excuse they call food have they?"

The medical officer just looked at me with a puzzled expression and said, "I don't know, there are no obvious signs and no marks or injuries on the body, it's a mystery at the moment. We will have to perform a post-mortem examination to ascertain the cause."

"Well, see to it doctor for I need to know how this man died. This is quite unsatisfactory, has the Provost Martial been informed?"

The guards and the MO just looked at each other in confusion so I said, "I am not happy with things around here, I will go and see the Provost Martial myself. You see to the body doctor and do what you have to, I will be along later to receive your report."

The bluff worked, sounding pompous and supercilious did the trick. To be fair, if brains were made of gunpowder and you took every single one of these MP's, there wouldn't be enough gunpowder to blow your hat off. IQ was certainly not an important requirement for joining the redtops. I walked right out of the prison compound. No doubt there would have been some difficult questions asked later, like who was the English colonel? Why was no visit entered into the prison log? Did anyone ask to see ID? Where was the colonel now? And, what's happened to Colonel Cunningham's uniform? All these things didn't concern me.

The next thing on my agenda was to find another body to use for a while so I could find out what had taken place. I knew exactly the place where my requirements would be met. No man's land. By the time I arrived it was going dark but I could still see the total carnage of what had taken place. It took me hours to find what I was looking for and I must say, over the years I have seen so many distressing sights but none worse than this, it was such a waste of human life. I knew the body of Major McCumsky would be here. Like him, I knew of his future, for I could always see the shadow of the grim reaper on a man and I saw it yesterday while I was talking to him. I came across his body, then took on the guise of Major McCumsky and went back to the British line. I shouted,

"Don't shoot, it's Major McCumsky."

"Halt! Who goes there?" the sentry said.

"I have just told you, Johnstone, it is me Major McCumsky. You idiot, you are supposed to say 'come forward and be recognized'."

Johnstone said, "I thought you were dead sir, where have you been?"

"Well I haven't been to heaven! I have been looking for that bloody football!" I said jokily.

"Did we kick it out today?" the sentry replied.

"Now you tell me," I said laughing as I came forward. Poor old Johnstone was as thick as two short planks and couldn't tell that I had been joshing all the time. When I was back inside the trench, I said,

"It's real nice to see that mug of yours again, Johnstone, now do me a favour. Go and fetch the officer on watch while I clean myself up."

A few minutes later, he returned with young Callum. The once fresh-faced junior officer looked as though he had now aged ten year's within the last twenty-four hours. The totally dumbfounded officer said,

"I don't believe my own eyes, is that really you sir? What is it about commanding officer's in this regiment? Were you issued with nine lives along with your uniform?"

He came forward and, unbecoming of a British officer, hugged me. I could feel him shaking as he pulled away saying,

"I would have sworn on a bible that I witnessed your death today but after what I have seen I no longer know what time of day it is anymore, I just keep seeing their faces covered in blood. You may well be able to see my body, although I am not sure if I am still here anymore, for I no longer feel compos-mentis."

What a sad sight to see. One of the most well-educated and intelligent young men I had ever had the pleasure of meeting was now a quivering wreak on the verge of losing his sanity, and who could blame the poor young lad? I tried to reassure him that he was not going mad,

"You are okay lad, it is when you stop questioning the total madness of what you are seeing, that is when I will take the hat round to buy a new uniform for you that fastens at the back. Now talking about the mentally insane, where's the new CO?"

Callum saw the funny side to my remark and gave a sad smile,

"I have not seen him since before the attack when he asked which was the best grandstand to watch all the fun from. I believe he left at half time when he saw we were not going to score. I think he's gone back to the headmaster's study, he may well get detention and a hundred lines for this mess. We have had so many comings and goings of senior officers today taking statements off everyone, I think they may well have interviewed Flanagan's cat, perhaps they will blame that or do you think they will make the English Colonel the sacrificial scape goat?"

I noted what young Callum had said and the witty manner he said it in. I do not think he was concerned whether I found what he said to be funny or not for he was beyond caring. I had not met Cunningham's replacement but if he was as slimy as the one I assaulted, he would know how not to take the blame and more importantly, he was one of their own. It was more than likely that someone of my rank would have to take the flack, I told Callum to assemble all the remaining officers in the CO bunker as soon as possible. I needed to know what went wrong for I had entered McCumsky's body far too long after his death for his total memory to be intact I needed to hear other people's account of this shambles to try impel the brain of the poor departed major. I now hoped with all my heart that his soul was at peace in the everlasting kingdom, for whatever wrong he done while on earth, in my opinion he had already served his sentence in hell in this world and deep down I knew that Paul McCumsky was a good man.

The officers were glad to see me if somewhat a little surprised. I informed them that I had been knocked unconscious and my memory was hazy as a result.

"I would like to hear everyone's account word for word, as this may well help to stimulate my mind and help me to remember."

I apologized in advance for I knew they had already been interviewed by officers from HQ. I sat back and listened intently as one by one they gave me their account of what had happened. The consensus of opinion was that the Germans knew at what point we were going to hit them and they were ready for us. That could only mean one thing; there was a leak at the very top. With that information I went directly to HQ. Just before I left I asked,

"Does anyone know anything about the arrest of Willie McBride?"

No one knew anything. As far as they were concerned, both McBride and Sergeant McNeil had been listed missing and were presumed dead. When I arrived at HQ, I had the CO awakened from his slumber to tell him of my report. He was not pleased to be woken at this ungodly hour, as he had put it, but seemed to calm down when he found out who I was. He informed me that off the record, I had been accused of insubordination, I was told exactly what McCumsky had said to Ashton-Jones and I agreed with every word and was proud of the major but I kept those thoughts to myself. I told the CO I would swear on a stack of bibles that I hadn't said any of those things to the colonel, which was true for it wasn't me that said it. The general seemed inclined to believe me. I then informed him of what had happened to me and that I believed there was a leak somewhere in HQ. He wanted me to be very careful going down that road for he had found out, to his own cost, that it can be very treacherous grounds when people close ranks as some of them have very influential friends in the government. He suggested that we meet at a more reasonable hour of ten thirty tomorrow and we could discuss the matter in detail. He found me somewhere to bathe and sleep and had my uniform cleaned and pressed.

At ten-thirty, I went back in my new clean uniform to the CO's office. Unfortunately, by this time, the cover up was well underway. To deflect attention from the apparent leak they would now focus on the court martial and the execution of Willie McBride. I was led into the CO's office to be met by the general I had woken in the early hours. General Blair introduced all those present saying,

"You've met your CO before, General Montague."

I had an awful urge to enquire after his teeth but I though it would be prudent of me to remain silent. Blair continued to point to Colonel Ashton-Jones saying,

"You two are already very well acquainted, oh by the way, you should read his report about you, it borders on hero worship, but then again, I do believe the Colonel thought he was penning your epitaph. The other gentleman is the new Provost Martial, Lt Colonel Cockburn, and by the way I am no longer in charge. General Montague is back in the hot seat, he has done the British army a great service reporting back to duty early from his sick bed after his horrendous injury."

I assumed the general was being a bit tongue in cheek, whether the others did was a different matter. Something was not right here though, I thought. The general continued,

"I have been asked to stay on as a judge for what would have been the court martial of Colonel Cunningham but unfortunately we can no longer shoot him for he is already dead." There was a hint of dry humour in his statement but again, it seemed like I was the only one aware of it. "But not to waste time, we will court martial a William McBride for cowardice in the face of the enemy."

I interrupted the general, "It's not William McBride sir, it's Willie McBride."

Then the pompous Ashton-Jones butted in saying, "Stop being pedantic to a senior office McCumsky, what difference does it make? William or Willie, he's a coward and he will be shot."

"It's Major McCumsky sir, and I thought the boy was to have a fair trial, your remark sounds very much like you have already found him guilty of the charges," I replied.

General Blair looked at the red-faced Ashton-Jones and shook his head and sighed, his expression seemed to say idiot, but he said nothing and allowed me to continue.

"The reason it makes a distinction, whether it be William or Willie, is known so well by General Montague for is that not why Colonel Cunningham knocked out your front teeth sir, because he brought you evidence that the boy was not William McBride at all but his younger brother Willie McBride who is still only seventeen, too young to be in the army, the same army that this boy has served in for two years."

I then told the complete story. When I had finished, General Montague looked totally shocked, he thought his guilty secret had died with Cunningham. Without thinking, he blurted out,

"How did you find out?"

Then without thinking, I said,

"Willie told me everything the Colonel had told him when I visited him this morning."

In hindsight, that was not the right thing to do for now Montague would clearly want Willie out of the way for sure. The other people in the room were a bit surprised to say the least about the new developments regarding the revelation of the lad's age and the fact that the CO had known all along. I was asked to wait outside the room while a discussion took place on this new disclosure. After an hour, General Blair came out to see me. He informed me that he had tried to stop the court martial but could not, for their argument was that the lad was a serving British soldier regardless of his age so he was subject to the British army law regarding the act of cowardice in the face on an enemy. He added

"I have persuaded them to let you act as his defending officer, the court martial takes place tomorrow morning at nine so I suggest you go and prepare the lad's defence and I do sincerely wish you luck for you will need it."

I said, "What about the matter I told you about this morning? Has that now been brushed under the carpet?"

The general said, "No there is, as we speak, a high level inquiry taking place into the matter and you and I can no longer speculate on what did or didn't go on for we are mere mortals, this has gone right to the very top. Do not concern yourself about that, try to find some mitigating circumstances to save this lad." He wished me luck again and I do believe he meant it.

I found myself back at the prison compound again, this time to visit Willie. I wanted to see if he would tell me anything that may help his case. When I told him that Sergeant McNeil was missing and presumed dead, and that his word was all we could count on now, I had hoped it would drive him to tell me what had happened but he still remained silent. I spent all day with him yet he would not utter a word. If anything, he had become more withdrawn when he heard about McNeil. I decided my best defence would be to tell the court how brave he had been in the past and that he had received a medal for his bravery for going back single-handedly into no man's land to rescue his sergeant. The charges against him would be totally out of character so he musthave been suffering from shell shock.

The court martial was convened just before nine the next morning. The charges were outlined against Willie and the proceeding commenced. You could have knocked me down with a feather when the prosecuting officer brought forward his star witness, none other than the fat faced military policeman from the prison that I had shared a minor conflict with when I was in the guise of Colonel Cunningham. How inappropriate could it be, when someone so obviously devoid of a backbone could now stand there with a straight face and a clear conscience and accuse a person of being a coward? He took the court through his story of how he had watched the defendant screaming that he would not go over the top. When he had finished, the prosecuting officer more or less said this was an open and shut case and that the man was clearly guilty.

Now it was my turn to see what I could do to stop this foregone conclusion. I started to question the rat-faced policeman,

"When you observed and listened to Private McBride screaming that he was not going over the top, why then did you not go forward and apprehend the soldier? For was this not your duty to suppress such actions? Could this not have lead to unrest with the other men? I put it to you Corporal that you, in fact, were too scared to go and stop it, in effect you were not enforcing your responsibilities, for you yourself were showing cowardice in the face of the Scots."

The prosecutor rose to his feet, "I object to this line of questioning, the defending officer is badgering the witness, the corporal is not on trial for cowardice, Private McBride is."

General Montague sustained his argument, which did not at all surprise me, for the court martial had been assembled to find Willie McBride guilty. No other verdict would be acceptable, that is why they had brought out their big guns in the form of the prosecuting officer. He was no ordinary officer; he was an experienced legal eagle, who on Civvy Street had probably prowled the courts of the Old Bailey. Now, my line of questioning would have come to an abrupt end if the rat faced MP had not offered an answer when he did not have to.

"I was too far away, by the time I got to the coward, he had already been restrained."

He had the look of a cat that had just got the cream, thinking that he could talk his way out of anything. What he didn't know was that was the answer I wanted all the time to come out of his mouth.

I said, "Before I go on, can I just ask the witness not to refer to the defendant as a coward, for that is for this court to determine."

I then repeated the same statement that I had used while I was in charge of the body of Colonel Cunningham,

"I have been into no man's land many times with that boy at my side, I have never seen him so much as flinch as he ran towards the German line. I can tell you he is no coward. Now as for you…"

The prosecutor's objection came in before I got the best part of my speech out but it didn't matter, the speech had achieved the desired effect, for the MP realised at once that he had heard those very words before. He looked into my eyes and saw something that made him feel very apprehensive, he was no longer cocky and assured, he was now visibly shaken. I said,

"How far away were you from the defendant?"

"I don't know, I can't quite remember exactly," he answered.

"Well, let's make an estimate shall we." I walked to the far side of the court, "Were you about this far away?"

He confirmed with a slight nod that he was approximately that distance away from Willie. I asked General Blair to stand next to me; I took off my leather belt and began to make a loud cracking sound by slapping it together, while stamping my feet as hard as I could. I then began to shout out,

"I am going over, you can't stop me. I am going over, you can't stop me." I then stopped the banging and stamping of my feet and asked the corporal "What did I say?"

The MP said with a slight smile on his face, "I am not going over, you can't make me. I am not going over, you can't make me." He then sat back in the witness chair like a boy who had just passed a very important test at school.

However, that expression soon changed when I asked General Blair to reveal to the court what I had actually said. The General said,

"I am going over, you can't stop me. I am going over, you can't stop me."

The corporal shouted at me, "I couldn't hear properly because of all the racket you were making."

Out of the corner of my eye I could see the prosecuting officer put his head in his hands for he knew what I was about to say.

"So our artillery were sending over marshmallows instead of shells that morning were they corporal? I suppose they were afraid of making any noise just in case they woke the Germans"

It was game, set and match with this witness. I had a friend once who was a bit of a legal eagle, he would have been proud of my performance I thought to myself as I sat back down.

"No further questions."

The prosecutor knew he was losing the case at this point so he decided to call Willie to the stand for he had heard that he would say nothing in his defence. When the prosecutor asked him to explain why he had to be restrained, Willie just said,

"I have no comment to make."

The prosecutor said that his silence confirmed he was guilty. I then got to my feet at once and said,

"Don't you see, his lack of comment proves he is suffering from shell shock, he is clearly afflicted and therefore not a coward."

The judges left the court to deliberate. The prosecutor came to me to shake my hand. He said,

"Lt Coronal Sharp, pleased to make your acquaintance. I don't mind saying that was a first class, totally professional job you did on my witness, I think it's in the bag for you now. Allow me to buy you a drink, they will be gone for hours. Where did you train for the bar?"

I told him the only bar training I had done was where he was going to take me for a drink. We had lunch in the officers' mess at HQ, although it was more like a five-star restaurant than a mess. These men certainly knew how to look after themselves while their soldiers were suffering on the front line. When General Montague walked in, he did not acknowledge Sharp or myself and proceeded to go to the far end of the mess. Two high ranking officers were waiting for Montague and as he approached their table, Montague saluted them and took a seat. Now I realised why these two had picked such an out of the way place to dine for their conversation was not to be overheard by anyone else. What they did not take into account was that an immortal being was also dining in that room and distance was of no consequence when he really wanted to hear something. So while I pretended to listen to Sharp talking, I eavesdropped in to the three officers conversation.

The officer with his back to me I didn't recognise but the one facing me, I was sure, was the Commanding Chief for the Allied Forces in France, that would explain why Montague was acting subservient. This man said,

"Sorry to interrupt your deliberation, how does this go by the way?"

Montague fumbled with his tie nervously and said,

"Not very well actually. Blair is convinced that the prosecution did not prove its case and with the soldier's good record and age, he should be acquitted and I have got to say myself, the Scot has done a great job on your man, tied him up like a kipper. I have no time for the man but even I had to admire his skill in the courtroom. At the moment I only have Ashton-Jones on my side and his judgment is only based on the fact of his hatred for the Scots."

The senior officer said, "This will not do Montague at all, we need to set an example to the Scots, we must make these Celts more scared of us than the Germans for we need them to go again."

Montague just said, "Impossible, it's totally impossible. That position is so well fortified; we lost nearly half the regiment last time."

The other man said, "I am afraid it's the only way we can convince the Germans that their inside man is really true to them."

Then the senior officer said, "Can you just imagine what we could do then? We could let the inside man inform them we intended to make our final push to end this war, we would just have to pick out a place and then they would strengthen that point with everything they had in reserve. We then would just simply slip in the back door; before they could react we would have them. We could win this war yet, before our damned colonial cousins really put their noses in. As we now speak, the Americans are drawing up long term plans for 1919."

Montague said, "I do understand, but what about the Scots? It will be cold blooded murder. They also know what to expect, it may be hard to convince the officers to go over the top, let alone the men."

The senior officer just said, "That is why the lad must die. We must make an example of him to ensure they follow our orders. I will also send some new English officers, and there will be a strong military police presence should any individuals need motivation. Oh, and by the way, send Ashton-Jones to lead them out with pipes playing, I think the Ashton-Jones family deserve a hero, even a dead one. Tell the Proviso Martial I would like to see him; I will leave it to you to persuade Blair." Montague saluted and left.

What cold-blooded bastards these English officers really are I thought, when Sharp woke me from my thoughts, "Are you not enjoying your food? You have hardly touched it."

"I'm sorry, it seems I have lost my appetite," I said. No matter what I said, it would not help to save Willie, they were going to kill him I thought to myself. "I'm sorry but I must leave, I need to speak to Willie." I said to Sharpe before leaving the mess.

Willie would still not tell me anything even when I told him he would die if he did not say something in his own defence. Somehow I had failed Willie and I didn't know why. The court martial reconvened at three. With a three to one majority, they convicted young Willie. He was to die by firing squad at dawn the next day so that night after his evening meal, Willie watched his last sunset on this earth. I sat up all night writing letters, one to the boy's mother telling her he had died in action as a hero and one to the British newspapers telling them about the injustice that had taken place. I tried to phone the heads in the government but I couldn't get through. I felt totally devastated by all this.

Just before dawn I received a visitor, he told me the full story of how he and Sergeant McNeil had to restrain the boy from going over, for McNeil did not want him killed before he received his discharge papers. The corporal had told all this information to Ashton-Jones before the court martial started and was told to be quiet or he would find himself in serious trouble for taking McBride out of the action without the correct authority. He was given eight weeks leave to go back home but he could not board the ship until he knew Willie was safe, because he felt sooner or later the boy would tell everyone what really happened to save himself. So that was why Willie had kept quiet, for fear of tarnishing the memory of Sergeant McNeil, for he knew that what McNeil had done was not authorized, if by some miracle the sergeant did return he would be in serious trouble for removing the boy from action. What a brave and totally unselfish thing to do, it mirrors what my Master did; 'No greater love hath a man, than to lay down his life for his friends'.

I ran as fast as I could to the courtyard where the execution was about to take place. The firing squad were in position and Willie was being tethered to a post by an English captain I had spoken to earlier that day. I looked at the firing squad and I could not believe it, they consisted of men from my own unit, these were trench mates of the boy. How exceptionally cruel by the power that be to have these men kill their own comrade. I ran forward and looked up to a balcony that led out from the officers mess. Standing there was General Montague, Lt Coronal Cockburn and Ashton-Jones, and no doubt after observing the murder they would tuck into a hearty breakfast. I called up to these men,

"This execution can not take place. I have in my possession a sworn statement that Private McBride was being restrained from going over the top, he is not guilty of cowardice."

Then Cockburn said, "It is too late to present new evidence, the sentence has been passed. You had your day in court now stand aside or you will be arrested."

"This evidence was deliberately suppressed by Coronal Ashton-Jones," I said standing in front of Willie. "If you are going to shoot him, you will have to kill me first." Two MPs ran forward and manhandled me away from Willie.

While this was being done, the boy said, "It's okay sir, don't fret, I have made my peace with God. I am ready to go for you see sir, it was written the day I was born that this will be the day I die."

I turned to look at him and could see in his eyes that he was prepared to die; he showed no fear just as he had done on the battlefield. Who was I to stop this lad from going to the paradise in the next world? So I stopped struggling and moved aside and said,

"Is there anything I can do for you Willie?"

He just said, "If you could find the time one day, could you go and see my mam and tell her I didn't die in pain but with a smile on my face." He then turned to the priest and said, "Pray for me Father."

The English officer in charge of the firing squad asked Willie if he would like a blindfold. Willie answered, "No thank you sir, I would just like to see the sun one more time before I go."

The officer complied with the request; he waited until the sun rose over the buildings directly opposite Willie's eye line.

He then said, "Present. Aim. Fire!!"

There was an almighty blast of gunfire that echoed around the courtyard but when I looked at Willie he was still admiring a magnificent sunrise, every shot had missed its target. It seemed his mates would not be the ones to kill him. There was total silence. No one knew what to do.

Ashton-Jones came down from his elevated position, and told every member of the firing squad they would be court martialed themselves if this order was not carried out. He walked towards Willie to take over from the captain. Then something amazing happened, Willie took charge of his own execution. He shouted to the men,

"Now come on boys, I have lived with you lot for nearly two years, you are better shots than this. I know what you are trying to do and don't think I don't appreciate it, for I do, very much so. But they have made up their minds, I am going to die there is nothing you can do to stop it; you will only get yourselves into trouble for nothing for I will still be dead. They will just get some fresh faced boys just off the boat that can't shoot straight for toffee and I could get hurt. You all know what a coward I am, I don't like pain so do a good clean job on me boys and shoot for the heart."

He then turned to me and with a sad smile on his face he winked, then spat on Ashton-Jones' newly-polished boots and turned back to the firing squad and said, "You understand the meaning of that don't you boys? Now shoot straight you bastards before he cleans it off." He then turned back to Colonel Ashton-Jones saying, "Not a bad aim that eh King Edward?"

Then in unison, without waiting for the command, the six men from Willie's own unit opened fire. The boys head shook violently and then his knees buckled and his head fell forward onto his chest. The earth should have shook, the birds should have stopped singing and time should have stood still in remembrance of that lad. But alas, the birds were singing and it looked as if it would be a lovely day, for the world did not know that one of the bravest men I had ever known had died in the guise of a mere boy.

The English captain said to no one in particular, "I don't know about shooting him, with a speech like that we should have made him a general for he could have persuaded the men to go into the jaws of hell and they would have. I think we have just killed a born leader. What did he mean when he called you King Edward sir?"

Ashton-Jones just said, "He was confused, it was just the last frightened ramblings of someone who knew he was going to die."

I interrupted him saying, "How dare you call him frightened, are you also blind as well as an imbecile? That boy has just orchestrated his own execution, only a very brave person could have done that. And regarding calling you King Edward, have you never read your history books? He was dying like William Wallace had done, by not betraying the common Scots and spitting at the English. I saw them both die and they were both brave and patriotic Scots, the only difference was one was born in Manchester."

Ashton-Jones just looked at me strangely; he did not reprimand me for my attitude towards him. He just told me to take the men from the firing squad back up to the front line with the rest who had come down earlier, he would follow later tonight. He then turned to the body of Willie saying,

"Before you go make sure McBride receives the internment befitting of a Scottish hero." So the way Willie had died had touched the stone heart of Ashton-Jones for even he had realized he had just witnessed something truly spectacular. So I went to all the taverns in the town to tell the remaining men that their leave was over and they were going back to the front but first they would be attending the funeral of a hero. After the service at the church, the six comrades who had shot Willie now carried his coffin draped with a flag of St Andrew and we took the long way to the cemetery passed our HQ and we beat the drum slowly and played the pipes lowly. As we lowered him down to his grave, the band played the last post and the pipes played a sad melody. We said our last goodbyes to Willie McBride, leaving the sun shining on his grave as we headed back to the trenches and to an uncertain future.

Before Ashton-Jones arrived back at the front, I assembled my officers and told them what I had heard for the plans of our attack. I told them I had an alternative that didn't entail us all dying. However, if it didn't work we all would end up dead. I asked if they were with me and they all agreed. Each officer went back to his unit to give the men the instructions. When the whistle sounded to go over the top, they were to disarm the English officers and also strip the MPs of their weapons. The English officers were to be taken to the CO bunker and the military police were to be sent back to HQ with their tails between their legs.

Just before dawn, the British artillery opened up to bombard the German lines. Just before it stopped, the officers whistled and the plan went into action. It was carried out just the way I wanted apart from one small variation. When the MP's were stripped of their weapons their uniforms were also taken and they were sent back to HQ naked. The Scots then changed their defensive position; they now had their backs to the Germans. I was waiting in the CO bunker with the English officers, a major amongst their number was shouting,

"You mutinous Scottish cowards, you will die for this."

Including Ashton-Jones, there were all together ten English officers. Apart from the major and the captain, the rest were made up of junior officers, some just off the boat from England and more than likely straight from public school for they looked no more than schoolboys. So much for the back up that Montague had promised, how in hell's name did he expect these poor young lads to make battle-hardened Scots go over the top if they didn't want to? I felt so sorry for them; they just couldn't comprehend what was happening to them. I had all the officers seated in front of me, the mouthy major was still complaining but Ashton-Jones was very silent which I felt was very strange at this time. Whether he was relieved at not having to go over the top at this moment I was not quite sure. I informed them what I had found out about our plans of attack and how someone on the General's staff had informed the Germans we were going to knock on the same door again but now, what started the other day, would be finished and we all would have been killed,

- but we would not have died in vain for now the Germans would believe that their mole was telling the truth. The mouthy major interrupted by shouting out,

"It's our duty to go."

I told him that if he had really made up his mind and wanted to die then he could go by all means but on his own. He said nothing and just sat back down. I then told them my plan.

"When we don't attack, the Germans will eventually send out a spotter plane. The pilot and the observer will be very surprised for hopefully by then, having been convinced by the MPs that we had mutinied and taken our English officers captive, Montague would then send forward the reserve regiment to retake the trenches. At first, the Germans will not believe it so they will send out a patrol into no man's land. They will then report back that we were now facing the other way. They will not believe their luck and will send up a second plane and this is where you come in gentleman. The second spotter plane will see ten roughed up English officers running for their lives and to make it look realistic you major mouth, you captain, the tall lad at the back and you ginger will all be killed."

The four men looked at each other dumbfounded. The major spoke up, "You can't do that, it would be murder."

"But hold on a minute," I said, "why are you complaining now when I suggest killing only four people to achieve our objective? You were willing to see many thousands killed just because the General's staff told you to. You see gentlemen, we need to convince the enemy that the British really do have a mutiny on their hands. If it works out, it could enable us to take the

German line and end this war so your death would not be in vain. However, don't look that worried gentlemen, I am not going to ask you to lay down your lives for your country, just your bodies, you see I am not as barbaric as you think I am. All I want you to do is to fake your deaths by falling down. You major mouth will fall first for with your gob your erroneous wailing will be heard back home in Blighty. You next big man, then the captain and then the saddest sight of all, young ginger here will be hit just before he reaches safety. You can act can't you ginger?"

The junior officer smiled and said, "I will give it a go, sir. I prefer it to dying." The rest of the men began to laugh.

I then continued with my briefing. "Knowing how outraged General Montague will be, he will have the men open fire. This I hope will be witnessed by the second spotter plane and now it will be your turn colonel. You must tell Montague what we are trying to do; you will need to get him to order our artilleries to open fire on us. We will then take cover and wait for the Germans to come for I do believe gentlemen, they will come for they will see it as their opportunity to end the war while we are in fighting. When they are almost on us we will open fire with everything we have got and when they start to retreat we will go after them. Now this is the most important part of my plan, we will find out whether the Germans are like your English generals, for as we are attacking the retreating Germans will be our cover. The success of the plan will quite simply hang on one point, are the German machine gunners more humane that our generals, will they kill their own men? For if they open fire that is what they will be doing."

Then Ashton-Jones broke his own enforced silence, whether feeling more confident now that he was not going to die, he began to act pompous again, "I object to the way you refer to your senior officer."

I punched the colonel full force in the face, his nose burst open and I made an apology, "Sorry sir, I didn't mean to hit you so hard but you do understand, we have to make it look as realistic as possible." I then put my hand into the blood coming from his broken nose, wiped it over the young ginger officer's ruffled hair and ripped his jacket, "Sorry son, we have to."

The lad just smiled. I gave the signal to my men and they went about making the English officers look like they had taken a battering. In reality, I think only the major received a smack. We then waited for the first German spotter. I asked Callum to keep a look out over no man's land and let me know if he spotted an enemy patrol.

Montague turned up with the reserve regiment, and they set up their position about a quarter of a mile away. I had estimated that they would have come nearer. I went to the English officers who were to indulge in a little amateur dramatics and we worked out by looking back to the reserves' position, after exactly how many seconds each officer would go down. My snipers would open fire as close as possible to them one second before they were due to fall. We all synchronized our watches and bided our time.

As we were waiting for the second plane, I showed a map of the Germans front line to Ashton-Jones, I told him what I believed we would capture; once inside their trenches we would go at them from both sides. I told him the reserve regiment should be split up and attack either side of the ground we had taken. If we did succeed in taking this amount of ground it would include an under-ground field hospital, many storage areas, rest rooms and even a kitchen; it would be a very significant loss to them. This land represents a very important part of their fortification, take this and the rest will fall; it could mean an end to the war before the year was out.

"So it is imperative for you do your part. How is the nose by the way?" I asked.

The coronal looked at me with bloodshot eyes. "You did that on purpose, you will have to hope this objective of your works or I will have you for that."

"Don't let your hatred of me cloud the issue, when this is all done I will walk you down the German lines and you will see for yourself that you were never going anywhere other than in a coffin. Your General friends had sent you out to die, for did they not give you the order to lead out the men? After this is all over ask your-self what is worse, a broken nose or death. Come here." Before he could realize what I was doing, I had pushed the spear head against the side of his nose.

He screamed, "What the..." then his pain was gone. "What did you do and what in God's name is that thing?"

I just laughed, "You answered your own question, it's something in God's name."

The second plane was spotted coming over, and I told the men to get ready. I reminded Ashton-Jones to make sure our artillery hit our position then we set the English officers free. Off they went, like the hares at a dog track, running as fast as their legs could carry them. The German plane was now looking down on us. The major fell so realistically that I had to question whether or not my sniper had actually shot him.

"Robbie, did you hit him?"

"Oh shit, was I supposed to miss him..., of course I didn't hit him, he's just like all English officers, a very good actor."

The other two went down just as good but the star performance went to young ginger. When he was suppose to fall he didn't, he held his back like he had been hit then he staggered forward a few steps before falling, it was so good again I almost believed it myself. It was such a convincing sight that two rankers ran forward to bring back the body of their obviously wounded young officer. The German pilot had seen enough and couldn't wait to get back to tell the good news that the British were fighting themselves. If he had stayed in the air another minute or so he would have seen the resurrection of the young officer, as he took to his feet and made a bow.

When Montague was told about the new strategy he was furious and asked why the men had not carried out the original attack. The colonel answered,

"Because it was a trap, we would have all been going to our graves and we knew you wouldn't want that. You see I had sent out a patrol to see if your intelligence was correct and I'm afraid to tell you it wasn't, for the position was far from being weakened, it had been strengthened. I knew you wanted this part of the line so when Major McCumsky came up with an alternative I went with it."

Then he asked for our artillery to go along with the charade. The General would not comply, saying,

"I would be sent to the bloody Tower of London for trying to kill my own men, I can't do it."

Whether he thought the idea wouldn't work and he didn't want to be associated with it I don't know. Ashton-Jones told me later that he believed Montague wanted the plan to fail but it didn't. As I thought, the German machine gunners would not open fire on their own men and by the time they started to fire it was too late, we were on them. When Montague saw that we had taken our objective, he split up the reserve regiment and Ashton-Jones took them over the top in a frontal charge as we came at them from the sides. By the end of the day, we had taken twenty percentage of the German line. I am not saying this victory was responsible for ending the war but the guns did go silent.

A month later on the 11 November 1918, the official reason for the armistice being signed in a railway carriage in the forest of Compiegne was because the German people were starving, so the Kaiser abdicated and fled to Holland. Not a word was said or a report was made about the capture of twenty percent of the German line for it humiliated both sides. The German high command didn't want it leaking out that they could have lost this war by being mislead into believing that the Scots had mutinied. The British high command were happy to go along with this for an investigation may have concluded that the Germans were not the only ones to be deceived, for the British may well have been hood-winked into believing that the Scots had actually not mutinied. So the powers that be just brushed everything under the carpet including the murder of poor young Willie McBride. Anyway, to win like that with the help of skulduggery wouldn't be English, it just definitely would not be cricket.

CHAPTER TWENTY ONE

The Safe House

Alex Smythe believed the time to be about ten-thirty in the morning. He had misplaced his watch and for the life of him he couldn't remember when he had last seen it. Alex used to be so precise about everything, not any more; he could just about remember what day it was. It was like living in an everlasting nightmare. About five minutes ago, he had made a call to the police on his mobile. He wasn't sure he had got through as the signal was very bad. He heard the operator on the line although he couldn't be certain that she had taken down all the information, most importantly the address, before the phone went completely dead. He just couldn't understand it, the battery was fully charged, he had tried several times since but to no avail. He made up his mind to act, if he didn't they would kill the lad.

They had tortured him for hours, he was sure the young man's body wouldn't take any more punishment. There was only Henry and Isabella in the house plus one of the French guys who was keeping guard outside the room where they had been keeping the lad securely bound to a chair. The rest of the gang of nutcases led by De-Burgh were doing a church by church search of the area near to the house where they had kidnapped the young man from. It was now obvious to Alex that the devil, or whatever unclean spirit it was, could not see the whereabouts of the spear if it was on consecrated ground so it had instructed its followers to search all the churches in the area. They had left Alex behind because he had proved useless the night before. Henry and Isabella went missing to get up to who knows what, but he couldn't care less that she couldn't keep her hands off the French man. Only a few weeks ago, if he had known his wife was being unfaithful his heart would have broken in a thousand pieces but not anymore, he realized that there were more important things in this world and in the next than his broken heart.

He decided it was now or never. There were two cars on the driveway, the first one nearest the road was one of the rented Fords, the other car was Henry's. He slipped outside and took the rotor arm out of Henry's car then he went back into the house to make a cup of tea. He carried the cup of tea up to the second floor and gave it to the French man who was guarding the door to the young man's room. As soon as the guy took hold of the tea with both hands, Alex hit him on the side of the head with his weapon. The man dropped the cup and the hot tea went over him. He just sat there all confused and pitiful, he was obviously dazed, in the movies he would have been knocked out cold then Alex would not have had to do what he was about to do. He pulled back his arm and hit the man full on with a gun. He heard the sickening crack of the man's skull, then the man collapsed. Alex looked around to see if the noise had disturbed Isabella and her lover but they were apparently too engrossed in their nefarious actions to take any notice of the noise Alex was making.

He stepped over the pole axed body to enter the room, the door was not locked for they knew the poor boy was not going anywhere under his own steam. He was tied to the chair; his head lay forward on his chest. Alex lifted the young man's head very gently to wake him. He almost had to look away in utter repulsion, the lad was totally distorted, he looked like the elephant man. He wasn't sure but he believed his jaw was broken but it was his eyes that broke Alex's heart, they seemed to be pleading as if to say, 'Oh my God, please not again'. Alex reassured him that no harm would come to him; he told him the others were out so they would have to move quickly before they came back.

He unbound the lad then very slowly helped him down the stairs as quickly as possible. He could tell that the young man was in agony, every step caused him distress. He did not know the young man but he admired him immensely, if he had been fully fit he would have been as strong as an ox. He was about three or four inches taller than Alex, who strangely felt no exertion from helping him. Either the young man was walking with his own efforts or something else was helping him.

In a room upstairs on the third floor, while Isabella and Henry were fornicating, a lizard-like creature appeared at the side of their bed. In a very angry and evil voice is shouted at them,

"While you enjoy yourself copulating, the bird has flown."

It then disappeared as instantly as it had appeared. They both lay there too shocked to move. When Henry eventually rose from the bed to retrieve his pants, he went to open the curtains to look for the rest of his clothes when he noticed Alex helping the injured prisoner escape.

They were making their way to one of the Ford cars parked on the front drive. He knew that even if he was to take the time to run down two flights of stairs it would be too late, they would be in the car and away so he picked up his gun, opened the window and shouted to Alex,

"Stop or I'll shoot him!"

Alex just turned and looked up at his wife who was now at the window with Henry. From her attire it didn't take much imagination to guess what they had been up to. Alex just said,

"Go screw yourself like you have just done to my wife you garlic-filled toad," which was not really that insulting under the circumstances.

Isabella screamed, "Alex, come back, you don't know what you're doing, you will get us all into trouble."

He just kept on walking to the car. Henry warned him again to stop or he would shoot. Alex said nothing he just stopped, slightly turned and gave the French man the Agincourt salute with two fingers. He then leaned the lad against the passenger door of the car and opened it. He was just in the process of helping the young man into the car when Henry discharged his weapon, more of a warning shot than intentionally wanting to hit him. From his elevated position, the trajectory of the bullet went down into the top of Alex's back. It was still travelling down when it passed through his body and then entered the head of OB who was now sitting in the passenger seat just below the standing Alex. The bullet finally lodged into OB's brain killing him instantly. Alex fell on the dead man's lap; he looked up to see the blood coming from the wound in the young man's head. He was now slanted to one side, Alex knew for sure he was dead; he thought at least he was out of his suffering. Alex knew he was now dying, but before he passed away he saw the police car coming up the drive; his message had got through. Explain two dead bodies you French prat, he though to himself.

Alexander Longsden-Smythe or plain old Alex Smythe may have lost his life on that cold morning in Cheshire but he won back his soul.

CHAPTER TWENTY TWO

Religion and Evolution

Like I have already said, I was born a Jew. Baptized by the Master in the Jordan and three hundred years or so later partly responsible for forming the Holy Roman Church. Do I wholeheartedly and totally believe in religion? The honest answer would have to be no. I totally believe in faith but I think sometimes religion can divide us. The Christian, the Jew, the Muslim, and so on. It must beg the question why so many religions when there is only one God. Why am I so disappointed with religion?

Well take the Holy Roman Church for instance. Bernard of Clairvaux was the most influential church father of his time. He was made a saint just forty five years after saying something that went totally against the Master's teachings regarding turning the other cheek. If he was a father of the church of Jesus Christ, should he not follow his lead? Yet in 1129AD, he said to the Knights Templar that it was their duty to kill for Christ. He went on to say that killing was a sin but malicide, the killing of evil, was not. Not only that, it was possible to gain Christ by dying for him. It was also possible to attain salvation by killing for him. This included the non-believer Muslims in Jerusalem. Now does that not sound familiar, is it not the same scenario today? The Muslim suicide bomber climbs aboard a bus full of innocent passengers about eight hundred and fifty years later to rid the same city of the non-believer Jews. Who do these people really think they are? That the creator of the universe, the Lord God Almighty, needs to help mere mortals, such as us to deem out punishment and retribution, remember vengeance is mine says the Lord. In every holy book he is seen as the father so consequently we are the children. If a child does an injustice to another child, does the father want a third child to dole out punishment? I don't think so. He would be well able to judge the offending first child and then act accordingly, so if the average man is capable of running his family so is God. He does not want or ask for our help. For every one of his children will have their day in court at the end of their last day on earth when they stand in front of their maker at the gates of heaven. There will be no more lies and falsehoods, no excuses or reasons. We will all be brought to account for our actions just like I will be for killing the two men who murdered my son, all those years ago in Ephesus. There will be no mitigating circumstances in my defence. Like I think St Bernard would have had to do, I will take my punishment.

Talking about punishment, I have known all the Popes starting with the first, Peter. Some were saints that walked as men, some were just very good men. But I am really sad to say, that one or two of them I would not have trusted as far as I could have thrown them. And let me say by their size, it would not have been that far. You may feel reader, I am some what captious about the church of which I am a founding member. I am and always will be a believer in the Holy Roman Church.

Nothing on this earth gives me more pleasure than going to midnight mass on Christmas Eve in the northern regions of Europe when it's cold and the snow is outside. But inside it is warm and bright, the little children singing beautiful carols, their faces full of excitement and anticipation for the forthcoming festivities. Strangers turning to each other with a genuine kindness, shaking the hand of the person next to them and wishing them a Merry Christmas. There was even a case during the First World War where enemy soldiers went into no man's land to wish one another the same, all in the memory of the birth of my Master. The best man and friend to walk this earth, Jesus Christ, our Lord. So consequently I have nothing against religion. The only bad thing is the individuals who use it and destroy it to their own needs, rather like the Labour Party; the ethos of the movement is good. A fairer distribution of wealth. It is again the individual within the party that destroys it; the human being is man's worst enemy.

The last thing I would say on the subject of religion is this. Over the years I have visited some wonderful ornate churches, synagogues and mosques, some just totally beautiful in simplicity. You just have to stand back and admire the work, that the people who have built these places have put in. I am not now going to say they have wasted their time but the question needs to be asked, do we really need them? Would the money have been better spent feeding the poor and needy? When the Master needed time to think and contemplate his fate, he did not go to the synagogue; he went into the wilderness for forty days and forty nights. Then again, in his hour of need, the eve of the day he knew he would have to suffer and die on the cross, he did not go into the Great Temple in the city of Jerusalem to pray for help and strength from his father, he went to a simple garden to pray. I am now not advocating you no longer go to your places of worship, for did he not say,

"When two or three of you are gathered together in my name in prayer, God will listen."

All I am really saying, is if you stand at the side of a magnificent waterfall, look up at it and marvel at the natural wonder that God, the creator made. It is then you could take the time to pray, for I am sure he will listen to you there as much as in any place built by man.

I will just add one more thing before I move on to another subject, evolution. In 1492AD, King Ferdinand II and Queen Isabella of Castile financed Christopher Columbus' voyage to discover a way of reaching India by sailing west. However, he underestimated the size of the earth; he came across a land mass which came to be known later as the Americas. In the same year, the evil pair made homeless twenty thousand Jews who had lived law abiding peaceful lives, minding their own business. Their only crime, they made interest lending money to people who at the time were very grateful for receiving the money. They found the terms of their contracts acceptable; it was only when the money was spent the contract was then unacceptable and totally outrageous. If that is a crime then all the chairmen and shareholders from main high street banks should be thrown into prison, not a bad thing I hear you say. I think you take my point. They are providing a service; they are not making you go into debt, only you can do that, if you take up their opition? But like money-lending Jews of King Ferdinand II's Spain, they are not committing a crime; these poor people were only given weeks notice to leave the only country they knew. They had lived in Spain for generations, they were just told to take what they could carry and leave. The poor unfortunate vendors were given no more than a handful of coins for land and houses worth a fortune. They were then horded onto ships only for the men to be robbed and the women raped by the sailors. Where did these poor, wretched people find refuge? I will tell you, with the Muslim people. So remember Jews, when you make an innocent Arab homeless, you are hurting the very same people whose ancestors helped yours. Muslims remember to hold fast with your acts of vengeance, for two wrongs do not make a right. Think on this, your religion as being the most tolerant of all religions over the centuries. We are on the verge of a new millennium; do not enter this century in the way that has been foretold, by attacking the twin towers of Christendom and Judaism with missiles of fire. Be wise and tolerant like your ancestor for to be any other would bring war and misery for all, resulting in the total destruction of the earth.

Evolution. Where does that fit into religion? The honest answer would have to be, I am not sure. I do have a theory though, but like everyone else it's only supposition. What if Charles Darwin's discovery was not evolution but devolution? I will go into more detail later. So let's start at the beginning. Do I believe that God made the earth in six days? Now the scientists and the educated men will tell you that it is impossible, that the earth was created six thousand years ago. But they would also tell you that it is not possible that a man could live for two thousand years. Well that's not true for I am living proof that to God nothing is impossible. So let's say, for arguments sake, that the world was created six thousand years ago and man is the offspring of Adam and Eve. Then what about what Darwin said, I have met the man and found him to be pleasant and plausible, definitely nobody's fool. I have seen his evidence, but what if that evidence was not authentic; just planted for Darwin to find by a very intelligent life form, the devil, to undermine our faith in the Lord? We have been told one story over the centuries and the majority of us believe in the teaching from the Old Testament. Then along comes someone else with something that sounds feasible, so it naturally throws confusion on all the original teachings we were told to believe in. This reminds me of a joke I have heard - A man goes into a museum and asks the attendant,

"How old are the bones of the dinosaur in the corner?"

The attendant says, "They are three hundred million and four and a half years old."

The man then asks, "How can you be so precise?"

The attendant then says, "Well they were three hundred million years old when they were discovered four and a half years ago"

Okay, it's just a joke but it does mirror real life. Nearly every morsel of knowledge in your mind was put there by reading a book or someone telling you.

What if Charles Darwin's theory was not his own, he was just reading the signs left by the devil? Then years later, to help corroborate Darwin's assumption along comes another scientist with his hypothesis regarding ape and man. He tells us that ape and man have over ninety-seven percent the same chromosomes, the chimpanzees have even more. Then does this not confirm Darwin's supposition? Although, there is another school of thought on that. The argument is, if the missing three percent is the ability to talk then does that not feasibly make the ape a completely different animal? Take two airplanes on the ground, identical in every way but one. The first airplane, was built without an engine, would that not make it a very cramped restaurant? Whereas the second plane would be a means of transport, taking people to different destinations by air. In essence, although looking the same it would in fact be a completely different animal. Can you see my point? When I have told that hypothesis to educated people over the years, their final argument is the old chestnut, if God really does exist why did he create a world with famine, earthquakes and war? I would then answer with my own theory and yes, it is only my supposition. God did create a world without famine, earthquakes and war, it was called the Garden of Eden. God has no conception of time, which is a man-made thing. When it was written, God created the world in six days; it could have been six hours, six hundred years or six million years.

Don't you see is it not relevant, God is everything including time; he is an eternity without a start or an end, the alpha and omega. So let's say God created the world six billion years ago in the time scale we understand. He then created man and woman, he gave them everything they needed but like a parent who hides away a Christmas present from their child, only for that child to find it before Christmas day. What should he do? He loves the child with all his heart, should he just give in to the child and let it have what it wants when it wants? The answer, although somewhat cruel, would be to take that present and give it away. In the long run, the child would become a better person; it would appreciate the benefit of waiting. It will also understand you can't have what you want when you want it. It will learn to be obedient; the lesson would be harsh but a good one. In some ways, it would be harder on the parent, and that is what I believe God felt like when he sent Adam and Eve out of the Garden of Eden. When eventually Adam and Eve died, they would have been welcomed back into a far better paradise than Eden - heaven. They would not be two spoilt children but parents that have seen suffering and hardship - and ultimately better people, worthy and able to appreciate paradise. What about their children? Well, because they began to feel the cold, they grew hair to keep them warm all over their bodies and to protect themselves from the dangerous species God had created in this new world. They took to living in the trees, yes; in essence they became the ape. So, you see, my theory is that Darwin did not discover evolution but devolution. He found evidence of Adam and Eve's offspring turning back into man, so they could once again walk upright to appreciate the good things in this world that God had created. Only this time, they would have to live as men in this new world with its famine, earthquakes and war. This is only my hypothesis and of course it is only supposition but is it not as good as the next man's theory? So what I am really saying is I don't know whether the world was created six thousand years ago or six billion years ago, I just know when I go into church and I sing that new hymn that ends with the line, "Then sing my soul, my saviour God to me, how great thou art, how great thou art," the hair on the back of my neck stands on end.

I know one thing for definite. That whenever or by whatever means, evolution or devolution, or made in six days or six thousand years ago, I know it was created by one true God, the Lord God Almighty.

CHAPTER TWENTY THREE

Quid Pro Quo

Father Diego Mendez had just put down the telephone to cancel his last appointment for the day; he wasn't sure how long it was going to take. He did know something; he felt very put out by the English priests expecting him to erase all his appointments on their say so at the last minute. Then the phone rang, on the other end of the line was Father Phil O'Malley.

"Please Father Diego; I've just been thinking you must be rather peeved at the moment with you having to cancel everything at the last minute to go to this man's apartment. Well we have a saying in this country, 'If you scratch my back I will scratch yours'. I suppose in this case you will be scratching my mate Father Jim's back, but we won't split hairs."

This was going right over the South American's head and he said,

"I don't understand all this back scratching."

Father Phil thought his explanation was fairly clear to him. Something must be lost in the translation; they were both men of the cloth so he would use their common language. So he said the words in Latin,

"Quid Pro Quo - A favour for a favour," he continued,

"Every year my bishop gives the Christmas collection to a different overseas charity. This year it could be a charity from your homeland, and I must add that I envisaged a pretty substantial amount. The attendees of the cathedral are a very generous bunch at the best of times but at Christmas they really loosen the purse strings."

Father Diego deliberated for a moment then said,

"I do collect for an orphanage in my own town, any donations would be gratefully appreciated so I take what I'm doing is for his eminence, the bishop?"

Father Phil just said, "Oh no, the bishop knew nothing about our little favour for Father Jim."

"Then why would his eminence make a contribution to my charity?" asked Father Diego.

"Oh, you are not up to speed on the internal politics of the church; they are the same as any large organization. When a man makes it to the top, he no longer has to perform the mundane tasks like thinking for himself. Someone else takes over the duty: that is where I come in. This is my bishop so I give him all his ideas. The trick is to make him believe they are his own."

When Father Phil had finished his lecture on the ins and outs of deuces protocol, Father Diego said,

"You are a very cunning man, have you ever thought of standing for Parliament?"

"It's funny you should say that, I have always had a yearning to be a South American dictator. You don't know of any military groups in the offing that need a man at the top?"

Father Diego didn't see the funny side of Father Phil's joke so when there was no laughter forthcoming, he told Father Diego it was a private joke between him and Father Jim.

"You see, Jim is very outspoken against South American dictators. Look send me all your information about your orphanage and when you manage to get a few days to spare, come up and see the cathedral. You will be able to meet Jim at the same time. I think you two will get along just fine. Anyway thanks for your help, see you soon."

Father Diego said goodbye and put down the telephone, he was now in a much better frame of mind. It was nice not to be taken for granted. He thought he would take Mrs Owen's communion on the way back, because he would be going near her home. He gave her the sacraments as often as he could as she was housebound and couldn't get to the church. He would take her some cakes as well. One of his many pleasures was to sit and have tea with her. Mary would never moan about her predicament, she just got on with life. So he went through the church to collect the sacraments. He then decided to go that way out so he could pick up one of the leaflets on the orphanage back home, they were in the porch. So he would leave by the front doors of the church. When he got to the back, he put the literature about the charity in his case; he would send it off to Father O'Malley. When he was doing that, he inadvertently put down the paper he had in his hand with the address of the apartment on it. He went out of the doors; he then began to close them. When he looked up at one of the gargoyles that adorned the walls of the church, he was sure for a moment it winked at him. Then he remembered the address he had left on the table at the back of the church. Instead of standing there and contemplating the task of closing the bottom lock, he just reopened the door and went back inside. He felt the draft of something pass his ears, and then he heard an almighty crash. He turned to see what it was. Where he had been standing seconds ago, and would still have been there locking the door if he had not gone back in for the address, he would be lying under the remains of the gargoyle and could well be dead now. He had never liked those awful things; he liked them even less now. It was a good job someone was looking out for him. He now realized what he perceived to be an evil wink must have been the thing cracking. He went back into his office to phone the builders to come and make sure everything was secure. He told him he would not be there; he needed to go out on important business, just to put the estimate for the insurance under the door.

If Father Diego had not been going out in the car, he would have taken a drop of the hard stuff. If Father O'Malley hadn't been so kind regarding the generous donation idea, he would have phoned him to cancel, but he now felt obliged to fulfil the errand. As he sat in the car he looked at the address and the instructions to get there. He thought for a moment then came up with a shorter way, he would drive downhill to the shopping centre. Then second left, then third right, that would bring him out fairly close to the mystery man's address.

Everything seemed normal with the car until he was coming down the hill to a set of traffic lights that were on green. He touched the brakes, just in case they changed at the last minute. He was right, the lights did change but now the brakes didn't respond. His foot was right down to the floor on the brake; instead of slowing down he seemed to be going faster. He had no alternative but to run a red light, narrowly missing a taxi, which opted to go early. Obviously the meter wasn't running, Father Diego thought. Why he was thinking like that at a time like this, he didn't know. He tried the handbrake but that was not working; he was in hot water now, and he knew what he should do. Take the next turning on the left, it would take him to a little bit of a motorway. He took the turning almost on two wheels, and after several near collisions he eventually arrived on the motorway. In between the north and south lanes was a piece of man-made green belt, it went down in the middle from both sides like a little valley. There was no pedestrian access just flowers and young trees that the council had planted to try and appease the local green lobby. Father Diego knew this was where he had to attempt to crash the vehicle, at least then only he would be injured. A passing radio traffic helicopter was now watching the drama unfold while relaying the action back to his station. Father Diego was now running along the gully at the bottom of the green belt, quickly running out of land - if he kept on this course, he was going to hit a concrete wall supporting the overhead roundabout. Father Diego took the only option available, he would drive on the slope into the young trees, and perhaps this would slow him down. The first did nothing to stop him, he just simply uprooted it. The second seemed to slow him down a little; he did manage to stop after destroying four of the trees. He came to a halt just ten yards short of the wall. 'That was some ride', he thought. The above helicopter had captured the incident on video camera; they would try to sell it later to the television networks.

Mercifully, Father Diego was unhurt; he was taken in an ambulance to hospital for a check-up. As for the car, that would never see the road again, it was a write-off. Funnily, this made the priest a little sad, he had that car since he came to England ten years ago. In a small way, it was like losing an old friend. The doctor informed the priest that he was very lucky; he had not sustained any external or internal injuries. He finished his synopsis with a throwaway remark,

"Someone from your gang upstairs must have been looking out for you."

"What?" said the confused priest.

The atheist young doctor thought he had over-stepped the mark with the little joke and went slightly red with embarrassment, like the best man in the wedding reception speech recounting an event that him and the bridegroom had got up to in the past that was just too near the bone for a family function; everyone laughed on the stag night but now it had gone down like a lead balloon. Then to the young doctor's utter relief, Father Diego got the punch line,

"Oh, I see, upstairs - heaven. You just may be right."

He then started to laugh and was joined by the doctor out of sheer relief; he couldn't afford another dressing down from the Trust CEO for being offensive to a patient, especially to a member of the clergy. Father Diego patted him on the back and thanked him. He then asked where the nearest payphone was, as he needed to make an important call. The young doctor was just about to direct him to the phone when he told him to use the one in the office.

"Call it professional courtesy, we are both colleagues in a way, we both look after people, and the only differ-ence is that I look after their health and you their soul," the doctor said.

He showed him into his office to make his call, this could possibily put him in line for a reprimand because it was not hospital policy to let non-medical staff use the external line but deep down he knew the real reason why he was letting him use the phone. It was because he liked this man and he knew the priest didn't find the joke funny, he had laughed out of courtesy, a very kind thing to do under the circumstances. After he showed such a lack of concern, the poor man was suffering from shock and all he could do was to be rude about his chosen profession. The young doctor thought he would have gone to his church if he had not been an atheist, a voice in the back of his mind said 'Don't let that stop you'.

Father Diego called Father Furpay, he told him about his near death experience. Father Furpay was honour bound to tell Father Diego the full story when he finished. He told Father Diego not to go to the man's home because it seemed to be putting his life in danger, Father Diego would not hear of it, he just said,

"What kind of priest would that make me to run away from evil? I will complete my mission for you."

Father Furpay told him to take some holy water or something to protect himself. Father Diego said that he had something far more powerful than that in his possession; he had the consecrated body of our Lord.

Jim Broadbent had been a London taxi driver for over twenty five years. He had a wife and four grown up daughters, three were already married and now the last apple was falling from the tree so consequently Jim was having to fork out for another big expensive wedding. He was so depressed, not by the fact of having to spend big once again for his daughters but, once again, the bridegroom's family would not be making any financial contributions. When he complained about it at home to his wife, Jean, she would only say, 'Oh no James, not again'.

What really pissed him off this time was when the bridegroom's father wanted to break the wedding protocol by making a speech. This had happened previously with his daughter, Helen. Her new father-in-law was from Liverpool, he thanked everyone for coming to his son's wedding and that really got to Jim. It was not the lad's or his daughter's wedding; it was his wedding, for it was his hard earned money that had paid for the bleeding thing. Could one of these guys have broke with tradition for once and put their hand in their pockets? No, not one of them. It was all left to big old muggings Jim, that's why he had to work twelve hours a day, seven days a week. But not all that was the real cause for Jim's melancholy. It was because this particular apple was the last one to fall from his tree and she happened to be the apple of his eye.

A tap on the window of his cab brought Jim out of his daydream. He looked out to see a foreign-looking priest; he stood staring right into Jim's eyes. When Jim returned the stare he saw fear in the priest's eyes. He passed Jim a piece of paper and a twenty pound note and said,

"Can you take me to that address as quickly as possible, but drive very carefully my son."

Jim thought to himself that this was not feasible; he was after all a London taxi driver. Before the priest got into the back, he did something that Jim had never seen before in all his years as a taxi driver. He opened a flask then threw the contents over the vehicle. Jim assumed it was holy water because the priest was blessing the taxi. If this was not a wind up by one of those hidden camera TV shows, then this guy was one very nervous passenger. Jim was a lapsed catholic so when he heard the priest talking in Latin, he knew he was praying. Jim just thought the sooner he could get rid of this nutcase the better.

Just before reaching the priest's destination, Jim suffered a heart attack brought on by an apparition of a big lizard-like creature that jumped on the front of his cab. Jim knew this was just an illusion but it set off pains in his chest. He couldn't see the road that well; the creature seemed to be in agony as its feet were on fire. Jim managed to bring the vehicle to a safe stop at the side of the road. He calmly turned to the priest and said,

"Father, can you help me, I think I am dying."

Father Diego got out of the taxi and opened the driver's door. He noticed a policeman across the road, and shouted for him to call an ambulance. Jim was slumped in his seat saying,

"Can you give me absolution Father before I go, I have not been inside a church for a very long time."

After hearing his confession and giving him absolution, he broke off a piece of the sacrament to give to him. Jim started to feel better almost instantly; the pain in his chest began to subside. He knew one thing now, if he came through this he definitely wouldn't be bothered about who was paying for what with the wedding. For he knew now that life was just too short to hold a grudge. The ambulance came to take Jim to hospital; it seemed he would be fine now. The taxi driver thanked the priest for his help and he handed him back the piece of paper and the twenty pound note. As he looked at the address, Father Diego realized that he was now standing on the road of the man's apartment.

The apartment's main doors were open. There seemed to be no one in attendance so Father Diego approached the elevator. He pressed the button marked 'three'. When the elevator door opened, he cautiously walked down the hallway of the third floor. He found himself standing outside Lazarus' apartment door. He made three sharp knocks on the apartment door.

CHAPTER TWENTY FOUR

Unlucky for some, Friday 13th

I suppose I cannot write my memoirs and not say something about what has been called the most evil date in history, Friday 13th October in the year of our Lord 1307. This was the day when the corrupt and notoriously insolvent King Philip IV of France had the grand Master of the Knights Templar, Jacques De-Molay, and some of his men arrested on trumped charges including necromancy, the devil's work. The Knights Templars, who were they?

They have become, since that cold Friday morning in October 1307, something of a conspiracy theorist's paradise. Some will tell you they were devil worshippers, some will say they were over-serious Christian military fanatics and I suppose most interesting and controversial of them all, the most recent book published in the nineteen eighties says the Templars were the keepers and protectors of the bloodline of Christ. Mystery has always surrounded the organization since its eradication in the fourteenth century. Did they have in their possession documentation that could bring down the Holy Roman Church? Or perhaps they had the gold chalice from the Last Supper containing the blood of Christ collected at the crucifixion. Most importantly, to the impoverished King of France, did they have in their vaults the treasure of King Solomon? I will now try to answer all the mysteries surrounding the Templars. Like did the brotherhood know that Philip was coming? What happened to the Templars' fleet of ships that had set sail a few days before the arrest and detention of the order in France? Did those ships contain the treasure from the vault of the Paris Temple? That October day, they set sail from the Templar naval base, La Rochelle; where did they go? For all intents and purposes it could have sailed over the edge of the world for it was never seen again. So once again it is left to me to solve one of the world's great mysteries.

In 1305, Philip had sent spies to join the Knights Templar. Was he concerned with the rumours that the brotherhood were all homosexual, that they were in league with the devil? I don't think so. His one and only agenda was to locate the treasure of King Solomon. The Templar Knights had come across the treasure when they were doing building work beneath the temple mount in the 1120's in Jerusalem. It was taken back years later to France and as Philip believed, it was being kept in the Paris temple house. His spies had built up an extensive damning report condemning the activities of the organization. One of the items in the report appertained to them worshipping an idol called Baphomet; this was only their mistranslation for Mahomet, the Prophet Muhammad. You see, they were more enlightened than anyone realized. They believed there was only one God and Muhammad was sent by him. It was very radical thinking, although true. In those days, if you said all the religions were the same, believing in the same God, you would be signing your own death warrant.

Don't get me wrong, the Templars had not always been good and honest. The brotherhood had started out with the right intensions, to protect the Pilgrims going to the Holy land, with their network of temple houses and castles right through Europe to the Holy Land. Pilgrims from England could deposit their gold with the Templars in London then in return they would receive a credit note by which they could draw money from any temple house to and from the Holy land. This would safeguard their money, preventing them from being robbed on the roads of all their funds for financing their trip to Jerusalem. All they had to do for this service was to pay a small charge. So you see, there was nothing at this time sinister about the organization, they were in fact banking and hotel chain all rolled into one.

Like I have said before about the organization, they can have the right values but sometimes the individuals within its walls can be corrupt. Even worse than that, a demon could have joined their ranks. That was the case in 1208AD with a certain Simon-De-Monfort. He had built up a reputation for being inhumane in his treatment of prisoners. The spear of the Lord had sent me into the area where he was operating. I had no trouble in identifying that the sadistic De-Monfort was possessed. I emitted the evil spirit from his body but unfortunately the reprobate knight was too far damned in his evil ways, or had started out unequivocally malevolent before the infestation took place. So I had no alternative but to send the man to meet his maker. That was why, from that time, I kept a watchful eye on the brotherhood.

A hundred years later I was once again inside the organization. This time in the guise of a recently departed knight from Italy, Peter of Bologna. Pope Clement V had received a copy of one of Philip's spies reports so he had decided to instigate an inquirer of his own. Although Peter of Bologna was a Knights Templar of some standing, the pontiff knew he was loyal to mother church. Peter was not really a spy; he was a member of a very secret organisation that, to the Templars superseded his allegiances. This order was called The Holy Eye. It was set up one hundred years earlier by Pope Innocent III and me. The society became the window into the Knights inner sanctum. The Holy Eye was also inside the hospital and the Teutonic knights two other military religious orders. When the Pope's extra eye inside the organization passed over to receive his rewards in the next life, a replacement was ready to take over his role. This is how the task came eventually to Peter of Bologna. Unfortunately, Peter died suddenly. Whether someone found out about him, I am not sure so this time I thought it wise to take over the function myself. So I took over the guise of Peter and found myself a knight once again at a very interesting time for the Templars.

I found out that they had very close links with the assassins, the Islamic equivalent of the brotherhood. The two Holy orders were slowly coming together in their thinking; they were trying to bring an end to the wars between the Christians and the Muslims. This information I did not pass on to the Pope for I did not know if I could trust him. It's like this, can you imagine if the Muslim world and the Christian world merged into one religion, it would mirror what would happen in your time now, when two multi-conglomerates merge for the wholesale benefit of the two companies - but sometimes the individuals at the very top do not want this amalgamation to take place unless they are guaranteed the top job. So you see, I could not tell the pontiff until I knew for sure whether he thought more of the church than he did of himself.

Although, I did convey to the Holy Father that the order were good and honest and had only the best interest of the mother church at heart. So the Pope informed the King of France to do nothing. Philip was exasperated. He told the Pontiff in no uncertain terms that with or without his holy blessing he was going to arrest the French Templars. When I heard this news I went direct to Paris to warn Jacques De-Molay. So there you have the answer to one of the mysteries surrounding the Templars. Were they warned of their impending arrest? Yes, when I told the Grand Master he would not flee, he said,

"The order has done nothing wrong so we have nothing to answer for."

I eventually persuaded him that Philip could not care less whether the order was innocent; he was only after the treasure of King Solomon. So with some reluctance he ordered the treasure to be taken to the Templar fleet docked at their naval base at La Rochelle on the Atlantic. Now, to answer another question from history. What happened to the treasure and the fleet? Well in 1291, Schwyz and Unterwalden signed a mutual assistance pact. The Templars secretly sent money to help form the union into the country Switzerland enabling them to gain independence from the Holy Roman Empire. History says they suddenly and mysteriously acquired one of the best armies in Europe from out of nowhere. It was no mystery to me. The money came from the sale of some of the treasure; this was used to pay for an army of mercenaries. Within the ranks of the army were thousands of experienced Templar Knights that had escaped on the fleet in the autumn of 1307 with the treasure. It's not surprising that the country became known for its international banking system; probably the most significant legacy the Templars gave to Switzerland was their banking expertise. The Templars treasure did help Switzerland in the short term but it would certainly not last forever. They had to use the money they attained from the treasure wisely. So this is why with the Templars help, the country went into the banking profession. There is a saying that is very apt, 'You can give a man a fish and he will feed himself for a day but teach a man to fish and he will feed himself forever'. So you see the brotherhood taught Switzerland to fish. The country went from strength to strength. In the wealth department, it became financially independent; it never needed to join in with Europe's petty squabbles. One of its best achievements was to stay neutral during the bloodiest times in the twentieth century, 1914-1918 and 1939-1945. So there you see what eventually happened to the treasure, but that does not answer the question of where the fleet went directly after leaving La Rochelle?

Legend has it that Robert the Bruce sat in a cave after being defeated by the English. Depressed and disillusioned, he came across a spider struggling to build a web. When he destroyed the web, the spider just went about its business starting all over again; the creature would not give up. This inspired Bruce to take on the English yet again. A real good tale but alas not true. Robert did not get inspired by a spider; he gained his inspiration from the arrival of the Templars' fleet at Argyll. For onboard those vessels were ten thousand battle hardened knights ready to help Bruce fight for independence from the English. They had two conditions. One was that the

English never found out that the Templars had helped him. You see they were still operating in England under a tax exemption agreement set up by Edward I, regarding money leaving the country heading for the Holy Land. If the English found out that would definitely go out of the window, followed very quickly by the confiscation of all the Templars assets in England - so before the Knights went into the battle of Bannockburn, which Bruce won, they were stripped of anything that could identify them as Templars. The second condition was that the Scottish boat builders change the look of the fleet. Some took the guise of being Spanish and Portuguese vessels while the others were made to look like Italian and Dutch ships. So you see, consequently they disappeared into the pages of history never to be seen again. After the victory over the English, some of the Knights stayed in Scotland, the majority went with the treasure to help the fledgeling nation of Switzerland.

While the fleet was heading for Scotland, I was arrested with the Grand Master and the rest of the remaining Templars. Pope Clement was outraged and demanded that we were all released. He told the King of France that he had no jurisdiction over the Knights Templar brotherhood. Whether or not they operated in his kingdom, whatever land the Knights lived in they were not answerable to that particular throne, their only accountability was to the Vatican. Philip stood firm for he had not found the treasure. While he was still in dialogue with the Pope, his men were looking through the Paris temple, going into the records and assets of the brotherhood. Even without the treasure, the King's accountant confirmed that the Templars assets were considerable. Philip was not going to give this back without a fight, he was desperately in need of the funds to put right a short-fall in his own accounts. He had been running the country badly since he took over from his father.

If the pontiff had a fault it was that he was a weak and easily bullied man. He was also slightly frightened with being on French soil. It felt to him like he was under house arrest. French troops were outside his gates; he had been informed they were there for his own protection against reprisals from the remaining Templars still not under arrest. However, he did manage one small concession; he had persuaded Philip to release me. He had informed the King of France that I was in the order of The Holy Eye and so therefore not a Templar. My peers in the prison were naturally sceptical when I was leaving. I told the Grand Master he must put together a defence, but again, he would not listen,

"We are not guilty, we have done nothing to answer for, and God will deliver us out of the hands of this evil son of France," he said defiantly.

My answer to him was simple,

"God only helps those who help themselves."

I was then taken before the King, with him was another man. I later found out he was the keeper of the seal, Guillame De Nogaret. He asked me if I had any damning information against the Knights, I told him I did not. The King was furious, I think if he had not already have told the Holy Father I was to be released, I am sure he would have thrown me back into the cells. De Nogaret whispered something into Philip's ear; this seemed to calm him down.

This man seemed somewhat familiar but not in his looks. He was about forty, slim and going slightly grey. He would have probably been considered handsome in his younger days. There was just something about his eyes that was so strangely familiar; if they had been in their natural colour of red I would have obviously recognized this demon. But like on so many occasions, this beast was hiding from me. It said very whimsically,

"You are not a very good spy if you have found out nothing my friend. Do you have another profession you can fall back on? For I feel this line of work is far beyond your capabilities. Now run along little puppy back to your Master. He has a nice warm kennel to keep you safe." The King began to laugh.

"I would be careful sir, for even a puppy can give you a nasty nip," I retorted almost instantaneously.

"Watch your tongue before I have you taken away to have your bark seen to," the King said.

Then he and De Nogaret laughed once again. So I bowed and left the palace. I then went directly to the Holy Father, I demanded of him to threaten the King of France and his men with excommunication. He said nothing; he just took me by the arm to the window of his residence to show me the French soldiers. He said sadly,

"I was invited to this country as a guest, do you not see now, I am as much a prisoner as are the Templars."

On March 18th, 1314, Jacques De-Molay and the preceptor of Normandy, Geoffroi De Charney, were led out on to a platform outside the Notre Dame Cathedral. There in the shadow of mother church, a hideous crime took place. The two Templar Knights were stripped to their shirts and burnt at the stake. The witnesses of this evil deed reported that the men seemed almost glad that it was all over, for they had been kept in prison for over seven years. During that time, they sat before papal hearings, the papal committee and the University of Paris assembly. There was torture, confession, then retracted confession. The two old men were just so exhausted that they could not fight anymore; they had lost their war with the evil King of France. Things could have been different if it had not been for a weak and inadequate Pope and a very devious demon. They would have won their day in court.

I would now like to tell you what happened that day on November 22, 1309. The papal hearing opened and for all intents and purposes, this was the real trial. The bench consisted of five judges who were all cardinals, to their right sat the Pope and to their left sat the King of France and his entourage.

A few days earlier, I had persuaded the Holy Father to let me act for the defence. I was no attorney but I did know a little about the legal system. The brotherhood did not trust me so they elected as their representative Reginald of Provins. So the day before the trial was set to begin, I went to see my co-counsel to discuss our defence plan to see if we could thrash out a strategy. Now how can I describe this man? He was the type of man you didn't mess with. He was not a big man by any means but he was powerfully built. Although I had never seen him in combat, other knights had said he was fearless and scared of no one, which turned out to be true. He had long brown hair, a moustache and beard and dark defiant piercing eyes. When I asked him what the defence would be, he informed me it would be a big surprise for someone. I asked what type of surprise, he just said,

"Now if I tell you what I am going to do, it would not be a surprise would it? Now I do not mean to be discourteous but you, my friend would be the very last person I would tell. Have you not already turned out to be wearing another face? Before I reveal any secrets to you, I would want to make sure that this is your real face and not another mask. For deep down I still feel you are not what you say you are."

I think he was referring to me being in The Holy Eye. 'Fair comment', I thought to myself. If the shoe had been on the other foot, I would have done the same so it was decided that he would make the opening defence statement. So the day of the trial, I received the first shock of the day when Reginald walked into the court to take up his position next to me. He had gone completely mad with his razor and shaved all the hair off his head. The only hair remaining on his face was what you call today, a goatee beard. With his piercing defiant eyes and newly shaved head, he looked totally menacing. If his appearance was frightening, it was nothing compared to his opening defence statement. For a few moments, he had the King of France shaking in his boots.

The court case opened in the normal way by charges being read out, the indictments were heresy, sodomy, blasphemy and finally that they as an order were denying Christ. The middle cardinal in the file, who was acting as the presiding judge, asked,

"How does the order plead to the charges set out before them?"

Reginald sprang to his feet, ignoring the judge. He turned deliberately to the King of France then said,

"We are not guilty of any crime, we plead not guilty to all the indictments set out by this court."

Then the prosecution opened up to outline their case. After he had finished, Reginald rose again to his feet and turned to the King looking almost like he was threatening his life.

"Not only do I stand here today to defend my order which I intend to vindicate totally of all the charges, but I am also here for another purpose. To indict Philip IV of France with the murder of Pope Innocent III. I would also like to know if the King of France has had his brain removed for I feel he must have had, if he thinks he's going to convince the crowned heads of Europe that these charges against my order have not been trumped up by himself for one reason only so that he could steal our assets like he has done with the Jews, who used to live in his country. It seems this is the only way this man can get his hands on money. For if he debases the coinage of his country yet again, it will be so light it will float from your hands before you have time to spend it." The majority of the court erupted in laughter.

The King of France was now quite visibly shaken, whether with shock, fear or anger, I was not sure. De Nogaret stood next to the King showing no emotion. Looking back now I should have noticed De Nogaret's manner, you could see that Philip was losing it but his right hand man was calm and collective. I should have seen that the demon had something up his sleeve. The presiding judge brought the court to order and said,

"The King of France is not on trial here."

Reginald sprang back up to his feet and said, "Exactly, what I have been trying to say is that he should be." He then sat back down immediately but not before the court was once again in a pandemonium of laughter.

Philip rose to his feet, turned to the set of judges and barked at them,

"Do something about this insolent dog, you incompetent fools,"

His face by this time was completely red; he had lost all control of his temper. He was not aware he had walked into a trap that Reginald had set for him. Not only had he lost his temper that day but by insulting the cardinals, he had lost control of his judges. He roared once again at the presiding judge saying,

"Do something you imbecile, he has just insulted me in my own court. If you do not stop him I will have him taken outside and hanged!"

The judge turned to the King and said,

"You may well have been able to manipulate the Vatican into holding this papal hearing in your land, but I will have to make one thing clear to you. While I preside over this Papal hearing, it is, and always will be Papal. You sir, will have no influence or any jurisdiction over these proceedings and furthermore, if you were to take out the attorneys for the defence and hang them then that would be murder which ultimately would make you a murderer. Now, unless my ears have given my brain the wrong information, is that not what the leader of the defence is accusing you of?"

The court once again broke out in laughter. I just sat back in total admiration for my co-council, not only had my learned friend, caught the prey but the rabbit had skinned itself and jumped into the cooking pot while dicing a few vegetables. The judge once again brought the court to order and addressed my colleague,

"You are very good at your job but don't think you can manipulate me so easily. Keep your opinions to yourself; I only want to hear a line of defence relevant to this case."

Reginald was once again on his feet with an instant answer,

"I beg to differ. My line of defence is relevant to this case. I have with me two sworn statements from Papal bodyguards stating that the soldiers they captured, while trying unsuccessfully to kidnap Pope Innocent III in 1303AD, confessed to being French. They said they had been sent by their King to capture the Pope to ransom him back to the Vatican. I also have a signed statement from the Pope's own personal physician that the shock of this kidnap attempt brought about the Holy Father's heart attack resulting in the early demise of the Pontiff. This and the expulsion and asset stripping of all the Jews was done for one reason only, the same reason we are in this court today - because the insolvent King of France needs money. Do you honestly believe I did not know I was signing my own death warrant when I made these accusations against the French King in his own king-dom? Look very closely at me gentleman, for you see before you a dead man walking."

He then slowly sat back down and winked at me. This time the court was in complete silence. For the rest of the day, he tore up and discredited every single witness the prosecution brought before the court. By the end of the day, it was all over except for the shouting. The King had left court long before the end. As the presiding judge was about to adjourn for the day I requested that my co-council should not be sent back to a French prison because of the threat that the King of France had made on his life. My request was denied by the judge so I made a further request that I could have one hour with my co-council to discuss our strategy for tomorrow. The arbiter of the trial just looked at me and smiled,

"You can have all night or a least until midnight. Not only that, you can use my chamber here and because of your friend's performance, I will buy you both dinner from the finest tavern in Paris. The French may not be good at making money but I can tell you, they know how to cook."

I thanked him and he replied,

"You can call it payment for an overdue chastisement of a spoilt child."

The judge's conversation with me seemed to be going over Reginald's head, and then I realized that the cardinal had been speaking in Latin. We were both taken under French guard to the judge's chamber. When we were alone, my co-council asked me what had been said. I could see in his eyes he did not trust me. I informed him that we were talking in Latin so the French guards could not understand us. He then asked me if I thought I could have confidence in the judges to come back with an honest verdict. So I gave my own opinion from what I had gathered from watching and talking to the presiding judge. I thought the Cardinals had gone into the trial with an open mind but had now been persuaded to believe in our side because of the strength and skill of his expert defence. I also told him that the court was packed with representatives from the entire crowned heads of Europe. They would have to acquit us now even if they didn't want to. I tried to assure him that we had won. There is no way they can convict the brotherhood now.

He just fixed those firm eyes of his on me and looked into my soul. When he did not receive the answer he wanted, he said,

"I wish I could trust you for I would like to, but unfortunately my belief in my fellow man died a long time ago when I was a young man in Jerusalem, when I saw so called Christians killing innocent women and children and Muslims and Jews, it didn't seem to matter to them. I will let you into a secret, I have killed just as many Christians as Muslims, and I have more in common with assassins, that the Christian world calls Infidels. I find these men honourable and like I, they only send evil men to meet their maker."

His confession to me was like him confessing to the church for he knew too well that I was one of the Pope's men, for I was in the order of The Holy Eyes. So you see, this man wanted to die. When he attacked the King of France, I thought he was being unselfish putting his life on the line, alas, he was being self-serving. So you see, there is no such thing as an unselfish act, for the reason for performing the action is taking something from it.

I could not find fault with this man so I made the decision to tell him who I really was, for this man was more like my brother than any man I had met during the years, for he was suffering the same pain as me. In his short life, he had come to the conclusion that, like I, he had lost his respect for mankind.

He obviously did not believe me when I told him who I really was until I left the body of the Knight for a moment to reveal my true self. He was visibly shocked. When he did regain his composure, he seemed almost at peace to believe in me. This also meant there was definitely another life after this. For over the years this man had been slowly losing his faith; if this man was to die he would be taking his faith once again intact back to his Lord.

The food came about ten minutes later. I thought it wise that I should test the food first just in case it had been poisoned. The food was fine; in fact, it was excellent like the cardinal said it would be. It was especially good for a man who had just spent over two years on prison food. After dinner, we discussed the rest of the trial. He gave me instructions of what to do if for some reason he did not turn up. The guards came for him just before midnight. That was the last time I would see that fine man in body and soul again.

In the middle of the night, I was attacked in my quarters at the Pope's residence and was overpowered by several men. I was put into a sack and thrown into the River Sienna. Before I entered the river, I heard the sound of a large object hitting the water. I knew at once that the object was my co-council, Reginald. When I hit the water, I found it easy to escape from the sack for it had been left open. For over an hour I stayed in the cold, murky water looking for my friend but to no avail. I then went directly to the Pope, still in my wet clothing, to show him what had happened to me. To my utter amazement, the Pontiff just said,

"I knew it! I knew it! I said at the time that line of defence was going too far. You can not accuse a King in his own kingdom of such a ghastly crime and not incur any consequences. You can never hope to get away with it. We will now all have to leave before our lives are threatened."

"What about the Templars?" I asked.

The Holy Father said while arranging to have his trunks packed,

"What about the Templars? Is it not their men who have caused all this?"

I just could not believe what I was hearing, the Pope was only thinking of himself.

"I knew once of a case when an innocent man was taken out and murdered. All his so-called friends could do was to run away and that included me. Well, this time,

Holy Father I will not run away, those days for me are over." The Pope looked somewhat bemused but kept on packing.

A few hours later, I was once again in court, only this time there was no co-council with me. As I opened, I looked around the courtroom. I noticed the Holy Father had regained some of his courage and was present. The King was also in his position. I coughed to clear my throat then started to speak,

"Yesterday, myself and co-council's very existence was threatened in this court. You all heard who made the threat, the man who calls himself the King of France. In the middle of the night, I was man-handled from my room, put into a sack and thrown into the river. Fortunately for me, I was able to escape with my life. However that was not the case for my friend, Reginald. He was thrown into the river and drowned. He was murdered by the French King's henchmen."

The court went into a rumpus of noise from the accusations I had made against the King. The judge did not need to call for order as, all at once; the court fell into complete silence. All eyes were fixed on the door behind me and I heard the distinct sound of footsteps walking up to the front of the court. My legs almost vanished from under me when I saw the man walking towards me.

It was Reginald.

He began to talk the moment he reached the chair beside me. He informed the court that he had been sent new evidence outlining that the statements appertaining to the kidnap of Pope Innocent III were in fact fraudulent documents.

"I would like this new evidence submitted into the records," he announced.

The judges were given the new paperwork to examine. The presiding judge informed him that an accusation had been made against the King of France that an attempt was made on our lives last night. My co-council answered,

"No attempt was made on my life. As for my friend I cannot say, but I can venture my opinion that we did have a lot of fine French wine to drink last night and perhaps my co-council was dreaming."

He sat back in his chair and winked at me. This time his eyes were no longer dark and defiant, they were blood red. A demon had now possessed the body of my friend and not only that, like Philip the day before, I had walked right into the trap so expertly set by the demon. As I now looked around the court, apart from the Pope and the judges, the only people not laughing were the Knight Templars. I sat back down totally perplexed. Looking directly at me now was De Nogaret. It seemed he was also a demon, for his eyes were also red. I assumed this was the evil creature that had set the trap. I thought to myself, 'What would Reginald have done now?' So I got back onto my feet and said,

"I believe that my co-council has been tortured into changing his mind."

When he was asked by the judge whether he had in fact been made to change his story, his answer to this was very dramatic. He rose to his feet and removed his shirt to show there were no marks of torture on his body. I explained to the court that torture marks were not always put onto the body but into the mind. I defied the King to send the strongest man he had into this court and I would make him say anything they wanted me to. I may well make the man scream, but after it was over there would be no marks on his body. The presiding judge said he would allow this experiment to take place in his court and he adjourned for two hours while I prepared for my example of mind torture. I asked the court carpenter to make me a box that had a hole at one end large enough to let a man's hand through. There had to be straps inside to ensure the hand did not move. Also, the box needed to be open at the top so that both the experimental subject and I could see inside.

When everyone was settled in their seats, the King had his man sent for. Now man was no understatement, he was a giant. When he sat down in the chair, it just about fitted him; I just prayed this man's hand would fit into the box. I asked the judge what he wanted the man to confess to and with this the King shouted,

"Make him admit he's had carnal knowledge of a demonic woman."

The court began to laugh as Philip sat back down, very pleased with the fact that he knew no man would admit such a thing. The judge brought the court to order and told them in no uncertain terms, that if there was one more outburst he would have the court cleared, for he said that this was not a side show but a very important experiment to see if one man could change another man's mind without causing physical harm in the process. The giant man slipped his hand inside the hole in the box. I then went about very slowly and deliberately breaking the man's fingers, only he and I knew what was taking place. The man only shrilled a little even though he was in great pain. Unfortunately, unlike his fingers, this man would not break, he refused to give me the answer I wanted. I then took the spear head from under my clothing and proceeded to cut off each one of his fingers. The brave man shrieked and although it was very obvious that he was in great pain, he refused to answer the way I wanted him to. I realized that in my feeble attempt to defend the Templars, I was causing unnecessary suffering to a very brave and innocent man. This was surely something the devil would find amusing, so, with the help of the spear, I stopped the poor man's pain and went about re-attaching his fingers. To my utter surprise, when the man saw his hand restoring itself in front of his very eyes he cried out,

"I, Guy De Seurey, do admit to this court that I once had carnal knowledge of a demonic woman," at that he fell unconscious.

He was roused by the court physician who then removed his hand from the box to show to the completely dumfounded court that there were no marks or injuries to him. The court was so amazed for they had all witnessed this man's misery yet they could now see he had not been harmed in any way, only in his mind. The prosecution said this was the work of the devil. I replied that I had now established my point about why my friend, Reginald, was now singing a different tune from the one he sung yesterday. I felt for sure that the judges would now not believe what my co-council was saying and they would be more inclined to believe what he had said yesterday. I felt so good that I had proved my point but I also felt very disheartened that my demonstration had caused so much inhumane suffering to the giant man. To prove a point on the back of an innocent indi- vidual takes the shine off your achievement.

By the time the court proceeding had been adjourned for the day, I had my co-council dismissed on the grounds of mental instability and I then went on to almost, single-handedly, destroy the prosecution's whole case. The only thing they had to go on tomorrow was the confession of some of the knights who admitted to the denial of Christ in their initiation ceremony. My defence therefore would have been that they had to learn to deny Christ for in the event of their capture by the Saracens, this would be the only way for them to come out alive and with the shortage of Knights in the east, the order could not afford to lose any. So if they learnt to deny Christ, this could save them to fight another day. They believed as an order that the Lord would understand why they had done it and would grant forgiveness. Whether I could have won with that argument remains to be seen for I never got the opportunity to find out. I knew too well that demons would try to stop me from returning to court so I had an all night vigil in my room. I had taken off the spear and hid it behind a loose brick in the wall for I also knew that a demon would try to have it destroyed.

During the night nothing happened so I relaxed a little the next day which turned out to be a big mistake. Leading into the court house was a small yard with gates at either end. When I entered through the first gate it was locked behind me. I was now in the yard with about twenty-five French soldiers; I knew right away they were not after my autograph so I drew my sword. Over the years I had become quite proficient with a blade but even I could not take on that many soldiers. My only satisfaction would be to deprive the King of quite a few of his henchmen by sending them to the devil. It was inevitable that they would win, it was just a question of could they finish me off before the any witnesses started to arrive. I was just about managing to hold them off when I made a miscalculation in a challenge and was caught by one of the soldiers with his blade. This made me stumble back a little and they were all on me like a pack of wolves.

I was eventually killed and my body was dragged to the palace dungeon on the order of De Nogaret, I assume. My body was clasped into a metal cage in the shape of a woman, it was known as the Iron Maiden. My body and soul would stay incarcerated for years until the device was used on the next poor victim. When I did not turn up at court, the presiding judge called a mistrial. After a few more years of hearings and papal trials, the order was disbanded and, like I said earlier, the two top Templar Knights were executed. The rest of the Knights were imprisoned for life. As for the land the Templars owned, it did not go to Philip as he hoped. Along with the possessions of the order, the land went to the Hospitaller. So as far as everyone was concerned, that was the end of the Knights Templar.

After my incarceration was over, I found out that the remaining knights were in the newly formed country of Switzerland. It was decided, with the then Grand Master and I, that a special troop of soldiers would be sent to the Vatican to help protect the Pontiff from kidnap attempts from the likes of a corrupt monarch. So you see, the Knights Templars never died, they're active today in the guise of the Vatican Swiss Guards.

CHAPTER TWENTY FIVE

What hope have the sheep?

Lazarus had just started writing a chapter about how he had stopped the Nazis and the devil from completing their nuclear goal in 1944, when he was disturbed by three sharp knocks on the door. He put down his pen, got up from his desk and closed his journal. He thought he would resume it later. He glanced at the clock; it was three forty-five in the afternoon. He then looked at his watch to check the date; he worked out that he must have been sitting at his desk for over eighteen hours. He looked back at the journal and flicked through the pages; he realized there was not much written evidence for his labours. Also, he had not come up with a solution for his and the world's dilemma. He could only assume he had been in some kind of trance just thinking and then writing intermittently. He closed the door to the study then went through to the hall.

He opened the door and standing before him was a little man about five foot four, he was dressed like a priest. He said,

"My name is Father Diego Mendez, I am here as an envoy for another priest, a Father Furpay."

He then handed Lazarus his passport and also a cutting from a catholic newspaper. The article had a picture with it; the picture was of the priest and two women. The story told of a church in London where the parishioners had collected for over a year to pay to bring the mother and sister of their parish priest over from Chile for a visit and to attend a celebration mass for Father Diego, who had been a priest for over twenty-five years. There was also a small metal container.

Lazarus gave the priest back his possessions without opening the container for he knew what it contained. He just didn't know whether it was consecrated or not.

"Very impressive, now what is this all about, Father? But before you answer, you look at though you could do with a drink."

"A whiskey and soda would be very nice, I have had a day you would never believe even if I told you," the priest said.

In return, Lazarus just said,

"Try me."

Then he went about fixing the drink for the priest. Along with the whiskey and soda water, he put a good measure of holy water in the drink. This will be very refreshing or give him one hell of a sore throat, he thought. He handed the drink to the priest. Father Diego took the glass with both hands and drank greedily from it. Lazarus was now convinced the man was who he said he was and he told Father Diego what he had put in the drink to check him out. The priest just said,

"If you don't mind and would be so kind, I could do with a refill with all the same ingredients but go a little easy on the holy water, it dulls the soda water a shade. Oh, by the way, the object I gave you contained the consecrated body of our Lord. You see, I was also check-ing you out - is it not becoming a terrible world when you can't trust your fellow man or really know if he is one?"

They both laughed then Father Diego told the complete story from start to finish. When he had finished the story, Lazarus just said,

"Referring to Father Furpay's reluctance in believing the young man when he told him about the devil, you know what makes me laugh about you clergy, and I have met many of you in my lifetime, you all seem to have one thing in common. You have spent most of your lives preaching to people about all the temptation of evil sent out in this world by the devil, then when some poor soul comes up to you telling you about the devil or some such thing that is bothering them in their lives, you don't believe them." Then in Latin he said, "What hope have the sheep when the shepherd stops believing in the wolf," and added, "A friend of mine once said, happy are those who have not seen but yet believe."

Father Diego thought Lazarus' friend was guilty of a slight plagiarism for he knew who the original author of the quotation was - not as well as Lazarus though but that's another story.

While Father Diego was still in the lounge, Lazarus went back into his study and proceeded to write a note in his journal. He then went back into the lounge and asked Father Diego if he would like another drink, and if so, to help himself from the drinks cabinet while he made a phone call to Father Furpay. After that he would take him home, he was in no danger now that he had completed his mission. He was now of no consequence to the dark one. As Lazarus was saying this, he was writ-ing a cheque for ten thousand pounds. He handed it to

Father Diego and told him it was for the repairs to the church. Anything that was over could go to any charity of his choice; Father Diego thought the English people were the most generous in the world.

Lazarus picked up the phone and dialled Father Furpay's number. He introduced himself as Larry, he told him he had Father Diego with him and informed him that Father Diego had told him the entire story. He then told him to listen and not to say anything, not his name or the name of his church because others could may well be listening. He then told him what was going to happen, the one thing is the beast cannot see the whereabouts of the holy relic while it stays on consecrated ground. But we have to assume that once the police have left this area in force, the devil's people will start to check out all the churches in the vicinity. So try to make the church look deserted, no lights on or anything but a note on the door saying you have been called away on urgent business and will be back in a few days. This may make them bypass you; they would then assume that the boy would have gone to someone for help and not to an empty church.

"I don't know if this is the right thing to do, I am not infallible, I will leave it up to you to decide what to do, but remember, someone or something could be listening."

Lazarus hoped the priest was intelligent enough not to do any of the things he had suggested; this would confuse any would-be listener. Then he told him he would drive to Stockport, when he arrived he would phone him and pick out landmarks. When he gave the priest a landmark which was within minutes of his church, he should then, and only then, give him the directions. If the church is locked, he would knock three times then he would put a piece of paper under the door with a Latin encryption on it. If it correlates with one in your possession word for word then and only then you can open the door. The priest then said,

"What encryption?"

"Father, we will get over this a lot quicker if you only listen. You can ask questions if anything is not clear at the end."

He then continued with his instructions. He told him to take the spear and examine it closely. Father Furpay would find that at the bottom, where the spear shaft would have been attached, will be a hole about an inch from the end where a silver chain had been fitted through it. At the very end, it had been sealed with a silver plug. He told Father Furpay to break off the plug and then the chain. When he removes the chain, he will find another silver plug embedded into the spear. This one is slightly different; the head has a screw type seal. He was to turn it clockwise to open it. Inside he would find a small airtight waxed pouch. The contents will be a Latin quotation.

"The same quotation I will give to you under the door. If it matches word for word you will know that it is me and you can open the door." He then said he would see him later. He took Father Diego home and headed for Stockport.

In the meantime, Father Furpay had thought on Larry's words to make the church look deserted. He had a second thought about that, if indeed someone else was listening, they would know that this was the right church with the note on the door so he came up with a completely different option. He would act as if nothing was amiss. When the church was supposed to be open, it would be. He told Jamie the plan and that he would have to hide when the church was open. He knew just the place. He explained where and what it was to the young man. The church had been built on the site of a Tudor manor about one hundred years ago. When the church was being constructed, a priest hole was found with a tunnel leading to the river, this was left in there and incorporated into the church's cellar. It was now used to store the altar wine but most importantly, it would have been consecrated to protect the priest hiding in there. So it was decided that while the church was open, Jamie would stay there, he would have to go there in a few hours because at seven until eight on Tuesday nights was organ practice. The church's doors were always open for that hour, for several of the church's parishioners would come into listen. Before they went down to the cellar to show Jamie where he was to stay, he dismantled the spear from Larry's instructions. This did not please Jamie at all; he spent the next two hours reassembling it to its former glory.

CHAPTER TWENTY SIX

The Devil and a Pope

Pope Pius XII, in my opinion, was one of the pontiffs who I believe were saints that walked as men. He was one of the few people over the centuries to whom I revealed my true identity to. I also feel he was one of those Popes who received a lot of unfair criticism that he of all Popes, did not deserve. They said during the Second World War, the Holy Father was in bed with the Nazis that he was turning a blind eye to what they were doing to the Jews. That could not have been further from the truth, for the secret organization 'The Holy Eye' which we set up in the thirteenth century was given precise instructions directly from the Pope. They had to do everything within their power, including laying down their lives, to save as many of the Jews as possible. The order set up an underground network that would smuggle the Jews out of occupied Europe to Palestine.

Now how did these people thank the one God who had saved them? They went about displacing the innocent Arab, through bitterness these people felt to the world. I for one cannot blame them for feeling resentful when they had witnessed the atrocities first hand.

Perhaps as people, this was the final straw that broke the camel's back. After centuries of vile persecution, they had decided as a nation no one was ever going to push them around again. I can understand that mind-set; nobody liked them so they didn't like anybody else. This time if they had to die, then they would die with a gun in their hand fighting for their homeland, not going like sheep to the gas chamber - that is the only thing I can say on the subject. I'm afraid they picked on the wrong people, it's like being bullied in the play-ground by the big boys so you decided you'd had just about enough of being a victim so you go out and find someone smaller than you to pick on. The Arab, who is mainly Muslim, ends up the victim. The irony of it is, it was the Islamic religion that helped the Jews over centuries, this is what grieves me so much about the world today, people's attitudes towards one another. 'I am proud to be French 'or whatever', or 'Those people should not be living in my country'. Don't you realize, it is just an accident of birth where you were born? Like I have been trying to tell you, it is not important who you are in the world but what you do when you live in it. Like I keep saying, life is just a test, it is the next life you are going to that matters.

So going back to the Palestinian question, it was wrong for the Jews to make the Arabs homeless, without a doubt. The question to be answered is does the land rightfully belong to the Palestinians? For like I said, didn't the Roman Emperor make the Jews home-less by banning them from entering Jerusalem nearly two thousand years ago? Both these evictions were wrong, both were done by force. What, in my opinion, should have been done? That every single piece of land should not have been taken, it should have been purchased. After the war, the allies should have found the then owners of land, i.e. the shepherds, the farmers or even the nomadic Arab, and then they should have made these people an offer they could not refuse. Where would the money have come from? Switzerland, for in their banks, they were holding a vast amount of Nazi gold appropriated from murdered Jews. Then like the Chinese restaurant in New York, the Indian takeaway in London and the Irish bar in Benidorm, these properties and the land they stand on do not belong to the people indigenous to the country where the places stand. They now belong to the Chinese, Indian and Irish men who purchased them.

So getting back to Pope Pius, why did people take up the impression that the Pontiff condoned the Nazis? Was it because he never came out publicly to denounce their demonic ways? The whispers started that perhaps the Pope's view of condemnation was due to worry; that criticism of the movement would result in the asset stripping of all the possessions held by the church in Germany's occupied territories. You see, ever since Henry VIII of England had reclaimed every single piece of land that Rome owned in his kingdom, the Vatican had sometimes held back with denunciation of individual monarchs for fear of incurring their wrath. Resulting in the same scenario as the confiscation of all their assets in England.

Well, this time they all got it wrong. The Holy Father was stopped by me, for it was I who informed him that a demon was inside the German leader. I told him I knew the way to take the demon from him. The only way I thought this could be achieved was if we could make him come to the Vatican. So you see it was I who was almost asking the Pope to befriend him. We had to get him to make an official state visit, it's like the saying 'Keep your friends close but your enemies even closer'. The only problem this time, I had underestimated my opponent. For it was not a simple demon inside Hitler, it was none other than the master of darkness himself, Satan - although I did not know this at the time, so when the German leader turned down the invitation time after time, I thought we could hold a long-distance exorcism.

So in a large secret room under the Vatican City, the ceremony took place with the Holy Father and eleven Cardinals and I. We went ahead with the ritual of exorcism. During the service, we demanded the unclean spirit to leave the body of the German leader; we evoked it to appear to us before its expulsion from Hitler's body. The thing did emerge from the bowels of the earth, hideously deformed like the others I had come across in my life. But this one seemed different in a way, perhaps more evil. Then I realized it was just a spirit, for it would not come in flesh for it sensed the spear of our Lord. Then all at once, every candle in the room went out. I felt a cold chill that went through my soul; there was an almighty flash of light then complete darkness. From out of the blackness came a red glowing light. Then a wind appeared from out of nowhere to blow the Pope and the Cardinals against the wall. They were now looking down on me; each one was about six feet from the ground, their arms stretched out like they had been crucified on imaginary crosses. For in each of their hands and feet, a nail had been hammered through them into the wall. The eyes and faces of every individual were contorted with pain, apart from the Holy Father who seemed to be peacefully praying. Then the apparition of the Roman soldier from the crucifixion appeared and said,

"Lazarus, I knew you were behind this mumbojumbo. Do you really think I could be hurt by all this crap? I told you once I would never eliminate you for I want you, my friend, to witness the defeat of your Master. You see, I have given both these futile tribes a weapon that will destroy this world and you will have a ringside seat. You or your Master can't stop me."

"You know that's not true. You haven't got the power to appear in front of me in the flesh for you know that I, a mere man, can stop you. This is all just an illusion; can you not feel your power over these good men is evaporating because of the power of prayer?" I said.

As I had been engaged in conversation with the devil, one by one each of the Cardinals had followed the Pope's lead and begun to pray. Slowly each nail in the Holy Father's body popped out and the Pope gently slipped down the wall. Then every individual Cardinal did the same. The apparition of the devil disappeared and the lighting and temperature of the room returned to normal. The majority of the Cardinals were in a jubilant mood believing they had just defeated the devil. I had the unenviable task to deflating these good men of the cloth by informing them that their celebration was somewhat premature. Not only that, I thought the world was in great danger of coming to an end. By the look of the Holy Father's face, he had already come to that conclusion. Then I felt from inside my clothing, the heat coming from the spear. So I took it off at once. I was not surprised to find it was red hot and had turned completely white.

I asked for a map of the world to be brought into the room. One of the cardinals immediately left, and returned a few minutes later clutching a rolled up map under his arm. When it was unrolled, it was totally enormous. Almost too large for any wall by its size, as you can well imagine it went into great detail. A Cardinal stood on each corner to hold it down. I slowly walked around it, at the same time watching the spear for any sudden changes. After my second circuit of the map, it became clear my destination was to be the Balkans. It was there I would come face to face with Satan. I would also witness first hand the power of what some people say was mans worst invention. This most destructive weapon may well have been built by man but I can definitely assure you that the idea and the plans came from the underworld, the land of the evil dead - Hell.

I departed from the Vatican the very next day to go to Yugoslavia; to get there from Italy was not an easy task. I had to pass through several battle zones. I was also fortunate that I was immortal, for a mere human being would have had to pay for the journey with their life, as for I, that was one commodity I could spare. I reached my destination on June 27, 1944. I soon found a host I could use to infiltrate the top secret underground testing bunker for the weapon. My guise was a recently dead German physicist named Karl Stein who insistently had been named Goldstein until a few years prior to that. You do understand the implication of the name, you see it doesn't matter what race or religion you are, when someone needs you to split the uranium atom by bombarding it with neutrons...

Dear Reader,

I am sorry but I will have to bring my book to a premature end.
I have just received a visit from a South American priest who
has just given me some very useful information appertaining
to the whereabouts of the 'The Spear of Our Lord'. If I can be
reunited with the relic, I could yet save this world. So consequently, I will have the time to finish this another day. So until
we meet again, wish me God speed.

Yours,

Lazarus

CHAPTER TWENTY SEVEN

What Is Written, Is Written

Lazarus arrived in Stockport just after eight. He had made up time fairly successfully considering he had to negotiate the London rush hour traffic. He came off the motorway and took the directions for the town centre. He ended up parked on a hill in between, what he assumed to be, two Victorian buildings. The one on the right was of a grey type stone; it looked like a hospital with all its small windows. The one on the left was of white stone, a shade grander than the adjacent building.

He opened the window slightly to shout to a passing middle-aged man with grey hair and glasses who was walking with his feet at a slight ten-to-two angle. His left hand was in his pocket, the right was swinging by his side. When the man came forward to the car window, Lazarus realized he was not middle-aged at all, probably not even thirty. The type of guy who, when he dies, will ask Father Time for a rebate for taking his youth away so very prematurely. For some reason he had gone red in the face from embarrassment with being called to the car. Lazarus then asked him what the building behind him was. The man answered, at the same time pushing up his glasses with his forefinger,

"It's the Town Hall me old cock, Stockport Town Hall."

Lazarus thanked the old looking young man, he thought he really had arrived up north with the expression 'me old cock' being said to him. He then phoned Father Furpay to tell him he was outside Stockport Town Hall.

"Good," said Father Furpay, "you are only a few minutes away from my church," he then gave Lazarus the directions.

Two French men were sitting in a car outside Father Furpay's church; they had just watched him lock the church doors after the end of the organ practice. Then, one of the French men asked the other,

"Well, what do you think David? I don't think they are hiding anyone in there. It's just too open. While I sat in there pretending to listen to that awful organ music, people were in and out of the vestry arranging flowers and cleaning the altar. It looks to me like nothing out of the ordinary was going on."

They were just about to leave when a green BMW pulled up outside the church doors. A man got out and started to bang on the door three times. But then the man did something strange. He didn't wait for a reply; he just took out a letter from his jacket and placed it under the door.

"That's it David, let's get him!" one of the French men said. They left their car and begun to creep up behind Lazarus. Before he realized what was happening, Lazarus felt a hand around his mouth and a blade entering his back. It was so painful and he knew at once that the wound that had been inflicted was fatal.

While the attack on Lazarus was taking place, Father Furpay had taken the note into the church to read it under the light. What was written on it was exactly the same as what was on the parchment retrieved from the spear head. The words were the ones that were inscribed on Our Lord's cross at Golgotha. Written in Latin, it said, 'Behold the King of the Jews'. Then in another handwriting the words, 'What is written, is written' had been added. The handwriting of those last five words was remarkably like the handwriting on the paper he had just picked up from the doorway floor. He went back out to the door and opened it.

The two French men pushed the dying body of Lazarus against the shocked priest who was then covered in what he thought was the poor man's life blood. As the man died on top of the priest, Father Furpay looked directly into his eyes. They showed no fear, far from it, they seemed to be smiling. As Lazarus died, he said to himself, 'How many times does a man have to die in his own lifetime?' The thought really amused him; he tried to say something and then died.

The man called David pulled the priest up from under my body of the dead man and then said,

"Where is he, the man you are hiding?"

Then, for no apparent reason, he head-butted the priest breaking his nose. He was then manhandled through the side doors into the main church; he must have looked a real sight to Jamie. Not only was he covered in Lazarus' blood, he was now bleeding profusely from his nose. Jamie didn't know what to do, he was halfway up the church so he decided to turn and make a run for it. The other French man took out a gun and discharged it in the direction of the young man. A silencer had been fitted to the end of the weapon so Jamie only heard the strange thud sound then felt the pain as both bullets lodged into his back sending him flying forwards. He was now lying on the altar floor facing the man who had just shot him, who was now slowly walking towards him. Jamie knew instantly what the man wanted.

Then from somewhere, the seriously injured young man received some strength. He rose to his feet, took the spear head from around his neck and looked up above him. About thirty feet, on a ledge was a statue, and in its outstretched hand it seemed to be holding a set of keys. Jamie knew what he was going to try to attempt but he also knew it was destined to fail. He threw the spear into the air when a miraculous thing happened. He achieved what he hoped he would, somehow the chain was now hanging around the keys to the kingdom of heaven. For Jamie now recognized the statue, it was St Peter. It was like a once in a lifetime thing, like when you ring the star prize on the side stall at the summer fair. As the spear head hung there like the Sword of Damocles, all Jamie could think was, 'I wish the boys could have seen that, it was better than OB's overhead kick'. He was then punched in the head and sent back to the floor, knocking over flowers that had been beautifully arranged by Mrs Jameson only an hour before.

As Jamie lay in pain on the altar floor, the French man who had shot him kicked him in annoyance at what he had done. The French man now turned to Father Furpay and told him to go and get some ladders. The priest said defiantly that he would do no such thing until he had helped Jamie. The man just turned to Jamie and without a second thought put the gun to the lad's head and fired, removing his brains. They now adorned the altar wall. After the killing he simply turned to Father Furpay and said,

"The boy is now beyond your help Father, now be a good priest and show my friend where you keep your ladders."

Father Furpay would not tell the men where the ladders were kept, no matter how many times the man hit him. He thought to himself he had just seen two people murdered, he was also in no doubt that when they got what they wanted he would be their third victim. He didn't care; he was not going to be a part even in a small way to help the evil men to get their hands on the sacred relic that had been in the side of the saviour of the world. So this man was wasting his time beating him for he wasn't going to tell no matter how long this went on. Unfortunately for Father Furpay, the man was not wasting his time, for inflicting pain on an individual was never a waste of time for a sadist.

Father Furpay's pain was to no avail for the other French man had discovered the whereabouts of a set of ladders. He was now in the process of placing the ladder against the wall just under the statue of St Peter. He began to climb at the same time that Lazarus was putting the barrel of a gun against his friend's head; the French man knew instantly what the object was that was now digging into his head. Lazarus whispered in French,

"The great white hunters were told to always check that the kill is actually dead before you have your picture taken with it, for it just may well get back up and bite you. Now take your dirty French blood-stained hands off the priest or I will have no alternative than to put a hole in your head that will match the one on your person that your leader speaks out of."

The man did as requested, Lazarus then hit him on the side of the head with his weapon, knocking him out cold. The noise didn't disturb the man on the ladder, if he did hear something he didn't react. He may well have thought it was his friend carrying on with his beating of the priest. Lazarus knelt down and said very quietly so as to not alert the man who was now ascending the ladders,

"Father James Furpay I presume."

The totally battered and bleeding, and definitely confused priest just said,

"I thought you were dead."

Lazarus smiled at Father Furpay and said,

"Oh, I have been Father, and to be quite honest, I recommend it. Once the pain subsides, you feel an overwhelming sense of utter peace, although in my case, that has never lasted that long."

All the information and the pain from the injuries he sustained from the beating proved too much for the priest and he blacked out. Lazarus noticed the priest's right arm was broken; also his jaw, nose and cheekbone all looked to be fractured. This poor man had taken one hell of a beating; Lazarus gently moved his head into the recovery position.

He walked slowly towards the man who was now at the top of the ladder trying desperately to reach the spear. Lazarus noticed the dead young man on the altar; he knew it must be Jamie. He felt sorry that he could not have helped the boy; he kicked the bottom of the ladder in frustration. The French man screamed then began to fall. Before dropping to the floor, he made a grab for the chain holding the spear, he was successful but not for long. The chain snapped as it had only been temporarily repaired by Jamie just over an hour ago. The movement dislodged the statue of St Peter. Lazarus stood back and watched as both the man and the statue fell on top of the body of the dead boy.

The church went completely black. There was a flash of light and then there was a blue light emanating from the body of Jamie and he began to rise. As he rose to his feet, Lazarus noticed the spear head had been rammed into him. Lazarus ran forward to the young man, he then asked him in Latin if he was feeling okay. Jamie responded in English with a remark that would have not been out of place in a James Bond film. He said simply,

"Shaken but not stirred."

Lazarus realized he had a comedian on his hands, what he didn't know was that this funny guy had been sent by God to assist or replace him. He went forward to him to remove the spear from his heart. Jamie looked shocked, for somehow he had not observed the spear head lodged into his chest. He was obviously feeling no pain although he did flinch when he felt it being removed, but almost immediately he perceived his body going into a restorative mode.

Lazarus took the spear and told him to follow. He went back to Father Furpay and proceeded to place the spear on to all the priest's injuries. Jamie watched in amazement as they began to heal in front of his eyes. The priest started to wake. Lazarus gently touched the side of his neck, this sent the priest back off to sleep. While the priest was asleep, Lazarus told Jamie who he was and who he now thought Jamie was. Jamie didn't believe it at first, he said,

"I'm not even a good person, I don't even go to church, I didn't even believe in God and I let my very best friend be taken in front of me by men who had just killed his parents. I knew they were not going to take him out for a drink. What did I do, I did nothing. I just hid and watched - why would he pick someone like me?"

Lazarus put an arm around his shoulder and said,

"My son, I did exactly the same and he picked me. For you see, you are weak and ordinary like me and that is what he wants. Just a normal human being to look after his fellow man, not a saint for men are quite definitely not saints. Just take a look at those two," pointing to the two poleaxed French men.

"Well what do we do now?" Jamie asked Lazarus.

"I think the first thing we should do is to leave here. The devil may well not be able to see us, but his acolytes will start to wonder where Batman and Robin are," pointing again to the French men. "You wake up Father Furpay and I will go outside to see if the coast is clear."

Lazarus then went outside to his car; he went into his pocket for the keys but couldn't find them. He noticed them on the church steps; he must have dropped them when he was attacked while trying to enter the church. He bent down to pick them up, and then he heard a whistling sound go over his head, then a thudded impact. He saw a splintering hole form in the church door. Lazarus knew what it was that had made it. He made a run for the door; he managed to get inside but not before taking a slug in the shoulder.

When inside, he bolted the door then went through to the main part of the church. Father Furpay looked shocked again when he saw that Larry was injured. He watched him sit down, take off his jacket and his shirt and ask Jamie to take out the bullet.

"What with?" Jamie asked.

"Use the spear," Lazarus replied.

Jamie took the relic then started to cut into Lazarus' shoulder to retrieve the bullet. If that was not amazing enough for Father Furpay that Jamie had become a battlefield surgeon who didn't need the correct instruments to perform an operation, the next thing he witnessed was totally unbelievable if he had not seen it with his own eyes. The wound commenced to heal itself. Within minutes, the shoulder didn't even look as though it had ever been injured. Father Furpay had a thousand questions to ask about his injuries and about Jamie's apparent death. Lazarus could tell that the priest needed answers but he didn't have the time to give them, he just looked at Jamie with a look on his face that said, 'You say something' so Jamie did,

"I know this looks crazy but he's a good man, we are on the right side with him so just do everything he tells you, I am sure he will explain later when he has the time."

Lazarus asked Father Furpay if there was another way out, "Just back through my house," Father Furpay said then remembered the underground exit, "Oh yes, there is another way but I've never used it. There is a priest hole in the cellar with a tunnel that leads out. It was widened during the war years to use as an air raid shelter. It goes under the church down to the river into the town centre," so they took that escape route out of the church.

Before going, he took the spear and made the injuries heal on the French men. He told them that God was responsible for their recovery. They should take the time to think before rejoining the dark one; he then bound them together with some rope Father Furpay had given him.

They left the church and went down into the cellar where they all entered the priest hole. Father Furpay had supplied torches. The passageway was completely filthy; every so often Jamie would jump up into the air when he came across one of the small furry occupants of the place. Lazarus smiled and said,

"Some immortal you will make being afraid of rats!"

Jamie just said,

"I don't like them that's all, they're all dirty, smelly creatures."

"They are meek and mild, more afraid of you, but don't underestimate them, they know how to survive. I think these animals will be the major incumbents of this planet when we are all gone. So one day just maybe the meek will really inherit the earth," Lazarus said.

Jamie couldn't help himself, he had to try and say something funny,

"Well, I don't fancy staying around if this lot will be the only staff available to work at McDonald's. Yeah, you can definitely revoke my immortality!"

Lazarus thought he could not take eternity with this wise-cracker and said,

"Is there nothing you don't make a joke about?"

Jamie answered,

"You have to, for life is too short not to laugh when you can. Although, come to think about it after what've you've just told me, it may well not be."

They eventually made it to the river after about half an hour. They walked along the embankment until they came to a set of steps leading up to the town. They emerged up into the town centre as three very dirty bedraggled individuals. They walked to the taxi rank. The driver was ready to object to them entering his newly valeted taxi but when Lazarus gave him a hundred pounds, he willingly agreed to take them to a monastery on the outskirts of London. If it was any more he would give it to him when they arrived. When they were inside the vehicle, he told the taxi driver to turn up the radio. He then began to whisper the entire story of his life to Father Furpay with Jamie listening. When Lazarus had finished his story, all that Father Furpay could say was,

"So you really knew Our Lord, what was he like as a man?"

Lazarus thought for a moment, for in all his years he had never been asked that question, so he said,

"He was a man and all men that knew him aspired to be like him and all women who knew him loved him dearly. He was handsome, witty and charming. Yes, I would go as far as to say he liked to tell a story and a joke or two - not as often as our young friend Jamie-boy mind you! He was the type of man who could never be tricked with words, when people tried to trap him he would easily slip out of the traps they set. If I could put it in a nutshell, he was what every man would want as a friend and I for one was proud to call him my friend."

Father Furpay seemed happy with the answer; he was a man well into his sixties. He was exhausted; the day had proved too much for him, he could no longer stay awake to ask anymore questions. Now it was Jamie's turn to start asking the questions like,

"What was the plan?"

Lazarus had told him to speak in Latin, Jamie did not know any Latin. All of a sudden he was conversing in the dead language as though he had been speaking it all his life. Lazarus told him he thought the world was coming to an end. Once again, Jamie couldn't help himself and said,

"Don't tell me that the day you inform me I am immortal, you then go and tell me the world's going to end!"

Lazarus just flashed him a look to say keep your mouth shut and listen. He then carried on saying,

"I think the earth is coming to her end, it's like she is cracking up, and she seems to be getting warmer. If it carries on at this rate, within a hundred years the ice caps will melt, submerging coastal towns and cities. Earthquakes and floods seem to be happening more frequently. I don't know whether I am responsible for that, for being selfish and not keeping watch all the time. For when I have come out of my hibernation, some disaster or another has happened. It may well be just coincidence, I don't know. Perhaps that's why you have been sent, someone who is not disheartened with this world. I have also another theory; the demons seem to be coming through more frequently. Perhaps they know that the end is on its way. Just imagine if one demon took over the body of the President of a super power, how long would it take for him to activate a nuclear war head? Don't you see, when two armies faced each other in the battlefield, it would only take one man to start. Then all hell would break loose and everyone would join in. Men have always been divided into countries and religions. I realize now, men should never be divided by anything. Take religion, I was born a Jew, and then I was christened by Jesus and was partly responsible for forming the Holy Roman Church. Yet, I no longer believe in one religion, I think men being separated will be the downfall of mankind. Jews against Muslims against Christians, that's what the devil ultimately wants. I think in the next few years you and I will be very busy for

I believe all religions and organisations, such as PLO and the IRA, could well be infiltrated by demons using the cause of religion. They would then make impossible demands which Governments could not comply with. So the result would be bloodshed of the innocent, then the other would want to take revenge. It would just go on and on, culminating in the end of the world. Then the devil would have achieved his ultimate goal through religion. How ironic!

I believe in heaven and would like to go there one day soon but deep in my soul; I know the place will not be full of priests, bishops and rabbis. No, in my opinion, it will be filled with just good people."

As he was talking, he heard part of a speech being given by Mrs Thatcher on the radio and it just dawned on him, he had been looking for the wrong gender, he realised this time the demon was in a woman. Lazarus asked the driver to stop at the next services; he then made a phone call to the Stockport Police telling them the men responsible for kidnap and murder in Heaton Norris were now surrounding a church not far from the town centre.

He would now take Father Furpay to a friend of his at the monastery where he would be safe. Jamie could come with him and learn what to do in the future, for he knew now where he was going and what he had to do when he got there.

The Epilogue

The Place: A Rented Villa in Turkey Overlooking The Aegean

The Time: Two Years Later

Lazarus enters his bathroom to shave, he looks into the mirror and out of the corner of his eye his attention is drawn to the glimmer of a shining hair at the side of his temple, close to his right ear. He takes out a pair of tweezers from the bathroom cabinet and extracts the unusual coloured hair, and when he examines it closely confirms that it is quite definitely grey. Lazarus now had the answer to a question that had been pre-occupying him over the last two years, was Jamie sent as an assistant or a replacement? The hair has confirmed it is the latter, he had often wondered what he would look like with grey hair. It makes some people look like Albert Einstein; others can look like the Hollywood actor George Peppard. As he surveyed his handsome tanned look, he felt for sure he would be more of a Peppard. He looked at the hair still not quite believing it had come from his own head, he felt so happy as this was the confirmation he had been hoping for, for the past two years. He was actually dying after all these years, it was finally happening. Never in the history of man has someone been so happy to receive the final call.

He would eventually meet up again with his loved ones and his thoughts then turned to Anna, the beautiful slave girl he had married so many years ago. He was sure he felt that tingling butterfly feeling in his stomach that you associate with being in love. Was it the prospect of seeing Anna again? Oh, how he had missed her over the years. He could still see her now in his mind as clearly as though it was yesterday, standing there in the harbour at Ephesus. Her hair: golden and shining in the sun. Her eyes: big and brown, that slightly drooped making them so much more appealing. Her mouth: perfectly shaped, full and the most luscious shade of red. Her outstanding figure: so perfectly proportioned with curves in all the right places. But her most astonishing feature was her skin colour, she was pure white. This made her stand out like an alabaster statue among the throng of people who had either natural olive skin, native of the Aegean, or the sun burnt skin of the slaves who had been bought over from cooler climates. This contradiction of features made her so unique and unforgettable.

I learnt later that Anna's Master's cook, who was also a Celt, had been a herbalist in Britania before she was enslaved, and had given Anna a cream mixture she had made up, which I now realise was the earliest form of sun block, and yes it was her skin colour that really did bring out her beauty. He thought in all honesty that if God had made a more perfect creature he had yet to see her.

Lazarus now lives in a place called 'Golden Sands', he moved there to be close to Anna's memory. You see, it was about two hours drive from where he first met her and every Sunday for the past two years he would make the pilgrimage to the ancient city of Ephesus. He would first go to the church of Virgin Mary to hear mass being said then he would wander around the city going to places where he and Anna had walked, hand in hand, just two young lovers, so much in love with one another that they were oblivious to the people around them.

Lazarus snapped out of his daydream and went into the kitchen to make a pot of coffee. Not because he needed, or felt like, a drink, it was the smell of the fresh ground coffee that he loved. He took the pot of coffee out onto the balcony overlooking the sea and he thought to himself, this is one of the most beautiful places in the entire world. As he looked over the Aegean he had an overwhelming feeling of loneliness, how he wished the love of his life was sitting here beside him, enjoying the panoramic views,

"Not to worry, it won't be long now, my love," he said out loud. Lazarus put his melancholy mood to one side and began to write.

Now as we leave Lazarus completing the book about his life I would like to clear up a few loose ends regarding what happened in England two years ago. Well, obviously, Lazarus and Jamie prevented the world's end or you would not be reading this today. With the help of the spear they located the demon that was just too close to the British Government for comfort and removed it. This went totally unnoticed by the British public. Yes, the human race would never know how close it came to the abyss.

The conservative government stayed in power, the only real thing that changed was that Mrs Thatcher stepped down. People say she was never the same person after she had been **stabbed** in the back by people she had trusted and worked with for so long.

As for Isabella Longsden-Smythe and Raul Henry, they were indicted with the murder of Alex Smythe and Dave O'Brian.

Antoine De-Burgh and his men were charged with the murder of Mr & Mrs O'Brian and the, yet to be identified, young woman whose remains were found at the Longsden-Smythe estate. When the judgement was made they were all found guilty. De-Burgh was sent to a hospital for the criminally insane and the rest were sentenced to life imprisonment. When the judge was reading out the sentences De-Burgh had to be restrained, he was screaming that the end of the world was coming. He told the judge he would be standing in front of the master of darkness before the year was out to answer for this outrage.

As for D.S. Sue Hogan her prediction came true, D.I. Mike Connor suffered a fatal heart attack eighteen months later. She was told in no uncertain terms by her superiors to attend the funeral service. She complied but on a very reluctant basis. When she saw the suffering the widow and her children were going through her heart actually went out to them. At the end of the service, she went up to Michelle Connor and embraced her tight, then something strange happened, it was like someone inside her had taken over her voice and she heard herself saying what a great policeman and a wonderful person her husband was. She then noticed how those hypocritical words helped Michelle and she realised, who was she to judge whether a person was good or bad? That was for some higher force... she was only responsible for herself *'to keep her own house in order not to sit and pontificate on others.'* She was also relieved to realise that day that her heart had not completely turned to stone as she had once believed.

As for Jamie the new immortal and, eventually, the new keeper of the spear - Lazarus had told him to stay in Stockport to be close to his loved ones for as long as possible, for all too soon his lack of ageing will become apparent and he would have to leave his home town. Before long people would start to wonder if he had 'a portrait of himself in the attic that was ageing instead of him'.

Lazarus had given Jamie a great deal of money before he left and with this money he had purchased a shop on the outskirts of Manchester which sold unusual items from around the world for the household. The speciality at the moment was varnished palm tree leaves, from 8 inches to 8 feet, sent over from Turkey by a close friend. No self-respecting conservatory owner would have been without one in the Manchester area in the 1990's.

From time to time Jamie would have to go at a moment's notice when Lazarus called, he told his staff he was going around the world collecting unusual things to sell in the shop. He needed someone he could trust to be left in charge so, he employed Stanie's younger brother John and he also employed Tez's sister Sharon. Their mutual loss eventually developed into love and Jamie knew what he would give them as a wedding present when they married and it would be to take over the business. For very soon he would be going to Lazarus for training in a new form of work.

In the past two years he had grown a lot closer to his mother, he had persuaded her to seek help for her drinking. It had now been twelve months since she had had a drink. She had signed up at the local gym and there was even a new man in her life. For the first time since his Dad had died Jamie could see she was really happy, knowing she loved someone would make it easier when the time came to leave.

So that was the past dealt with. Now for what the future could hold. In the same way that I have been taking you back in time I also have the power to take you forward in time for a glimpse of what is yet to come. This written picture of the future may not come true, that is entirely up to you as an individual and the rest of mankind collectively to change your ways and change them now. I am afraid, dear reader, that if the human race keeps walking down this road of hatred and bitterness to one another then there will be only one conclusion and I think you know what that will be *(like John told Lazarus all those years ago in Ephesus "when the evil people of the world outnumber the good that is when the Anti-Christ will come to end this world and not you or the spear of Our Lord will be able to stop him, you will see the signs that it is coming. When earthquakes, hurricanes, tidal waves and the like start to happen all to frequently you will be able to see the earth turning in on itself and start to crack).* So I tell you, reader, you still have time to turn off this path that is leading to the earth's destruction. I will make one last supplication on behalf of your own guardian angel, turn the other cheek and live in peace with your fellow man or, this will come to pass.

The Place: North Of Baghdad, Looking Out Over The Euphrates

The Time: 03:30 ON 05-05-2065

A Jeep pulls up near the Euphrates River just before dawn; a young man who looks in his early twenties leaves the vehicle, and from the open back of the jeep he takes out a wheelchair. He assembles it very quickly then wheels it round to the passenger side of the vehicle and opens the door. He proceeds to help a very old man into the chair, when the old man is settled he wheels him very slowly to the edge of the river and then says,

"Well, is this really it then Larry, the end of the world?"

The old man turns very slowly to look at the young man and answers.

"Don't tell me you are really bothered Jamie, have you not seen enough revulsion in your short life? Did the violence and atrocities of the wars you have seen in Yugoslavia, Afghanistan, Iraq and the religious civil war in your own country not sicken you to the bone? And before that did you not witness first hand, the repugnance and greed of the rich getting richer? Pop stars, actors and all manner of other celebrities throwing their weight behind worthwhile causes, demanding government abolish third world debt but, then contradicting their principles by moving to tax havens to avoid paying the correct amount of tax as their earnings exceed expectations. Have you not witnessed company directors buying other companies and then merge them together in order to make wholesale redundancies in order to increase their own slice of a very large pie? Best of all, you have the Lawyer claiming his clients' human rights have been breached when he could not care less, he only wants to dip his hands into the rich gravy train called legal aid. I look around and I am sickened by rich people making more and more money when there are so many starving in the world – *like fat squirrels amassing a fortune of food for a winter that will never come!* And look what people have done in the name of religion, does that not sicken you to your very core? I just hope people have done what I have told them to do. Go back to their synagogues, churches and mosques and don't take their religion, just their faith."

Jamie interrupts Lazarus in full flow.

"Hold up old man there is no need to preach there is only you and I here, anyway I nearly forgot I have something for you. It's two of your most favourite things in this world."

Jamie runs back to the Jeep and brings back a Havana cigar and a bottle of claret with two glasses. Lazarus takes hold of the Havana, he then begins to smell it while Jamie is opening the claret. As he hands the glass of claret to Lazarus, Jamie says, trying to lighten the sombre mood that seems to be rising and almost contaminating the atmosphere with an overwhelming feeling of disappointment,

"I didn't bring you anything to eat, for the life of me I wasn't sure what was the appropriate provision to take to an end of the world party, for as you can well imagine, I have not been to one before. Oh, but just as a matter of interest what would have been your favourite food of choice?"

Lazarus takes hold of the glass and ever so slowly moves it to his nose and takes in the aroma of the red liquid, then after a few seconds he answers Jamie

"I have sampled many specialities of countries all over the world and I can put my hand on my heart and say this, it is chicken breast stuffed with banana served in a creamy coconut curry sauce. There was a little restaurant called the Blue Ocean in a place known as Altinkum which is in Turkey, and many years ago the chef was called Ilhan Gok and this meal was his house special, and I can truly say without a doubt it was the best meal I have ever tasted in my entire life!"

Lazarus then lights the cigar and after enjoying the Havana in silence for a few minutes he turns to Jamie and says with an air of satisfaction tinged slightly with an apologetic tone,

"Thank you, thank you very much my friend that was really thoughtful of you. I am afraid I did not reciprocate the gesture. I have brought you nothing my dear boy but, out of curiosity what would you have liked?"

Jamie thought while taking a sip of the claret and then said,

"There was a Chinese takeaway near where I lived on Belmont Bridge in Stockport and if I was to have one last meal it would be a mixed curry with fried rice, now that reminds me of a joke. A man and wife are in bed after a long night working in their Chinese takeaway when the woman says to her husband 'What would you like me to do for you?'"

Lazarus interrupts the joke. "I have heard it so many times Jamie, the punch line is: *if you think I'm cooking at this time of night, you can forget it!* You know why you tell jokes about the act of love-making, it is so apparent my dear boy because you have never really been in love have you?"

Jamie felt slightly put out by this remark and just gave him a puzzled look and said,

"Come on then, what is real love Larry?"

Lazarus thinks for a while and then says,

"Love is when you think more of a person than your-

LAZARUS THE UNTOLD STORY

self, you feel a butterfly sensation in your stomach whenever you see them, you are happy and proud of what they achieve and you feel their pain and disappointment when the slightest thing goes wrong for them."

As quick as a flash Jamie replies, "If that is the definition of love then I have been in love for many, many years but it wasn't with a woman, my one true love has always been Manchester City Football Club."

Lazarus and Jamie lock eyes and both begin to laugh hysterically. Not because the remark was that humorous, but because laughter was a gift given to the human race by God. Now the race was almost over and the end was in sight; as the super powers faced each other in a deadly stand off. The world knew deep down that the final curtain was being lowered. So the mood was sombre and frightening so probably this was the last time the gift of laughter would be used. They eventually stop and Lazarus dries his eyes and raises his glass and says in Latin,

"illi super morior, EGO tutus vos" which translates to *"for those about to die, I salute you"* he then clips the side of Jamie's glass and sinks the wine in one huge mouthful. The world ends, as some say it began with a big bang.

Apocalypse 18.1
Babylon, capital of the kingdom of the Anti-Christ, and the earth was lit up by his glory and he cried out with a mighty voice saying, "She has fallen, she has fallen. Babylon the great has become a habitation of demons, a stronghold of every unclean spirit."

John 1:1-18
Into that darkness a light shines, an amazing light and the word, the very expression of God becomes flesh.

Author's Notes

If you've reached this point by taking the conventional route of starting at the beginning then you deserve my congratulations for sticking with it to the bitter end. This now entitles you to make an opinion on my work, although I would appreciate any feedback whether positive or negative, for you see this is the first time I have put pen to paper this way, and I can hear you say 'that's blatantly obvious'. When I started this the only persons opinion that counted was my son Nathan, you see, I first started telling stories to him when he was just a baby in his cot. I remember pushing my index finger through the bars and watching with pride as he wrapped all his tiny little fingers around mine, I can still see the smile that seemed to go from ear to ear, as I told him my version of this little piggy went to the Chinese chippy. As the years moved on so the stories progressed in more detail, the tales told about a hero, who just coincidently was named Nathan. He was a knight who would fight dragons and all kinds of nemesis, and like most super heroes he had a sidekick named Matthew. Who just so happened, coincindently once again, to be the name of his cousin two years his junior. The two boys would go through the ages on adventures righting wrongs. So when I finished my story about Lazarus the first person I read it to was my son, who was about 12 at the time. So like most sons he believed everything his father would say. So real was the tale to him that I had to take him to the place where the devil appeared on Belmont Bridge, to Christ Church graveyard and to the Church where Jamie became immortal. Then what made me so proud was that he went away and wrote a poem about his guardian angel. So I would now like to end this book by sharing his work with you, many thanks once again.

Yours Murph

My Gaurdian Angel

By Nathanial Luke Murphy

I know he's there, I'm sure he's there,
I can feel his guiding hand.
He's been with me through thick
and thin as I walked across this land.
He's there when the morning breaks
and at the passing of the day.
He bears my pain and feels my
strain, watching City play away.

When I'm feeling sad and life's
unkind I look over my shoulder
and feel him close behind.
I know he will be there, I'm sure
he will be when I finally pass away.
I will see his face and touch his
hand on that oh so lonely day.

Printed in the United Kingdom by
Lightning Source UK Ltd., Milton Keynes
142056UK00001B/3/P